Descendants of Hugh McAlester

Hugh McAlester
BIRTH Sep 24 1780
Scotland
DEATH Aug 24 1842
Tennessee

Sarah McAlester (Donnelson)
BIRTH May 16 1783
Scotland
DEATH July 23 1865
Tennessee

Mathew McAlester
BIRTH July 3 1804
Scotland
DEATH Nov 9 1834
Tennessee

Jane McAlester
BIRTH Feb 18 1806
Scotland
DEATH Jun 12 1880
Tennessee

Rebekah McAlester
BIRTH Sept 1 1807
Scotland
DEATH Jan 27 1830
Tennessee

Andrew McAlester
BIRTH March 18 1809
Scotland
DEATH Apr 19 1866
Tennessee

Joshua McAlester
BIRTH Jun 27 1811
Scotland
DEATH July 19 1835
Tennessee

Mary McAlester
BIRTH Oct 20 1812
Scotland
DEATH Aug 12 1896
Tennessee

Jesse McAlester
BIRTH Dec 20 1813
Scotland
DEATH Dec 27 1878
Texas

Rachel McAlester (Burns)
BIRTH Sep 27 1819
Scotland
DEATH Feb 5 1902
Texas

Angus McAlester
BIRTH Jun 25 1839
Texas
DEATH Nov 25 1863
Georgia

Sarah McAlester
BIRTH Mar 25 1841
Texas
DEATH Aug 14 1921
Texas

Jacob "Buddy" McAlester
BIRTH Dec 16 1842
Texas
DEATH June 3 1864
Virginia

Martha McAlester
BIRTH Oct 27 1843
Texas
DEATH Mar 17 1932
Texas

Ben McAlester
BIRTH Sep 4 1845
Texas
DEATH May 11 1928
Texas

Margaret "Maggie" McAlester (Scott)
BIRTH April 19 1850
Texas
DEATH June 28 1933
Texas

Creed McAlester
BIRTH April 28 1872
Texas
DEATH July 31 1950
Texas

Kirby McAlester
BIRTH Nov 9 1873
Texas
DEATH Nov 9 1873
Texas

Anne McAlester (Stuart)
BIRTH Jun 1 1875
Texas
DEATH Sept 9 1955
Texas

Ruth Mitchell (McAlester)
BIRTH Aug 27 1905
Texas
DEATH Jun 6 1992
Texas

Alamo Letters

JAMES & PAMELA NELSON

CONTENTS

CHAPTER ONE
The Gold Cup Race

May 8, 1820

The four-week-old colt dashed across the field, a streak of red, his white-stockinged legs a mere blur. He reached the hedge at the far end and skidded to an awkward stop. He shook his head, white blaze flashing in the sun, and emitted a high-pitched snort. His dam, a darker shade of chestnut, raised her head and nickered. The baby bucked, lashing out with his hind legs, and then trotted back to his mother, reaching far out with his forelegs, head and stubby tail held high, seeming to float above the ground. With a conqueror's air, he thrust his head under his mother's belly and began to nurse. She nickered again and gently nuzzled her foal's back.

Two men had just stepped inside the high pasture after opening the wooden gate. The Earl of Norfolk, the richest man in the coastal Lowlands of Ayr near Glasgow, Scotland, turned to his horse trainer. "My son

Magnus tells me, McAlester, that there might be something special about this foal. A man would be blind not to see that my boy is right." Lord Norfolk, his white hair tousled by the wind, spoke in the clipped tones of the upper class—Oxford English. Tall and lanky, he was expensively dressed in a brown cashmere vest over a white silk shirt, tweed knickers, fine woolen socks and high-topped black shoes.

His trainer, Hugh McAlester, a true Scottish Highlander, was at least as tall as his employer. His proud stance belied his poor clothing: a broadcloth work shirt and long pants, worn and baggy at the knees, and scuffed shoes. Driven by high English rents from the Highland home where his family had lived for generations, Hugh, thanks to his skill with horses, had earned enough to buy a small farm near Ayr, Scotland.

He nodded. "Yes, sir, Your Lordship. Ye see how, at such an early age, he can already extend a trot. And he can run like the wind. But it's too soon to tell if he'll keep all that promise as he grows."

The foal stopped nursing, kicked in his mother's direction, and dashed to the opposite side of the field. The Earl raised his field glasses, focusing on the red blur. "My God, McAlester, I've been around horses my whole life, and that's the nearest thing to Pegasus I've ever seen! If he lives up to his promise, I want you to train him for the Gold Cup Race."

"Yes, Your Lordship. I will train him well." He smiled. "Is Pegasus the name you'd like us to use?"

"Most certainly, Hugh, the name suits him well."

Unknown to the Earl and Hugh, Jesse, the youngest son of the trainer and his wife Sarah, followed his father to the stable, and walked to an area outside the fence, a place that was quite familiar to him, where he remained motionless. When the colt ran, he smiled, knowing instinctively the colt would grow up to be a winner. He could hear the conversation between the Earl and his father, and memorized every word, knowing those words could be useful in the future.

Hugh knew the Earl had fallen in love with the magnificent four-week-old colt that would forevermore be known as Pegasus. Although His Lordship had purchased Pegasus' mare, bred her to one of his retired stallions, and the mare had delivered the colt in his stable, His Lordship had left him with Hugh for training, and Hugh's training was an exercise of will.

Jesse knew his father was not one for harsh treatment. He also knew his presence, and especially the presence of his dogs Samson, Ike, and Pete, during the training process would get him in extraordinary trouble. He signaled the dogs to sit and be silent. Watching the training from the left side of the barn, he could anticipate each step his father would take.

Hugh said, "Come here, Pegasus!" and the colt, seeing the piece of an apple in his hand, ran to him. Hugh said, "Here you go." The colt gently nudged him while crunching the apple.

Hugh's method of training horses was to respect them and reward them for a good performance. He used milt for the horse to smell. The milt was a newborn colt's afterbirth, which Hugh dried and kept in his pocket, knowing the horses he trained always responded to the scent.

Jesse saw the milt, but thought it was dried liver, which he used to train his dogs.

Hugh retrieved the halter and let Pegasus smell it, along with the milt. Then he gently rubbed the colt's back and placed the halter on the beautiful animal, while letting him smell the milt and the apple in his pocket.

In the following days, Jesse and his dogs were always in place for the training.

Hugh approached Pegasus with the halter in hand, slipped it on the colt, and reached into his pocket for a piece of apple, which the animal immediately scooped out of his hand. Still chewing on the apple, the colt followed Hugh, who led him by the halter, keeping it slack to minimize the pull on the young creature. Jesse and his dogs moved quickly and silently out of sight when Hugh approached the left side of the barn.

After several days of leading the colt by a halter, Hugh leaned on him to determine his strength and acclimate him eventually to bear a rider.

Just as Jesse expected, when Pegasus was old enough to bear a man's weight, his father rode the beautiful thoroughbred for short stretches, always rewarding him with treats, usually apples, and speaking kindly to him. At last, Pegasus was old enough to be taught to walk, trot, and canter with a man on his back.

The Earl came almost daily, and often brought his son Magnus with him. After all, it was Magnus who knew how valuable the horse was in the first place. Hugh watched both men's reactions as he put the colt, then the yearling, the two-, three-, and four-year-old through his paces for them. The Earl loved Pegasus and delighted in his progress and beauty, while Magnus did not hide his boredom, sometimes rolling his eyes and looking to heaven when his father gave Hugh a special compliment.

"You're doing a great job of training him, McAlester. Get Pegasus to a peak of perfection. I want to enter him in the Gold Cup Race when he's five years old."

I hope Magnus never gets his hands on the colt, Hugh worried, but never let on.

Jesse continued carefully observing the training of Pegasus and the words between his father and the Earl.

As the years passed, Hugh watched worry creases deepen in the Earl's forehead.

"Your Lordship, is there something fretting you, sir?"

"It's Magnus, my boy. He didn't want to come today. Said all this bother about a horse is tedious. I'm afraid he's after the lassies these days, and he keeps bad company. They've taught him to gamble."

"That's serious, Your Lordship. Does he have access to your fortune?"

"No. Thank God, I found out in time. I gave him an allowance as a youngster, and I'm keeping him on it now. I hope that will curb his madness. Gambling is a destructive vice, you know."

"Yes, I know that well enough. It's been the ruination of many a good man."

"But that's not all, Hugh. They've encouraged him to drink. Most nights he comes home late, stinking of whisky. I'm at my wit's end. He's my eldest and my heir. I fear they've ruined him."

"I hope for your sake that's not true, Your Lordship." Jesse heard every word, and started following Magnus.

April 29, 1825

Only eight days remained before the Gold Cup Race. Every evening, the pubs were full of rowdy and boisterous men making bets on the horses that would compete in the momentous event. But at ten in the morning, Magnus McGruder was one of the few patrons in the smoky Talley Ho Pub. He sat on a barstool, his head in his hands, the very picture of despair.

By now, he was notorious for his heavy drinking, for the erratic bets he placed on horses no one else favored, and for his violence if someone made a snide remark. He had grown into a big, coarse man with an evil temper, especially when he'd been drinking, which was most of the time.

Jesse was not allowed inside the pub, so he watched through a window, being careful to avoid being seen.

Despite knowing the crown of all races was coming up, Magnus had no money with which to bet. He had spent all of his allowance, and his credit was exhausted. No one would lend him a farthing. In desperate need of money, his mind clouded by alcohol, he devised an equally desperate plan. *I'll gather a few of my father's cattle and sell them at market. I'll be on my feet in no time. But how to carry out such a plan?* His father ran a large herd of Aberdeen Angus cattle on the Norfolk Estate. If he could steal just three or four at a time, no one would notice the difference. *I'll need someone to help me.* It would have to be someone who knew cattle, someone who wouldn't scare them as a stranger might. *Ah! Of course! Duncan Campbell, the manager of the estate. He's a cattleman born. But how to persuade him?*

Magnus let his head fall into his hands once more. He was thirsty, but knew he'd better lay off the whisky so he could think better. *Scotch… alcohol… brandy… of course! Old Duncan is truly fond of brandy! I'll invite him to visit me in my rooms tonight and we'll polish off some of Father's Napoleon brandy. I'll have to make sure Father doesn't see him coming and going.*

A man in dark clothes followed Magnus as he left the tavern. Jesse was not far behind the man, who grabbed Magnus by the shoulder. When the drunken aristocrat spun around, he grabbed him again, this time by the throat. "You pay what you owe, McGruder!"

With no response from a shocked Magnus, the man tightened his grip until his victim gagged, and managed to reply in a weak, high-pitched voice, "I can get the money after the Gold Cup. Just don't kill me."

"You'd better, or you'll be a dead man."

Jesse was fascinated by this encounter, and the news that Magnus was in deep trouble. He continued to follow Magnus from a safe distance.

Duncan kept track of Norfolk Estate business from a small office in his house on the estate grounds. He had broad shoulders, jet black hair, and wiry eyebrows. Magnus, his head a little clearer now, knocked on the doorframe. "Duncan, can you spare a minute?"

Duncan had been calculating profits from the previous month's sales and looked up in surprise. "Magnus! And what might you be doing here so bright and early in the morning?"

"I've got an idea I need to discuss with you, Duncan." Duncan's face took on a guarded look.

"What sort of idea?"

"I'll tell you tonight. Come to my rooms by the back door, and make sure my father doesn't spot you. You'd better come after dark and walk over."

"Hmm. That doesn't sound right, Magnus. You shouldn't hide your business from your father."

Magnus scowled and balled his fists. Then, knowing he needed gentle persuasion not violence, he relaxed, and spoke in a soft voice. "Duncan, even a good son needs to keep some things from his father. I need your help."

"In that case, tell me now, Magnus."

"I'd rather discuss it over a good drink. My father just got in a shipment of Napoleon brandy. Would you care to sample it with me tonight?"

Duncan's mouth began to water. "Well…I don't suppose it would hurt anything to give you a hearing for a wee dram of Napoleon brandy. All right. I'll see you right after dark, and I'll make sure the Earl doesn't know."

Jesse had listened to the conversation from a window that had been left slightly open.

That evening, after nightfall, Magnus heard a gentle tapping on his window. Moving the curtain aside, he saw Duncan and motioned him to the door. He greeted the older man quietly, but once inside, Magnus became the hearty host. "Sit down, sit down, Duncan! Before we talk business, why don't we enjoy some of this nectar of the gods Father so kindly supplied."

Duncan's feelings were divided. On the one hand, he didn't trust Magnus. On the other, he longed for the promised drink. Magnus produced two balloon snifters and poured at least a cup of brandy into each. "Cheers!" He swirled his glass briefly and took a gulp. Duncan took two.

They spoke about the Gold Cup Race for a while, Duncan finishing off his brandy and receiving more. When Magnus noticed Duncan beginning to slur his words, he revealed his plan in detail.

"But, Magnus, those are your father's cattle!" Duncan held out his glass again, and Magnus poured in another full portion.

"Just consider the cattle an advance on my inheritance." His face twisted into a sneer. Duncan leaned closer to Magnus, "I don't see how I could agree to such a scheme."

"The old fool doesn't keep a close eye on those cattle. You do. If you don't draw his attention to our little business, he'll never miss 'em."

Duncan gave the Earl's son an owlish look and boldly asked, "What would my share of the profits be?"

Magnus, his voice dripping with honey, replied, "What would you think about twenty-five percent?"

"Thirty percent would be fairer," peering at Magnus with a sly but drunken expression, eyelids drooping.

"Agreed." Magnus refilled the glasses with a flourish. He lifted his snifter and cried, "I propose a toast!"

Jesse, listening through an open window, was amazed at the despicable greediness of Magnus.

Each spring for the past twenty-one years, as manager of Norfolk Estate, Duncan Campbell's duty had been to count the livestock. He had made a detailed list of the cattle, including their age, gender, and a general description of each. Duncan would then give the completed list to the bookkeeper for the Earl's estate. But after a week of secretly selling the cattle, Duncan began to develop cold feet. *Too many people know we've been selling off cattle. What if one of them tells the bookkeeper what we've been doing?*

He hurried to Magnus's rooms and found him still in his nightshirt, though it was the middle of the afternoon. "Magnus, what am I to do when I've got to turn in me numbers next week? It's me head if they find out we've been sellin' the cattle." He had planned to finish selling, take his money, and disappear beyond the seas, leaving Magnus to answer for the crime. But the risk of discovery had robbed him of his courage.

Magnus squinted up at him from an easy chair. "Who's to know that it isn't the Earl selling off his own cattle? If no one gets suspicious, neither the bookkeeper nor my father will take it into his head to go count the cattle. I say let's finish what we've started."

May 6, 1825

At dawn on Friday, the day before the great race, the cattle buyer, the only person other than the two conspirators who knew of the scheme, began pounding on Magnus's door. "Magnus, Magnus, come out!"

Surly at being disturbed so early in the morning, Magnus yanked the door open. "What in God's name are you thinking, waking me up at this unholy hour?"

The buyer, hat in hand, his face pale, stammered, "I-I'm s-sorry to bother you, sir."

Magnus looked left and right, but saw no one nearby. "You'd better come in and tell me what's wrong." He closed the door behind the buyer and began to shout. "What is it? Out with it, man!"

The buyer hunched his shoulders, avoiding Magnus's eyes. "The last bunch of cattle was stolen. Thieves took them in the night."

Magnus at once realized the gravity of the situation. "You didn't keep watch over them? I'll beat you to death, you bastard!"

"But, sir—"

Magnus cut him off and pounded him with vicious blows. "I'll kick your teeth out, you dog!"

The buyer, hands protecting his head, ran for the door.

"Off with you and your bad news!" Magnus's final kick just missed the cattle buyer's disappearing arse as he ran out the door.

Magnus gripped his aching head and groaned, desperation filling him like a fog. Someone had figured out what he was doing with his father's cattle and had simply stolen the last batch. Profits from the scheme so far were scant; he'd had to pay Duncan, and settle some of his gambling debts. He pulled a bottle of whiskey from the liquor cabinet, tipped it, and drank four swallows. "I'm ruined now. I've made some money from the first two cattle sales, but it's not enough. Not enough."

He collapsed in the easy chair, drank the rest of the bottle to help him think on his problem, but instead fell into a drunken slumber.

Later in the day, he roused himself, hardly knowing where he was. He had a new plan. He would fix the Cup. *All I have to do is to bet a pile against Pegasus, and I can make my fortune. But I'd best be quick.*

Like everyone else, he knew that Pegasus was the heavy favorite for the twenty-first annual Gold Cup Race.

Thomas Cooper lived in the cottage behind the Earl's sprawling mansion. He was both the caretaker of the Norfolk Estate and had the additional responsibility of grooming and exercising Pegasus after he had been moved from the McAlester stable, as was customary. Magnus realized that Thomas had ample access to the stallion and his feed, and could come and go without being observed by Hugh. He smiled. *Thomas is the only lad that McAlester trusts around Pegasus.*

He pulled on his jacket and went to find Thomas, who at that very moment was pouring grain in the horses' troughs for their evening feeding.

Unfortunately, Jesse was not following Magnus because the boy was doing chores for his father.

Magnus shouted, "Thomas, get over here! I've a job for you."

Thomas rushed to Magnus, who whispered, "I can help the two of us make money from the Cup."

"That'd be right fine, sir, but how?"

"I need you to give Pegasus something before the race, to slow him down. And after that, make sure you don't bet on him."

"I don't know how I kin help…" Thomas paused as if considering.

Magnus understood. He fished several gold coins earned from the sale of his father's cattle out of his pocket and dropped one in Thomas's grimy hand. "I think you do know of something, don't you?"

"Well…"

Magnus dropped another gold coin.

"I don't know…"Another coin followed the first two.

"I've got something to give old Pegasus that'll make him run sideways."

"Excellent. Now, remember, mum's the word. A fish wouldn't get caught if it didn't open its mouth." A fourth gold coin followed the others.

Thomas was unsure of the connection between fishing, racing, and gold coins. But after Magnus had explained the plan, the caretaker decided to try his poison on a pony used as a companion to Pegasus. He cut a hole into a small apple and poured a little poison inside. "Come get your apple, Ole Smoky. This'll set your innards right!"

A short time later, the pony became listless and fell asleep. Thomas grinned wickedly. "Is that slow enough, me Lord?"

"I reckon Ole Smoky could outrun Pegasus, come race time." Magnus's evil smile and sinister, half-drunk glare clearly revealed his malevolence.

He turned to walk away, and as he departed heard Thomas say, "Pegasus is about ten times your size, Smoky, so I reckon to be safe, I'll give him the whole bottle."

May 7, 10:45 A.M.

Knowing the race was due to begin at noon, Thomas concentrated, half-coring the apple and carefully mixing a hefty dose of poison with the inner pulp. He replaced the top of the apple and laid it aside to begin vigorously rubbing Pegasus down as he always did before a race.

Pegasus snorted and pawed the ground, anticipating the apple.

"Ye'll have yer apple soon enough, old boy." Thomas palmed the poisoned fruit and held it for the eager thoroughbred. "Eat it all, Pegasus."

Billy Porter, the jockey, scowled as he approached. "Don't overfeed him, you dolt!"

"Your arse," mumbled Thomas under his breath, as he helped Billy mount the tall chestnut.

May 7, 11:30 A.M.

Jesse moved easily through the crowd. His father had told him a thousand times, "God gave you one mouth and two ears for a reason." He listened closely to the gossip, especially to any conversation that could provide information about the race for his father. Jesse knew that liquor quickly loosened people's tongues. The remarkable thing was his memory. He could always repeat verbatim what he had heard.

Basil Bryant, owner of Greystone, a handsome bay entered in the Cup, whispered, "Our jockey lad was so drunk last night, they had to carry 'im home from the pub."

Jesse listened intently.

"Well, and how's the laddie today?" asked his neighbor.

"Damn my eyes, he seems in good form. Don't know how he does it!"

Jesse moved on and, ever alert, heard the voices of Magnus and Duncan, who were standing a good distance from the crowd. He crept behind them. When Magnus opened his mouth, the smell of liquor and tobacco permeated the air like a rancid cloud.

"That old Hugh will never know what hit 'im,"

Duncan replied in a near-whisper, "You expect that poison will work quickly on Pegasus?" and turned to see if anyone was nearby.

He immediately recognized Jesse, who was behind them. "Magnus, there's a little bugger from the McAlester clan right there." He spit a stream of tobacco toward Jesse.

Magnus lurched toward Jesse, shouting, "You damned tadpole, I'm gonna brain you!"

Jesse deftly moved aside, dove under the stands and made his escape.

Magnus cursed. "If the little bugger tells old man McAlester what was said, there'll be hell to pay. After him, Duncan, or I'll cut your gizzard out myself!"

Duncan desperately scanned the crowd for any sign of Jesse, but in vain.

May 7, Noon

Blue sky and golden sun illuminated the scene for the Scottish Gold Cup, held the first Saturday in May, every year since 1804. The race was run on grass and was contested for a length of two miles in two heats.

The grandstands buzzed with excitement as the racehorses were led into the starting gate.

The jockeys, astride their horses, nervously eyed the starter.

Hugh yelled at his jockey, "Billy, get a good start and head for the inside rail!" Pegasus, the magnificent five-year-old stallion, snorted and pawed the grass.

The starter's pistol fired, and the horses surged forward. The McAlester clan screamed, "Let's go, Pegasus, give 'em hell!"

With a sudden burst of energy, Pegasus leapt to the inside rail. Billy yelled, "Go, Pegasus! Go!"

Without warning, Pegasus pitched toward the rail, hurling Billy into a grotesque heap on the ground and breaking his neck instantly. The crowd gasped as one, and pandemonium broke loose among the closest spectators. Pegasus, eyes wide with terror, blood bubbling from his nostrils, was engulfed in pain when Hugh arrived.

Hugh's voice trembled. "I'm sorry...to have to...do this, boy!" He drew a pistol from beneath his coat, took careful aim inches from Pegasus's head, and pulled the trigger.

A meaty fist slammed into the side of Hugh's face, and Duncan Campbell screamed, "You're gonna pay for killing Pegasus!"

A primeval roar erupted from behind Duncan, and Matthew McAlester, Hugh's eldest son, jumped on Duncan's back. "Get off 'a me father!"

Duncan, a startled look on his face, turned toward Matthew. The last thing he saw was Hugh's scarred, bear-sized fist coming toward his face. The crowd surrounding the fight grew very quiet as Duncan Campbell collapsed, hitting his head on a fence post.

Sarah McAlester, Hugh's wife, raced to the scene along with Bonny, her Westie terrier. "Hugh, stop! You're gonna kill 'im!" Her words were too late. Duncan lay on the grass track, blood pouring from his mouth and nose, a few of his teeth lying on the ground.

"Murderer!" shouted the crowd gathered close around the scene.

Hugh, regaining his senses, realized that Duncan was dead.

"Murderer! E's kilt 'im," screamed a bystander. Bonny, always ready for a good fight, growled and bit down hard on the troublemaker's ankle. He screamed in pain. "Get off 'a me!" which only encouraged Bonny to bite down harder.

Hugh shouted at the crowd encircling him. "Back away from me now!" He turned to his wife. "Sarah, get the children to the wagon. Go!"

Magnus pondered the situation. *Now that old Duncan's dead, the only other person that knows about the poison is Thomas, and I know how to remedy that situation*. He smirked while fingering his sheathed knife.

Matt and Sarah were still reeling from the shock of the fight and the death of Duncan Campbell. In a panic, Sarah screamed, "McAlesters to the wagon!"

She saw a doctor, medical bag in hand, moving rapidly toward the racetrack, heading straight for Billy.

Hugh yelled, "Don't stop! It's in God's hands now!"

Behind him, Billy Porter, Pegasus, and Duncan Campbell each lay in growing pools of blood on the grass racetrack.

CHAPTER TWO
Escape

T he crowd surged toward Hugh, who stumbled toward the wagon, his face a mask of horror, shock, and sorrow. Most of the family had already climbed aboard, the horses already hitched and ready. Keeping them hitched with the wagon turned toward the exit was a habit with Hugh, who knew how to beat the mass exit after a race. He now thanked God for his foresight. Jane, the eldest daughter, counted the McAlester children while her father boarded. She was nineteen years old. Her older brother Matthew was twenty-one. Rebekah was seventeen, Andrew sixteen, Mary fourteen, Joshua thirteen, and Jesse twelve.

"Jesse's the only one missing, Papa."

They heard a yell. Samuel Stuart, the McAlesters' neighbor, ran toward them. "Hugh, get goin'! There'll surely be a bounty on your heads. I heard talk that Pegasus was poisoned and there's a mighty purse to the man can prove it."

Hugh moaned. "My God, Samuel, I'm done for." He waited no longer, but bellowed, "Pull away, Ben, Lady!" and the team of draft horses, already tense and uneasy, roared into action.

Samuel, left behind, shouted after them, "Don't worry! I'll look into the matter. May God go with you!"

Sarah noticed Bonny running alongside the wagon. "Bonny, up!" Sarah reached down and, with a heroic leap, the dog jumped into her arms. She placed the dog on the front seat. "Stay, Bonny!" When Sarah spoke, all creatures paid attention.

Hugh urged the team into a fast trot and turned to his wife. "Sarah, I didn't mean to kill 'em. Duncan got the best of my temper."

Sarah gave her husband a terrified look. "What in heaven's name are we going to do?"

Hugh turned to peer behind the wagon, noticing that a few young men from the crowd were running after them, but seemed to be tiring. "You lassies, Jane, Rebekah, and Mary, quiet back there! Josh, Matt, Andy, come up close so I can talk to you. Where's Jesse?"

"Papa! Papa! I'm…here!" It was Jesse's voice, panting with exhaustion. He had barely kept up with the fleeing wagon, the dogs racing with him.

"Whoa, Ben and Lady!" Despite the danger, Hugh brought the team to a halt, and Jesse joined the other boys in a huddle behind the front seat. Hugh urged the team forward again at a trot. "Boys, we're in dire straits. All creation saw me kill Duncan, and the Earl will surely think I poisoned Pegasus to fix the race, and murdered his man when he found out. His men will shortly be after us. We've got to think of something to delay or stop them."

Jesse, still panting for breath, spoke up. "Papa, I've been needing to tell you…that Mr. McGruder…and Mr. Campbell…were whisperin' about you…and about poisoning Pegasus… before the race."

Hugh stared at Jesse, understanding dawning on his face. "Tell me exactly what they said, Jesse."

Jesse repeated the exact exchange of words.

Hugh nodded. "Thanks, Jesse. It's my fault. I should have had a round-the-clock guard on Pegasus. McGruder got to him somehow. Now, even if...even when the Earl finds out who did it, he'll want to blame someone other than his son. That'll most likely be me."

Sarah laid a hand on Hugh's arm. "Surely, there couldn't be a price on your head so soon!"

"There is if they think I fixed the race and murdered Duncan!"

"But Duncan's death was accidental. Anyone could see that. After all, there are laws in Scotland."

Hugh shook his head. "Laws, yes. But Pegasus was favored to win. Even if I could get a fair trial, people would not soon forget the money they lost betting on Pegasus." He twisted backward on the seat. "You children keep a lookout behind us. It won't take long for the Earl's men to saddle up and follow."

Sarah moaned. "But where will we go, Hugh?"

Jane, holding on for dear life to keep from bouncing out of the rear of the wagon, said, "Let's go to America for a fresh start, Papa!"

The team seemed to feel the urgency and tried to break into a canter. Hugh strained to hold them back. Once they were back at a smooth, fast trot, he grabbed his pistol with one hand.

"Sarah, take the reins. I have to make sure I have powder and ball. You boys, listen to me. The men who'll come after us won't bother to take us captive. They'll kill us on the spot. I hate to shed blood unless I have to, but in this case, we have no choice. It's kill or be killed. You understand?"

He heard a chorus of "Yes, Papa!"

Hugh began scouting the sides of the road, and seeming to find what he was looking for, he halted the team. He leapt from the wagon. "Matt, hand me that coiled rope in the back corner. Boys, all of you, get down. Sarah, drive the wagon behind that thicket of trees over there on the left."

The wagon rattled slowly forward, while the father and his sons prepared for battle. Followed by Matt, Andy, Josh, Jesse, and the three dogs, Hugh backtracked a short distance along the road to a place where sturdy oak trees stood on each side. He quickly tied one end of the rope to the tree on his side, high enough to clear a horse and saddle, but intended to hit the rider at about chest level. He made two more passes around the trunk, and then tossed the rope coil across the road. "Andy! Matt! Get over there, but see that you're out a'sight. Make two passes around that tree at the same height with the other end of the rope. When the riders come in sight, get ready. When I say 'Now!' pull the rope tight. Both of you hold onto it. Josh, back me up over here."

Jesse crouched next to his father, the dogs beside him, their heavily muscled bodies tense and ready. He patted their heads. "Samson, Ike, Pete, hold now." They panted only from time to time, nearly recovered from the run. They all kept their eyes fixed on the road.

The ground trembled. Dust clouded the air. A horseman was hurtling toward them. He held a pistol in his hand, and fired as soon as he had Hugh clearly in sight. The bullet whistled past his ear.

"Damn! Now!"

The boys and their father pulled the rope tight. The rider collided with it, was swept off his horse, and landed with a thud.

Jesse aimed his pistol and killed the man with one shot. To be certain, he cried, "Get 'im!" The three dogs mauled the body.

Two more riders appeared, with pistols aimed at Hugh as soon as they rounded the corner. The second rider tried to stop in time, but the third rider slammed into his horse, throwing both men to the ground. The boys knifed them, their weapons finding vital organs. The men died in the dirt, emitting gurgling sounds.

Hugh lost no time. "Good job, boys. Now we need to move fast. Get those bodies off the road and haul them down to the river.

"Girls, Sarah, sweep the dust over the blood and tracks on the road." He untied and recoiled the rope.

Jesse's lead dog, his muzzle still red with gore, silently watched his master for approval.

His master obliged. "Watch 'em up, Samson, Pete, Ike." The three dogs rose in unison to face Jesse.

The simple command startled Hugh. "By God, Jesse, how do you get them to do that?"

Matt stared at his brother, while Andy and Josh began dragging the corpses toward the river. "I sure don't want to ever make you mad!"

Sarah, in shock from the violence, joined her three daughters to cut branches from the bushes and sweep the road of all evidence of the slaughter.

Hugh issued another command. "Andy, Josh, weigh those bodies down with rocks and sink them. Matt, lead their horses down to the river— upstream from the bodies. They'll want a drink. See if the three of them will follow the one you lead. Unsaddle them, hide the saddles, bridles and their other things in the bushes, and turn them loose. They'll probably head back toward their stables. It might take a while for the next batch of pursuers to find them."

Hugh gave Jesse a tender embrace. "I'm so sorry you had to shed blood at such a young age." He could see that the whole family, even the other boys, was surprised and perhaps a bit intimidated by Jesse's quickness and coolness.

Once they had finished the grisly and necessary work, they piled into the wagon and headed home. Hugh turned to Sarah. "How can a twelve-year-old boy kill like that?"

Sarah looked coolly into Hugh's eyes. "His Highland blood and his raising, I expect. But he must be taught: 'Thou shalt not kill.' That's Exodus 20:13."

Jesse, sitting behind her, quoted, "'If any harm follows, then thou shalt give life for life, eye for eye, tooth for tooth, hand for hand, foot for foot.' That's Exodus 21:23-24."

"I'll be damned, Sarah. Where does he get that?"

"You will be damned, darling, if you keep speakin' like that. Hugh, you know Jesse reads his scriptures every night."

"Scriptures or no scriptures, McAlesters are warriors and descendants of William Wallace."

The team maintained a steady trot.

"You children be quiet for a while and let me think. Sarah, we've got no other choice. Jane, you're right. We're going to America. Last week, I heard Douglas McBride and Samuel Stuart talking about a ship tied up in Greenock. They said it was bound for America, leaving in ten days or so. If it hasn't left yet, we'll aim to board it.

"I know we haven't thought everything out, Sarah, but me and the boys will surely hang if we stay here, and Lord knows what they'll do to you and the girls."

The mood shifted at once. Rebekah and Mary began to sniffle and the boys, all except Jesse, looked frightened.

"I'll protect you!" Jesse put the dogs on full alert as they trotted alongside. They cocked their heads, looking as if they understood the conversation.

They rounded a corner and the McAlester farm came in sight. Hugh kept the horses at a ground-eating trot until they passed through the front gateway. "We've got to be out of here quickly or we're dead or worse. Sarah, pack what we can carry and get the girls to help you. I'll help the boys with the horses. Matt, Andy, get the two stallions. Josh, get the mares ready for travel. Jesse, get all the saddles, bridles, blankets, reins, and ropes to this wagon, and anything else we can carry to the other one. Get one of the other boys to harness and hitch the spare team to it."

Sarah planted her fists on her hips. "Hugh McAlester, if you think I'm going halfway around the world without my precious things, then I'll just stay right here."

Silence all around as the children turned to see their father's response.

"Everybody, you heard your mother. Let's be quick, but pack whatever your mother wants to bring."

Sarah nodded, relieved. She and the children hurried to the house.

Matthew, Andrew, and Joshua approached the barn. Matt spoke up. "Papa, we're through helping Mama."

"All right boys, let's get those horses."

"Matt, tie Shadow to one of the wagons."

"Andrew, make sure you keep those stallions separated."

"Papa, I'll control the stallions, but we need to get them to the ship now!"

"Josh, tie Stormy off to the side of the wagon."

"Papa, are we still going to Greenock?"

"Yes, son."

Sarah slid a small chest among the other things in the second wagon. "Hugh, it seems you already have a plan."

"Boys, girls, heed this—you always have to think ahead."

Hugh handed Matthew the rope attached to Comet's halter and cautioned him. "Matt, be vigilant. Comet's stronger than you think."

The caravan got underway.

Stormy, Comet's dam, struggled against Josh, who was holding her away from her colt. "Be careful, son. Don't let Stormy get away from you!"

"Hugh, the mare wants to be close to her colt. We're going to have the only colt in America sired by Pegasus."

"Let's hope he can fly as high."

"Mama, could Pegasus really fly?"

"As close as anything on this earth, Mary."

Stormy gently nuzzled Comet, who, reassured, nickered softly to his dam and stopped struggling.

After traveling several miles, Jesse suddenly shouted and pointed. "Look Papa! Look over there!"

A tall column of smoke rose in the sky behind them. Their home was going up in flames. "Oh, Hugh! There's no returning ever again!"

"Don't worry, Sarah. We'll be all right. I've got enough money for the voyage. I'll have to think of something to earn some more for the food and fodder." He hugged her close, imagining the scene of pillage and wanton destruction they had left behind.

Sarah took comfort in her small chest, safe in the second wagon.

CHAPTER THREE
Gibraltar

The McAlester wagons rounded the shoulder of the last hill and the family saw the afternoon sun sparkling on the bay that stretched before them. Hugh heaved a sigh of relief. Sure enough, the ship lay along-side the dock, her name, *GIBRALTAR*, painted in large block letters on her prow. "I hope this is the one bound for America, but no matter where it's going, we'll be on board."

The dockside bustled with activity. Hoists on the ship, fore and aft, lifted bales of cotton onto freight wagons.

"Look, Papa, a young man is in charge." Jane shaded her eyes as the wagon drew nearer the dock.

Rebekah, watching as her older sister leaned forward to get a better look at the young officer, asked with a sly grin, "Jane, is it love at first sight?"

Jane looked away with a sharp intake of breath.

Hugh's head swiveled as he scanned the wagons and wagon masters, especially those leaving after unloading their wares. The wagon that had just loaded bales of cotton drew his eye. One of the horses seemed more suitable for the rendering factory than for heavy work. Hugh could count every rib, and the poor beast's hipbones threatened to break through the hide. Its teammate looked like a pony. Hugh could picture the little mare pulling a cartload of children.

She struggled valiantly to help her emaciated partner haul the heavy wagon up the hill. Hugh steered his wagon closer to the departing one, hopped down, and hailed the driver.

"Sir, I'm noticing ye have difficulty with your team. Would you consider buying my two wagons and teams for 300 gold sovereigns? The wagons are solid and the teams highly trained. If treated well, they'll earn that amount and more for you in a few months."

The driver squinted knowingly at Hugh, his eyes mere slits. "Sir, you seem to be in a hurry to board that ship. How about two hundred gold sovereigns?"

"You know even one wagon and team is worth what I'm asking for both. I ask two hundred and fifty gold sovereigns."

"Two hundred and twenty-five."

"Two hundred and thirty."

"Oh, all right. Two hundred and thirty it is." The driver pulled a leather satchel from underneath his seat, counted out the coins and handed them to Hugh.

Hugh quickly stowed them in a large leather pouch, "I thank you, sir! Now as I said, treat my horses right and they'll make your fortune."

Meanwhile, Matt, now leading Comet by the halter, approached the ship with Hugh trotting to catch up and the rest of the family trailing behind. They arrived at shipside. Hugh had seen it at a distance and now estimated the four-masted freighter to be some 135 feet long, 30 feet wide and 24 feet deep. She would have a hold, a middle deck and an upper deck—surely plenty of room to accommodate his two stallions, two mares, and a tiny colt, not to mention nine humans.

The handsome young officer whom Jane had earlier noticed was supervising the loading. As they arrived, he shouted, "You men quit your loafing! Get the rest of this freight loaded. We need to weigh anchor and sail."

Hugh stepped in front of him and held out his hand. "Sir, I'm Hugh McAlester. This is my family and we need passage on your ship. Is it true you're bound for New Orleans in America?"

Startled at the sudden intrusion, the young officer accepted Hugh's hand. "I'm Lieutenant John Allen. Yes, sir, we're bound for America." His eyes slipped past the man whose hand he was shaking. Jane McAlester stood there, the breeze lightly lifting her blond hair, her blue eyes focused on him. She smiled and he stood there wordless. He watched, entranced, as she ducked her head and blushed—embarrassed, no doubt, to be caught smiling at a stranger.

Hugh's next question brought his attention back to business. "Lieutenant, do you have room on your ship for my family and horses?"

"I-I...yes, sir, Mr. McAlester." He seemed to be considering where he could house the family and what he would leave behind to accommodate McAlester's possessions and horses, wanting to please him and his lovely daughter.

Hugh was insistent, seeing the Lieutenant's hesitation. "Sir, is the Captain available?"

"I'm sorry, Mr. McAlester, but the Captain is indisposed."

"When might I meet him, then?"

"I'm not sure, sir, but I am duly authorized by the ship's owner to make all decisions in his absence."

"Lieutenant, then I would like to book passage on your ship for my family, horses, and our possessions, which can be found in those two wagons."

One of the sailors struggling with a heavy load passed Hugh mumbling, loud enough that he heard the words, "Damned Captain has been drunk for a week!"

Hugh turned in surprise to question the man, but he was already climbing the gangplank.

Lieutenant Allen had already answered Hugh's request in the affirmative, and now asked a question of his own. "Sir, do you want us to load the horses?"

"My boys and I can manage my horses; if you'll have your men unload the wagons."

"How do you propose to get them aboard, Mr. McAlester?"

"Why, walking them up the gangplank to the ship, of course."

The Lieutenant shook his head. "I'm sorry, but as you see, we have no loading ramps for horses in this small port. That gangplank is too narrow and will not withstand the weight of a full-grown horse. We'll have to winch them aboard."

Hugh looked incredulous. "I'm not comfortable with my horses hanging in air."

"I've had plenty of experience with winching horses aboard a ship and I promise they will be safe."

Impressed with the young officer's knowledge and expertise, Hugh asked, "How will my horses be stabled on board?"

"Four crates. They're six by eight feet, sir. We've transported fine horses before. Each crate or box stall has two windows in line with a horse's head, so it can see out the sides. The crates are padded inside, outfitted with mangers with their frames padded, too. We also pad and wrap the horses' knees and hocks for their safety during rough seas. The floors of the boxes are crisscrossed with leather strips to prevent slipping. And we do have some straw left over from the last horse shipment to pad the floors."

"Whew!" Hugh mopped his forehead with his handkerchief. "Ye really know what you're talking about. All right. Let's get our two stallions and two mares winched on board. Matt, lead Comet up the gangplank once Stormy is up there."

"Yes, Papa."

The Lieutenant couldn't help but gaze at Jane, his heart pounding. He cleared his throat. "You men on the ground here! Get those wagons unloaded and everything stowed in the cargo hold."

Jane gave Lieutenant Allen a furtive glance, then turned toward her family. She thought, *He's over six feet tall or more, beautiful blue eyes and coal black wavy hair—he definitely shows promise.*

Hugh asked, "Do you have enough to feed nine extra people for a long voyage?"

"We're sailing to Liverpool from here, sir. With the funds your fare supplies, I will purchase food there."

An hour passed, and all goods, horses and passengers were aboard and the Lieutenant was opening his mouth to order the sailors to cast off the lines fore and aft when he spied a small group of well-armed men on horseback riding down the hill toward the ship.

"Who in tarnation are they, Mr. McAlester? They look hostile."

"They are. I've been accused of a murder I didn't commit. My house, barn, and all my property they didn't steal, have been burned down by those men. They're here to kill us or worse, sir."

The Lieutenant took a step back, sized up Hugh from head to toe, and then met Jane's eyes. Her face was a mask of pleading. "Your lot surely doesn't look like a band of murderers to me!"

By now, the Earl's men had ridden up to the dock. From the group, a small, boisterous man, looking much like a bantam rooster, dismounted and approached the ship.

"We're here to arrest the murderer, Hugh McAlester!"

Jane screamed, "No! He's no murderer!"

Lieutenant Allen puffed calmly on his pipe and stared down at the party of men. One of the group, a large man, started to dismount but paused and stared at the deck, wide-eyed with fright, seeing the Lieutenant's lit pipe hovering over the touchhole of a cannon.

Allen gave an order. "Men, train this cannon on that bunch of men below there."

Two sailors swiveled the cannon and cranked its muzzle so that it pointed downward.

"I'm in complete command of this ship, gentlemen," said the Lieutenant with a touch of sarcasm, "and the cannon here is loaded with grapeshot. Leave now or I'll blow the lot of you to hell and back."

"I told you we should have come here first," whimpered the smaller man.

"I'll pluck you like the chicken you are!" The larger man thumped the smaller one on the head, got firm in his saddle and wheeled his horse. "Let's get out of here!" Without waiting for the bantam rooster to remount, he led the pack in a fast getaway.

Hugh watched the Earl's men spur their horses up the hill, with the little man trailing behind but gaining fast. He turned to Lieutenant Allen. "Sir, America is a big and wild country and could sure use good men like you." He lit his own pipe and began puffing as if nothing had happened.

"Is that a formal invitation, Mr. McAlester?"

Laughing, Allen turned to the waiting sailors. "Men, cast off the lines fore and aft and hoist the sails."

In minutes, the *Gibraltar* began to pull slowly away from the dock.

Jesse, watching from the bow of the ship as she came about, whistled shrilly. In response, Samson, Pete, and Ike leaped off the dock and swam toward the ship.

Jesse, waving a small piece of dried liver, yelled, "Faster, boys!" and the dogs doubled their efforts, furiously swimming toward Jesse.

Mary, the youngest daughter, pointed toward the dogs struggling in the bay. "Look, Papa! Jesse's dogs are coming too!"

Hugh looked troubled and scratched his head. "Lieutenant?"

Allen shouted at the deck hands who had just coiled the ropes. "Lower one of the skiffs on the starboard side and pick up those dogs. Look lively now!"

Fortunately, the wind had not yet caught in the sails, so the ship continued drifting slowly seaward. The two deck hands lowered the skiff and two oarsmen rowed vigorously and soon met the swimming dogs. One after the other, the dogs placed their forepaws on the side of the boat and an oarsman pulled them into the skiff. Once all three were aboard the skiff, it returned shipside and was hauled up to the deck. Samson, Pete, and Ike jumped out of the skiff, trotted to Hugh and vigorously shook off the salty bay water, soaking him, and putting out his pipe.

Once they had cleared the harbor, Lieutenant Allen assembled the crew and the new passengers and made introductions all around. No one mentioned the Captain.

After the formalities, the Lieutenant issued a command: "Man your stations." He then turned toward Hugh, smiling at Jane, "I would love for you and your family to join me in the dining room tonight for dinner. Say about six o'clock?"

Hugh, smiling, replied, "We'd be delighted, sir."

Jesse's three terriers took a half step forward and stared intently at the Lieutenant, drawing his attention. The Lieutenant laughed. "I'll make sure you boys have something special to eat." Samson licked his chops as if he understood.

Led by the second mate, the family descended the stairway to their cabins on the second deck. Rebekah teased her sister. "Jane's got a beau!"

Jane blushed and ducked inside the nearest cabin.

Captain William Langley bolted upright in his bed and asked, as his fingers searched furiously through his coat pockets, "Where's me gold sovereigns?" He tugged at his coat pockets and discovered that the bottoms were slashed open. "Blimey! I've been robbed!" His mind groped unsuccessfully for any memory of the theft. "What was the name of the last pub?"

Lieutenant Allen gently knocked on the door and called, "Captain, Captain, are you awake?"

"Stop the bloody banging and come in."

Allen slowly opened the door just as Captain Langley drained the bit of rum in the last bottle and threw it against the wall. The Lieutenant was experienced at dodging bottles and broken glass.

"Sir, will you be joining us for dinner?"

The Captain began coughing and slowly stood up. "Johnny, how long have I been in me cabin?"

"Sir, we brought you in two days ago."

"Did I have any coin on me?"

"I'm sorry, Captain, we found you passed out on the dock. I was informed by the fishmonger that two men dumped you there."

"I'll be damned, Johnny, a poor old soul can't even have a drink without being robbed."

"Captain, we've taken on nine passengers. Very decent people: Hugh McAlester, his wife Sarah and his seven children."

"What fare did you get?"

"Captain, I was waiting for you to decide."

"Well, it shouldn't be hard to figure out the fare for nine people."

"Captain, they have five horses and two loads of household goods. They'll be taking on hay and grain in Liverpool, sir."

"Good heavens, man, where are we supposed to put the slaves when we pick them up in Jamaica?"

"Sir, I was hoping we could make straight for New Orleans and unload the McAlesters and their property."

"Lieutenant Allen, why in God's name would I ever do that?"

"Captain, you can have my share of the profit from the Jamaica ventures if we go to New Orleans first. You can draw on the account when we get to New Orleans."

"I may be drunk, but I'm certainly no fool. What's her name?"

"Captain, it's true there is a lady in question. However, I've taken a liking to her father, Hugh McAlester. He has asked me to join his family in America."

The Captain shook his head and cast his eyes downward. "Is that right? I suppose you've told him of your involvement in the slave trade."

"No, sir, Captain. I was hoping to get a fresh start in America and be done with that dirty business."

"That dirty business, as you call it, has put food on the table and provided handsomely for you."

"Yes, sir, Captain, but if it's all the same to you, I've made up my mind to quit the trade."

"And just how am I going to explain this to the crew? You are fully aware that they are getting a share of the profits from the sale of the Africans when we get to New Orleans."

"I think we can come to an agreement in this matter." Allen handed the Captain a purse full of gold sovereigns.

The Captain greedily pawed through the coins, biting one to make sure it was genuine. "Johnny, this is not enough for the crew's share."

"When you collect the fare from Mr. McAlester, it should be enough to square things with the crew."

"What if this Mr. McAlester refuses to deal on the square with me?"

"McAlester is an honorable man. I'm sure he'll be more than willing to meet your price for the fare."

The Captain's face softened. "That's my Johnny! Always thinking." He shifted the gold coins from one hand to the other. "I'm going to miss you, my boy. There's never been another like you."

"Captain, may we consider this matter settled?"

"I've got to think this through. I'll need another bottle to help me with my consideration."

"Sir, I've taken the liberty to restock your supply while you were sleeping."

"Good lad. Dinner at six?"

The Lieutenant saluted sharply. "Yes, sir, Captain. Will that be all?"

Allen closed the door and thought about the Captain's dishonorable discharge report. *Captain William Langley was charged with willful neglect of duties, destruction of British Navy property, and endangerment of his crew. The findings are as follows: Captain Langley left his post as commander of the HMS* Royalty *in order to consume alcoholic beverages for several hours; as a result of his drunken state and negligent conduct, the ship ran aground in the West Indies while under Captain Langley's command. Captain Langley and certain members of his crew, including Lieutenant John Allen, were interviewed regarding this incident. Thereafter, Captain William Langley was found guilty of willful neglect of duties, destruction of British Navy property, and endangerment of his crew and accordingly is hereby dishonorably discharged from the British Navy.*

He walked briskly from the Captain's cabin into the depths of the ship. Hugh McAlester was busy feeding the horses.

"Mr. McAlester, I trust that your accommodations are agreeable?"

Hugh set down the bucket of oats at his feet. "Lieutenant, I want to thank you for allowing my family and stock to come aboard on such short notice."

"It's my pleasure," Allen replied, smiling as he thought of Hugh's lovely daughter.

"Let me have your hand in friendship, Lieutenant. I only hope someday that I can return your kindness to my family."

"Mr. McAlester, I always try to do my duty."

"You have gone well beyond your duty, Lieutenant. Please call me Hugh."

"Hugh, I've had the opportunity to speak with the Captain and he will join us for dinner this evening."

The dining room was a narrow space with a long table in the center and benches against the wooden bulkheads. The galley, somewhere nearby, emitted savory aromas. The meal was simple: a hearty mutton stew with potatoes and other root vegetables, and fresh-baked bread. A sailor acting as waiter served fresh water to everyone, and those men who wanted to imbibe were served beer.

The Captain never arrived at dinner. Despite his absence, the conversation was lively, and the ten diners exchanged much vital information. Hugh volunteered to tell the family's history, how heavy English taxation had forced them to leave the Highlands and settle near Ayr. He also told the story of Pegasus and the tragedy at the Scottish Gold Cup Race at noon that very day.

Next, he told of their flight and the near-miraculous haven of the ship. Hugh noted the attraction between Jane and the Lieutenant.

"Lieutenant, please tell us about your background."

Allen stared at his plate for a moment and then spoke. "I was raised by a single woman in the slums of Renfrewshire, Paisley, Scotland. I was a street urchin until the age of ten, begging for food and for a mite to help me mother. Captain Langley came across me—I had wandered from Paisley to Glasgow and was begging on the shores of the River Clyde. The Cabot Merchant Ship and Freight Company out of London had just hired Captain Langley and he was out scouting for a crew. He needed a cabin boy, and, for some reason, he bet on me. He's been my father ever since."

"Then you've been with him for years! What a pity we can't meet him tonight."

"Yes, Mrs. McAlester. It truly is a pity." The Lieutenant stared into the distance, looking genuinely troubled.

"So what happened then?"

"It took years, but I rose from cabin boy to sailor, to first mate, then Lieutenant."

"Tell us more about Captain Langley."

Lieutenant Allen blushed, clearly reluctant to reveal the truth about his adoptive father.

He bowed his head for a moment, and then began, "Captain Langley left the British Navy to pursue a career in civilian life. The Captain had been hauling freight under the direction of the Cabot Merchant Ship Company ever since. Since it's getting late, I will stop now."

The congenial dinner guests dispersed after the meal, and Allen, duty bound, went to the Captain's cabin to check on him, fearing the worst. He knocked and received no reply. To his sorrow, he found the Captain passed out on the floor with several empty bottles scattered around him. He dragged him to his berth, lifted him upon it, covered him with a blanket, and walked out.

Winds were favorable, and on the second day, they docked in Liverpool. Lieutenant Allen busied himself with buying necessary supplies for the long voyage across the Atlantic, and added farming implements, shoes, boots, clothes, hats, and most important of all, guns, ball and powder for the settlers of America. He had informed Hugh that the trip to New Orleans would probably take seven to eight weeks.

With the money he had earned from the sale of the two wagons and four draft horses, Hugh was able to purchase twenty bales of hay and ten bushels of oats, which he calculated would last the length of the voyage. Next to the four boxes occupied by the horses, the Lieutenant added another box in the *Gibraltar* main hold to house and secure the feed from vermin and any other animals lurking aboard. They left Liverpool harbor in fair weather and with following winds.

The Lieutenant stood hatless in the bow of the *Gibraltar*, the wind hard against his face and body, tossing his black hair. He considered the problem of the Africans. Yes, the slavers in Jamaica were expecting the *Gibraltar* to dock there in about six weeks' time, but the Cabot Company had no inkling that the *Gibraltar* was involved in "that dirty business," since the trade in cotton and other raw materials from America was making a healthy profit for the firm.

So far, Captain Langley and he had managed to get away with it.

But John's eyes had been opened. He no longer set greater value on clandestine monetary gain than on human lives. During the two-week stay at the port of Greenock, he had traded in Ayr, selling and buying, and had passed by a pub where a group was singing. He had paused to listen. He recognized their song as John Newton's "Amazing Grace," a tune he had always found haunting. Its message invariably aroused pangs of conscience now that he, like Newton before his conversion, was involved in human trafficking. When the song was finished, two of the singers began to mingle with the crowd and hand out pamphlets.

Turning to a bystander, he asked, "Who are these people?"

"They're Quakers. Pacifists. Have a look at a pamphlet." He handed one to John. "You'll see. They're absolutely opposed to the slave trade. They're called abolitionists."

Just then, one of John's crew members from the *Gibraltar* began shouting and jeering at the Quaker group. "You bunch of lily-livers!" he yelled. "Trying to take away a man's good profits. Those blacks are no better than animals anyway." Two more crew members joined the first, and they began shoving the singers as well as insulting them.

John admired the self-control of the Quakers, but he couldn't allow these pacifists to be abused by his own shipmates. Using his most commanding voice, shouting above the crewmen's curses and insults, he issued a command.

"You men, stand down! These people have a right to their opinions. Let them be! That's an order!"

His crew members stared as if he were crazy, but they stopped harassing the Quakers.

John had a quick look at the pamphlet. Its message and the Quakers' calm demeanor in the midst of the near-riot convinced him of the rightness of their cause. There would be no more trading in human lives as long as he was aboard the *Gibraltar* or any other ship.

CHAPTER FOUR
Atlantic Crossing

The *Gibraltar* was well out in the Atlantic, the winds continuing favorably. The Captain, subconsciously feeling the rhythmic swells of deep ocean travel, awoke around dinner hour, pleased to find his liquor cabinet restocked. He knew, therefore, that the Liverpool stop was behind them and the ship was on the high seas. With wobbly legs and fortified with rum, he walked out on the main deck, intending to descend to the middle deck and then to the hold to see how many slaves the ship could carry when they stopped in Jamaica. He had no intention of abandoning his profitable scheme or returning Allen's money.

As he approached the stairway to the hold, he heard a horse's snort. "I'll just have a look at these horses," he mumbled to himself. When he unlatched and lowered the rear panel of the box stall, the black stallion inside squealed and kicked his hind legs.

"I'll teach you not to kick me!" He grabbed a long gaff, normally used for hauling in large fish, and stabbed the stallion in the flank. The horse roared in pain, bleeding profusely.

Taking aim with his hind hooves, he kicked the Captain out of the stall. One hoof struck Langley on the forehead, the other full on the chest.

The second mate discovered Langley lying flat on his back, unmoving, and saw the stallion severely bleeding. He rushed to the dining room where Allen was at dinner with the McAlesters. He whispered the unfortunate news into the Lieutenant's ear.

Allen stood. "Excuse me, Mr. McAlester, uh, Hugh, but there seems to be an emergency I must attend to."

"Of course, Lieutenant. Is there some service I could render?"

"If I may have a moment of your time, there's a most urgent private matter. Could you follow me, sir?"

"Certainly. Do any of my boys need to assist us?"

"That won't be necessary." Allen's nearly panicked manner disturbed Hugh.

As the two approached the box stalls, the crew members were gathered around the prone body of the Captain.

"It's that evil horse that done it—killed our poor Captain."

Hugh was instantly fearful for the safety of his family, as well as his horses, which were his livelihood.

The crewman kneeling by the Captain stood and faced him. "Dead as a doornail. Forehead caved in. Chest kicked in, too. Captain got in a good strike against that devil horse though. Should've stabbed him through the heart!"

Hugh, in shock, moved to the stallion's side and saw the gash in his flank, still bleeding. "The Captain must have stabbed him first. The horse wouldn't attack for no reason!" He heard a rumble of muttering from the crew.

The Lieutenant moved decisively toward the men. "You fellows disperse. Go to your bunks. Mr. McAlester and I will handle this."

A fierce-looking crew member growled, "Lieutenant, what about our money? Who is going to pay us now that poor Captain Langley's dead?"

Allen took another step toward the men, some of whom backed up a little. "Men, I have always dealt with you fairly and I promise that you will get everything coming to you," He laid one hand lightly on his pistol.

Not quite certain of his meaning, the crew began whispering among themselves. The second mate spoke up. "Well, Lieutenant, you've always been on the square with us before, so I expect we have no choice but to trust you now." He led the way toward the forecastle, the crew's quarters, and the men began to follow him.

Allen and Hugh carried the Captain back into his cabin, set it to rights, and laid Langley's body out on his bunk, his head on a pillow, hands crossed on his breast.

Then Hugh returned to the cargo hold and doctored the gash in the stallion's flank, knowing it would heal, but that the wound's site would be marked with a patch of white hair, marring the horse's sleek black coat.

That night, Jesse set the dogs on high alert, leaving them as guards outside the McAlester cabin doors. There were no further disturbances during those dark hours.

The next day, all the crew members passed through the cabin to see their Captain lying in state. Then one of the crewmen sewed the body into a canvas bag, which was carried to the starboard railing and weighted down.

All crew members and the McAlester family gathered for as much of a burial ceremony as they could muster. Hugh acted as minister, reading appropriate passages from the Bible, such as Isaiah 40:31:

But they that hope in the Lord Shall renew their strength.
They shall rise with wings as eagles,
They shall run, and not be weary,
They shall walk, and not faint.

Then, as he led the crew in the Lord's Prayer, they tipped a plank and the body slipped into the sea and sank out of sight with barely a ripple.

In a brief meeting with the crew, Lieutenant Allen agreed to pay the crew for their involvement in the slave trade, and then charted a course heading directly for New Orleans.

Rebekah, one of Jesse's older sisters, loved to feed the horses. Late one afternoon, she thought she was alone in the stables with her beloved mares, the colt Comet, and the two stallions. She had begun doling out oats for all four adult horses when she heard a slight rustle in the straw behind her, a sound unlike any horse would make. Before she could move, powerful arms seized her and jerked her around. One of the sailors, one she had seen leering at her before, lifted her body and crushed his lips against hers, stifling her cries. He punched her in the face, threw her to the floor in the corner of the box stall, and began loosening his britches and tearing at her clothes, ripping off her skirt and petticoat.

Recovering from being temporarily stunned, she raised herself on her elbow and screamed, *"Help! Help! Someone, please!"*

Jesse was getting a breath of fresh air, the dogs with him. When he heard the scream, he instantly recognized Rebekah's voice coming from the horses' stalls and ran there, arriving just in time to prevent the sailor from raping his sister.

Jesse immediately commanded the dogs, "Sic 'im!"

Rebekah grabbed her torn clothing and ran into Jesse's arms, as the three dogs knocked the sailor down and quickly turned him into a bloody mass of mangled flesh. Rebekah, hysterical, clung to her brother. After she was calmed by Jesse's presence, he dragged the bloody body outside the box and covered it with straw from the stall, similarly covering the blood on the stall floor. The mare was pressing her body against the side of the box away from the site of the mayhem and was trembling. He held the milt for the frightened horse to smell and soon she stopped shaking.

Jesse led Rebekah to their mother's cabin, where she ran into Sarah's arms, sobbing. "Mama, one of the sailors tried to assault Rebekah, but the boys and I stopped him."

Sarah held and stroked her daughter. "Dear Rebekah, this should have never happened to you!" She washed Rebekah's face, gently dabbing her cut and swollen lips.

Hugh, alerted to the assault, fetched the Lieutenant, who assembled all hands on deck and revealed what had happened. With Jesse by her side, Rebekah consented to show her battered and bloody face. Allen warned the men about the repercussions of any further violence to the McAlesters. Most of the men hung their heads in shame at the attack, but a few were furious that their mate was dead at McAlester hands.

"Same as the Captain," Hugh heard one man say. "These people are a jinx and a plague on our ship."

A majority of the crew took charge of the body, held their own version of a brief ceremony, and committed their comrade to the sea.

Another week of tension followed, but Samson, Pete, and Ike patrolled the corridor nightly, and no sailor dared come near the McAlester cabins.

At last, one day, the sea turned the color of mud, and the Lieutenant informed Hugh that they were in the outflow from the mighty Mississippi River. Soon they came in sight of New Orleans harbor, and everyone could see the jumble of ships' spars from a distance. Under Allen's command, they docked successfully.

CHAPTER FIVE
New Orleans

After instructing the second mate to unload the ship and to take extra care with the McAlesters, their horses, and belongings, Allen went to the office of the New Orleans representative of the Cabot Merchant Shipping and Freight Company. He reported the deaths of the Captain and the crew member, as well as his intention that the ship be returned immediately to the Cabot Company in London. He asked that the Cabot representative pay off the crew. When the representative raised his eyebrows, Allen pulled out an official-looking document signed by Captain Langley and witnessed by himself and the second mate as Langley's last will and testament. The will gave the entirety of the Captain's wages to the crew. As a final action, Allen tendered his immediate resignation. He ceded his official rank of first mate to the second mate, recommending him as having been steady, resourceful, and knowledgeable during the voyage.

Meanwhile, the McAlesters had temporarily housed their horses at a clean and well-kept stable near the port, and paid the second mate to watch over their belongings until they returned. Thrilled to be on solid ground, they began to explore New Orleans on unsteady legs.

They toured the French Quarter where a new church, to be dedicated to St. Louis, was under construction. They bought pralines from vendors in the French Open Market and munched them as they inspected stalls filled with colorful wares. Since they moved as a family group, it did not take long for Allen to find them.

"Let's get some lemonade under the awning over there." He pointed at an outdoor refreshment stand with long tables and benches to one side of the market. When the family was happily sipping lemonade, Allen handed Hugh the leather purse containing the gold sovereigns he had paid for the sea passage for the McAlester clan.

"I found this, Hugh, and I believe it belongs to you."

Suddenly, Sarah remembered to count heads. "Oh, no! One is missing!"

Mary said, "Mama, it's Jesse."

The McAlesters immediately searched for Jesse. They heard a loud roar and, following the noise, they came upon a mob scene.

Hugh saw people screaming and jeering with fists pumping and knew it was a fight.

Various men shouted, "Kill 'em!" "Sic 'em!" "Grab his throat!" Hearing the shouts, Hugh realized a dogfight was in progress. Then he heard a voice that chilled him to the bone.

"Samson!"

Hugh pushed and shoved his way through the crowd for a better view and finally found Jesse, along with Ike and Pete. Samson was otherwise detained.

Hugh took Jesse by the collar. "By God, Jesse, you go from one damn fight to another with those dogs."

Jesse gulped, looking ashamed. "I'm sorry, Papa."

Samson lay on his back with a giant beast of a dog on top of him. The crowd pressed closer, screaming, "Twenty gold dollars on Ripper!" "Twenty-five on Ripper!" Money was piling up fast for the big cur.

A vile man dressed like a peacock, eyes bulging, belly full of liquor, exhorted, "Kill 'im, Ripper, my boy!"

Although even a keen observer might think this was the end of poor Samson, the dog had a death grip known as the "Stifle Hold" on Ripper, who started to whine, to the puzzlement of the crowd.

Large piles of scrip and gold dollar coins lay scattered on the ground in front of a burly, red-faced man, who seemed to be in charge of the betting.

Hugh, clearly exasperated with what he was seeing, gave Jesse an order. "I want you to stop this right now!"

Before Jesse could reply, the Peacock began screaming hysterically at the sight of Samson's final assault on Ripper. He yelled at Jesse, "Let 'im go, or by God I'm going to kill your dog."

The crowd, hoping for more violence, pushed in closer to view the scene.

But how to get Samson to let go of Ripper?

"Snuff," someone yelled, "Give the brute a pinch of snuff and when he sneezes, he'll let go."

Ripper began crying piteously and his owner pulled out a pistol, taking aim at Samson's head.

Jesse, watching the Peacock, said, "Sic 'im, boys!"

Immediately, Ike and Pete lunged for the arm and torso of the dandy, and the pistol discharged harmlessly into the air.

Samson finally let go of his foe, and Ripper and the crowd beat a swift retreat. The burly man quickly gathered the winnings, taking a share for himself, and ran as quickly as his heavy body could, knowing that the law would soon arrive at the scene.

As Jesse gathered his winnings, Hugh admonished him for leaving the family and engaging in a dogfight. After all, they could ill afford to have a member of the family arrested.

"Jesse, you must stay with us for our protection and the safety of the public. And another thing—how did you come to bet on that fight?"

Jesse realized that Hugh was softening. "Papa, I didn't like that big ole cur bullying Samson."

"Jesse, how in God's name do your damn devil dogs know how to fight like that? Please, I'm asking you for your family's sake to stay by our sides and don't look for trouble."

Before Jesse could respond, a stranger asked, "Say boy, what kind of dog is that?"

Samson looked at the man quizzically. "Oh, he's nothing special. Back in Scotland, we call 'em Blue Paul Terriers."

Their name was derived from the famous pirate John Paul Jones. Born John Paul, he added the surname Jones to elude local authorities. He brought the dogs from abroad and bred them when he visited his native town of Kirkcudbright in the year 1770. At forty pounds and nineteen inches tall, these majestic animals had a velvety coat and were powerfully built. Their large heads bore small ears that were usually cropped and stood alert at all times. Both forelegs and hind legs were stout. Gypsies in Scotland kept the dogs, which they fought to the death for sport and their own entertainment.

"He's a fighting rascal and looks game to the core." The stranger bent down to examine Samson's bleeding body. "How much would you take for 'im?"

Hugh, clearly astonished, looked intently at Jesse.

Jesse scrunched up his face, "Mister, I couldn't part with him for any amount of money."

"How's about two hundred gold dollars for 'im?"

"Mister, I could not let him go for any amount under three hundred."

"Done." The stranger counted out three hundred gold dollars and one by one handed them to Jesse.

Hugh gasped, "Jesse, what are you doing, selling your beloved pal?"

"Papa, I'm so sorry I got us into trouble and I just wanted to help the family. Please take all of the money to pay for the trip to Nashville."

"Jesse, this is...we can use the money, but I'm sad that you sold Samson."

"Don't worry, Papa." As Jesse whispered his goodbyes to Samson, the dog cocked his head as if he understood the words.

The next day, during preparations for the trip to Nashville, Jesse was very helpful, caring for the horses and ensuring they were being watered, fed oats, and curried down.

Hugh and all the McAlesters were eager to leave New Orleans. They had booked passage on a steamboat called the *Natchez*, with a nine-day trip to Memphis, then an additional five days to Nashville.

While the stock and goods were loaded onto the *Natchez*, suddenly Jesse appeared, arms waving wildly, with all three of his dogs following him, dashing for the steamboat's gangplank.

Hugh yelled, "How did you get Samson back?"

"Papa, I've sold him several times, but for some reason, he always comes back."

Hugh, clearly exasperated, shouted, "All you rascals, get on board!" which delighted the crowd watching the loading.

CHAPTER SIX
Natchez

As the *Natchez* departed, the McAlesters, John Allen, and the other passengers waved to the crowd gathered on shore to watch the steamboat start its journey to Memphis.

Jesse explored every nook and cranny of the steamboat. Below the deck, he opened a door slightly to peer inside, and saw a group of men playing cards in a smoky room.

A man with a goatee said, "Come on in, boy. You might learn something."

Jesse ventured in and watched the men, realizing they were playing poker and gambling, and observed the man with the goatee raking together his winnings. Jesse left the room but came back the next day and thereafter became a regular visitor in the poker room.

A few days after the steamboat's departure, Samson started barking loudly; within seconds, Ike and Pete joined in the raucous chorus. Jesse ran from the poker room to the deck, recognizing Samson's bark of distress.

On deck, a small young girl was climbing the railing to get a better view of the Mississippi River. In her struggles, her hat had blown off and fallen into the river. With no understanding of the depth of the river, nor its fast-moving current, she tried harder to climb the railing, hoping to retrieve her hat. She was on the verge of falling off of the steamboat when Jesse arrived.

He yelled, "Stop!" and rushed to the girl, pulling her from the railing to a secure place on the deck.

Hearing the commotion, some passengers had arrived to watch Jesse's heroism. Among the group were the girl's parents, who had been searching everywhere for her.

The mother rushed to the girl, embracing her fiercely, and said, "Oh, Eliza, my child, you are safe."

The girl's father said to Jesse, "Young man, you saved my daughter's life," and pumped Jesse's hand with great enthusiasm.

Jesse replied, "It wasn't me—it was my dogs," pointing to Samson and his pals who were panting and anxiously waiting for compliments, treats, or both. Having obtained Jesse's permission, Eliza's father bent down and praised the dogs and rubbed their small ears.

The rescue was the talk of the steamboat, and Samson, Pete, and Ike were welcomed everywhere on board, even in the dining area, becoming the official mascots of the *Natchez*.

The day after Eliza's rescue, Jesse received a formal dinner invitation from Eliza's parents, Arthur and Cynthia Billingsley; the invitation included Jesse and the entire McAlester clan.

After the McAlesters had taken their seats, the conversation began to flow.

"Mrs. Billingsley, thank you for the invitation. The table is elegant and the food smells delightful."

Mr. Billingsley picked up his fork and the other diners did the same. "Mr. McAlester, why are you and your family traveling to Nashville?"

"To build the best stable of horseflesh in this country."

"Are you buying your breeding stock in Nashville?"

"No, sir, they're on board."

"It would give me great pleasure to see them."

"Mr. Billingsley, I will be delighted to show them to you."

"How about tomorrow morning?"

"Tomorrow morning it is."

The next morning before dawn, Hugh gently woke his sons and said, "Get dressed and follow me. Don't wake your mother. You know how she is this time of day."

He led the boys to the cargo area of the steamboat to get the horses in good form. The boys were accustomed to tending the horses, but not at such an early hour. However, they knew their father needed their help and they worked hard. Soon the stalls were cleaned, and the horses were fed, watered, and brushed so that their coats shone.

Then Hugh said to his sons, "Good work, boys—go get cleaned up and have yourselves some breakfast."

When Mr. Billingsley arrived, earlier than Hugh had expected, he was glad that the horses were in good shape for their introduction.

Watching Mr. Billingsley inspect each of the horses in a gentle manner, Hugh knew that this gentleman was a true horseman.

"Best thoroughbreds I have ever seen, Mr. McAlester."

"Thank you, sir."

"I have a small farm near Nashville. It would make a good place for your business. It has a large barn and a small house. I'll give you a very good price. Would you be interested in seeing it?"

"Yes, sir."

Ex-Lieutenant John Allen and Jane were frequently seen strolling around the deck, his arm bent at the elbow where she gently placed her hand, while they spoke animatedly or were totally silent, as if they read each other's minds.

One day Allen, on bended knee, held Jane's hand, "Jane, I love you and will always honor and protect you. Will you marry me?"

Her response was a joyful "Yes!" With their faces bright with light, love, and smiles, Allen picked Jane up and danced around the deck.

The passengers who had gathered around them applauded and someone yelled, "Hip-hip-hurrah!"

The Captain performed the marriage ceremony the next day, and after the kiss, Hugh hugged the groom, shouting, "John, welcome to the McAlester family!" while Sarah, with tears of joy streaming down her face, wrapped Jane in a tight embrace.

Meanwhile, Jesse continued his visits to the card room every day. He knew there was something suspicious going on because the man with the goatee, who everyone called "Faro," won so many more games than the other players, who rotated in and out of the dark room where the whisky flowed freely. When Jesse got his eyes adjusted to the room's dim lighting, he intently watched Faro. After a few days of scrutiny, Jesse realized the man had cards up his sleeve and very deftly pulled them out with his long fingers at the appropriate moments.

Jesse decided that justice must be served. Taking matters into his own hands, he offered to top off Faro's whiskey. Faro, unaware and oblivious to Jesse's intentions, shoved his drink in front of him, splashing whiskey on the counter. Jesse grinned and turned the glass away from Faro, pouring a liberal amount of prune juice into it and masking it with whiskey. Faro finished three of Jesse's prune juice drinks before he started to shift uncomfortably in his seat. His stomach began to gurgle and as he winced and moaned, a foul odor began to fill the room. "Deal me out!" he exclaimed as he bolted from his seat and dashed to the privy.

Jesse was unable to contain his laughter. The gamblers joined in the revelry with bawdy comments until tears streamed down their faces.

Jesse left the card room in his usual manner, but went to find his father. When he found him in his cabin, he said, without preamble, "Papa, there's a good-for-nothing cheating card shark on board." After further questioning and Jesse's quoting verbatim the conversations of the card players, Hugh arranged a visit with the Captain. At the meeting, Jesse reported his observations to the Captain.

The Captain sent a member of his crew, dressed in his street attire, to play poker the next day in the ship's card room.

The crew member confirmed the cheating to the Captain, who then ordered Faro, whose full name was Johnny "Faro" Walker, to be held in his room until the *Natchez* docked in Memphis. All his money was confiscated, for redistribution to its rightful owners. When the steamboat docked at Memphis, Faro was escorted off and ordered to never return.

Compared to the journey to Memphis, the journey to Nashville was uneventful, but the McAlesters were treated royally, especially by the Billingsley family and by the poker players who would have lost their shirts but for Jesse.

CHAPTER SEVEN
Nashville

A few days after the McAlesters had arrived in Nashville, Mr. Billingsley sent Hugh a message inviting him to view the farm. Hugh, surprised by the formality of the invitation, stammered for a moment while he searched in his pockets for a tip. He could see that the messenger understood his discomfort. Finally, he pressed a half-dollar coin into the man's hand. "Please tell Mr. Billingsley we look forward to seeing the farm."

On the agreed-upon day, the McAlesters and John, who was now considered a member of the family, rode to the Billingsley farm in two well-appointed carriages, each pulled by a team of four matching chestnut horses, and driven by two of Billingsley's men, assigned to escort the McAlesters on their trip that day.

Sarah turned to Hugh as the carriage sped smoothly forward on the well-tended road. "Mr. Billingsley is such a good man," she said. "We've been comfortable in the hotel in Nashville, but I'll be so glad to have a real home again."

"We'll see."

The family members, filling the carriages to the edges of the seats, were enthralled with the view of the countryside, which glowed with fall color like an artist's palette. They passed vivid red and orange maple trees, yellow locusts, rusty red oaks, and evergreens. Jesse and his brothers, who were very observant, saw wildlife of all kinds: deer, rabbits, a fox, and wild turkeys. Their journey from Scotland to America had been lengthy and difficult, and they often felt homesick. But when the family arrived at the farm, they knew at once they were home. Even Hugh felt the pull of the homestead and the land, but he worried about getting his family's hopes up since he did not yet know the purchase price for the farm.

After emitting "Oohs" and "Aahs" as the carriages stopped before the house, the family jumped out to get a closer look. Hugh and John headed directly for the barn and Sarah, Jane, and Rebekah for the house, with the rest of the children shouting and laughing, scattering everywhere. Hugh was openly impressed with the barn; he found it spacious and perfectly set up for horses.

"John, I couldn't have built a better barn myself!" He pointed out all the practical features to John, who listened closely, realizing that his father-in-law truly wanted him to be a part of the family business.

Mary called, "Papa, come see the pasture."

The pasture was leveled, fenced, and well sodded. Hugh thought, *This place is perfect, but can I afford it?*

At the house, Sarah threw her arms around Jane and Rebekah. "What a wonderful home even bigger than ours in Ayr!"

Jane pointed, "Look, Mama, at all the nice rooms."

Hugh, his inspection of barn and pasture finished, rounded up the others and herded them into the house. Before he was halfway into the living room, Sarah embraced him. "Hugh, I already feel like this is my home. I've been saving money for years for such an occasion." She opened the small chest she'd brought from Scotland, to reveal approximately twelve hundred dollars in gold coins.

"Good Lord, Sarah, I never imagined you had saved so much!"

The ride back to Nashville was quiet; each one hoping desperately they could afford the beautiful farm, yet fearing their funds would not be enough.

The next morning, a bellboy announced to Hugh that Mr. Billingsley was waiting in the hotel lobby. Hugh finished dressing, re-combed his hair, making sure that errant cowlick was tamed, and descended the stairs. Billingsley was waiting at the bottom. He shook Hugh's hand and invited him for a cup of coffee. Hugh accepted, his heart accelerating. Once they were sitting opposite each other at a little marble table, before steaming cups, Billingsley spoke.

"Hugh, I've owned that place for a number of years, but have never lived on it. I got it in payment for a debt some time ago. I've always kept the place up; it was too nice to let it go to rack and ruin. I've been waiting for an opportunity to sell the farm to a good family, hoping they would have horses. When I met you and heard your plan, and then saw your horses, I realized you will be the perfect owner."

"I thank ye, Mr. Billingsley," Hugh said, his anxiety making his Scottish brogue much thicker, "but I didn't know if we kin afford it."

"Please call me Arthur."

He quoted an extremely reasonable price.

Hugh choked on his next sip of coffee, but once he recovered from his initial astonishment, he summoned the words. "I'll take it! If we could meet at my bank at nine tomorrow, I'll make the arrangements for the funds to pay you for the farm."

"I will meet you there and bring you the Deed to your property."

They stood, and Billingsley slapped Hugh on the back. "You're an honest man. I knew it from the start. I know you'll prosper on that farm and I'll be your best customer for those magnificent thoroughbreds." The two men shook hands and the deal was done.

It took Hugh three days to locate two teams of workhorses to his liking, after which he bought two nearly new wagons. These would serve him well for the hard labor necessary to run the farm. Some fields would be plowed and planted with corn, others in oats or milo maize, some left to grow hay for the winter. The pastures had to be kept clear of large weeds and sprouts.

Then, too, Sarah would need to have a garden plot plowed to grow vegetables for the kitchen. The workhorses and wagons would come in handy for all that. The next day, the McAlesters loaded their two wagons with all their earthly possessions, as Sarah hovered over them, admonishing them, "Be careful!" many times during the course of the moving day.

Hugh, John, and the boys hitched up a team of two horses for each wagon. Matt and Andrew rode the stallions and led the mares, and Josh watched Comet closely to see that he stayed close to his dam. The rest of the family—Jesse, John, Jane, Rebekah, Mary, and their mother Sarah—piled into the two wagons, sitting anywhere they could, with Jesse's dogs barking excitedly.

Sarah shouted, "Let's go!" holding Bonny, now a world traveler, in her lap. Then the family headed for their new home.

On the way, they sang in harmony with almost everyone on key, "Froggy went a courtin' and he did ride, uh huh. With a sword and pistol by his side, uh, huh. He went up to Miss Mousey's door, uh, huh. A place he never been before, uh, huh. Froggy went a courtin' and he did ride, uh huh…"

While the family was settling into the house, a wagon arrived unexpectedly. Hugh hurried to the front porch.

The driver pulled up to the front of the house, "Mr. McAlester, I brought you some furniture from Mr. Billingsley."

"How much do I owe him?"

"Not a penny—that's what I was told to tell you."

Hugh blushed with pleasure. "Please tell Mr. Billingsley how grateful we all are for his kindness!"

The driver touched his hat. "I surely will tell him, Mr. McAlester."

The younger McAlesters, who had been watching from the window, hurried to the wagon, followed by the rest of the family. Sarah directed the placement of all of the wagon's contents inside the house.

As the years went by, the farm became a paradise, with Sarah's vegetable garden yielding abundant vegetables most of the year, and the boys hunting, providing venison, rabbits, and wild turkey for the women to prepare. Hugh's breeding plans produced more and more beautiful thoroughbreds, which were trained and purchased, and cattle grazed in the upper pasture.

One day, Mr. Billingsley arrived at the McAlester farm with a man who looked familiar to Hugh and John. Billingsley introduced him. "Mr. McAlester and Mr. Allen, this is Senator Andrew Jackson. He is interested in looking at your horses."

Hugh eyed the lean figure of Senator Jackson, his prominent red hair streaked with white, creating an interesting effect.

"Mr. McAlester, I've been informed that you are a Mason. You must join us in the Grand Lodge in Nashville."

"Senator, that is most gracious of you, and I heartily accept."

Jackson would become the seventh President of the United States on March 4, 1829 and serve until March 4, 1837. He died of chronic tuberculosis, dropsy, and heart failure at his Nashville, Tennessee plantation, the Hermitage, on June 8th, 1845.

After shaking hands, Hugh said, "My pleasure. Gentlemen, follow me." He tried to suppress his excitement so he could present his horses properly, but his sons did the job for him.

On the way to the barn, Jackson stopped abruptly, seeing motion in the corner of his eye, and turned to look at the pasture. He was mesmerized by the boys racing their magnificent thoroughbred horses, their coats gleaming in the sunlight. While the two horses were at a full gallop, the riders stood in their saddles, then returned to the normal riding position. Their maneuvers continued when the riders slipped to the sides of their horses without slackening their pace. The other two boys were putting their horses through the training process: walk, trot, canter, and gallop.

Hugh pointed toward the pasture. "Senator, my boys. They were born in the saddle."

"Very impressive, Mr. McAlester—both your sons and the horses."

The Senator bought two horses that day, and a colt to be sired by Comet, with the stipulation that Hugh train it himself.

Sarah, holding a hoe, shook her head. "Hugh, we sure need some rain—my garden's wilting."

"By the look of those clouds, we'll get some soon."

That evening the thunder rumbled boisterously, sounding like a series of cannons, followed by lightning that illuminated the house like a million stars. The downpour that followed cleared the dust in the road and washed it off the vegetation, nourishing it with heaven's blessing.

The following morning, Sarah rose early, stepped out on the porch and inhaled the perfume of the air, freshly cleansed by the storm. Beads of moisture glistened like diamonds on the trees. "Lord, thank you for your many blessings," she said softly, then returned to the kitchen to bake biscuits and bread. Before long, her handiwork filled the house with fragrant smells.

Rebekah, roused from bed by the aroma, yawned and went outside to do her daily chores: gathering eggs and picking vegetables for the day. Although half asleep, she noticed tracks in the mud. She carefully delivered the eggs to her mother and began cleaning the vegetables in the kitchen bowl.

"Mama, somebody was outside last night."

"None of us heard anything except the thunder, and there's no such thing as a ghost. Don't fret yourself."

"But, Mama, it left footprints in the mud—it had no shoes."

"Daughter, show me."

The two went outside and Rebekah pointed. "See here, Mama?"

Sarah had to admit that Rebekah was right. "Shouldn't have doubted you, dear."

At breakfast, Sarah asked, "Did any of you go outside after the terrible storm last night?"

Everyone was busy eating, but eventually she heard denials from all the members of the family. "Someone was here last night," she explained. "There's muddy tracks."

His unfinished breakfast still on the plate, Hugh jumped up, retrieved his shotgun, and yelled, "Come on, boys, let's find this trespasser!"

Sarah shouted, "Don't track mud into the house!" and finished her breakfast.

They found the footprints and followed them but found no one. Then they searched the barn, the pasture, and everyplace else. After their futile search, they returned to their cold breakfast.

A couple of days later, Jesse and his brothers left at dawn to hunt and before long they had spotted and shot a wild turkey. When he retrieved it, Josh examined the bird, shot through the head. "Good shot, Jesse—

Mama will be happy."

Jesse spotted something in a nearby ravine and pointed to it. "What's that?"

Josh gazed along his brother's extended arm. "A squatter is living there on our land."

"Look, that's the ole blanket Mama threw out."

The boys scoured the woods until Andy observed a shadowy figure, bent nearly double, running through the underbrush. "There he is!"

The trespasser, when he saw Jesse's shotgun aimed at him, stopped and raised his arms. Jesse lowered the gun. "Why, he's just a child."

The brown-skinned boy, ragged and dirty, trembled and begged, "No shoot, *por favor.*"

Josh stepped forward. "Don't worry, we aren't going to hurt you. You look hungry. Why don't you come with us and we'll get you something to eat."

The boy cringed, but Jesse handed his shotgun to Josh and put his arm around the kid's shoulders. They escorted him to the house, even though he knew the way.

Jesse brought the boy into the kitchen. "Mama, Rebekah, we found your ghost."

Sarah took one look at the boy and pulled him into a motherly embrace. "Why, you poor child! Just a wee laddie! You look starved." She made a plate of food for him and turned to her youngest son. "Jesse, get one of your shirts and a pair of pants for him. I'll cut them down to his size. And bring your old pair of boots that don't fit you now."

The kid, whom they now knew as Tomás, cleaned his plate in seconds. Hugh smiled at him. "Tomás, you can sleep in the barn yonder."

Tomás looked up at Sarah and Hugh with tears of gratitude in his eyes. *"Gracias!"* Tomás turned out to be a hard worker, and he and Jesse became good friends.

Hugh was in the barn one day and saw a rope that looked strange because it was plaited, and asked, "What's this?" as he picked it up to examine it. "I've never seen anything like this."

Tomás said, "My *padre* showed me."

"Can you make another one?"

"Sí, Señor McAlester."

He ran to gather the materials.

"Jesse, this is the best rope I've ever seen. People would pay good money for these." Day by day, Jesse learned more Spanish words, and Tomás more English.

One day while picking berries, Tomás noticed movement in the brush. As he peered into the undergrowth, a black bear cub, berry juice liberally smeared on his small face, squealed in fright and ran back toward his mother. Mama bear wheeled in her tracks and began roaring, blowing and clacking her teeth while hurtling toward her cub. Just when Tomás' small body seemed in peril, Samson, Ike, and Pete sprang into action. Mama bear lunged toward Samson, who had placed his body between Tomás and the bear. Mama bear swatted Samson about ten feet through the air, just as Ike and Pete closed from the rear. They tore large chunks of flesh from the bear's hindquarters, and Samson leapt into action, sinking his fangs into her nose. With both the cub and Tomás seeking refuge in their respective trees, all of the action was below them.

Jesse, hearing the fight, rushed to the scene just as the dogs sent Mama into full retreat. "Tomás, get down out of that tree so the cub can escape with his mother."

"Sí, I was only picking some berries, when I encountered the bears. I promise to be more careful when I enter the woods again."

"Samson, Ike, Pete, get over here! Boys," while scratching their ears, "thank you for saving Tomás' life." Jesse checked the boys for cuts and broken bones. "I don't feel anything broken, but we need to doctor those cuts when we get back to the house."

Tomás, ever alert in the future, always took the dogs whenever he ventured into the woods.

As the years passed, Jesse became more interested and involved in the breeding and training of the horses, asking his father many questions. "Papa, I have a plan to raise a tough and beautiful new strain of horses by breeding one of our stallions to a sturdier mare."

"Why on earth would we do that? We raise the best thoroughbreds in this country."

"To make a new breed of horses—tougher and stronger."

"There's no need for that, son."

"But, Papa!"

October, 1835

Andrew Jackson, now the President of the United States, returned to the McAlester farm accompanied by Mr. Billingsley, along with an entourage of unknown faces.

"Hugh, you may have heard there's a war going on in Texas. Our spies have told us the Mexican army, under orders from General Perfecto Cos, is occupying the city of San Antonio. This situation could change this country in a mighty way. Texas will require plenty of horses, and I believe you're the right man to supply them."

Jesse listened intently to the President's words. "Mr. President."

"Jesse, please call me Andy."

"Sir, I have been hearing of the unrest in Texas. I know that a letter of introduction to General Sam Houston would be most helpful for a man interested in joining the fight."

Hugh, clearly astonished at this turn of events, began apologizing to the President for his son's impertinence.

"Hugh, I appreciate Jesse's interest in the Revolution in Texas."

"Jesse, since Hugh, General Sam, and you have been raised in the Lodge in Nashville, and I have been the Worshipful Master, there is no need of written correspondence," Jackson said. "I will tell you in private all Sam will need to hear as a means of introduction."

"That's very kind of you Mr. President, uh I mean Andy, sir," Jesse replied, eliciting laughs from the members of the group.

A few days later, he brought up his vision again. "Papa, have you thought about my horse breeding plan? We could make a lot of money selling them for the war in Texas."

"No! I don't want to degrade the pure line of my horses. I can't have my life's work ruined by breeding my stallions to mongrel mares. Don't bring it up again!"

Jesse wouldn't back down, though. The argument heated up until Sarah rushed to the barn and yelled, "Stop it—both of you! I can hear you from the kitchen! Stop this or you'll have to cook your own food!"

Hugh looked ashamed, but Jesse looked even more determined.

About a week later, Jesse announced at breakfast, "I'm leaving tomorrow for Bexar, the place President Jackson talked about. They'll need special horses there to fight the war."

The McAlesters, along with Tomás, who was now eating at the table and sleeping in the house, fell silent in shock for a moment. After they recovered from their amazement at Jesse's announcement, everyone shouted at once: "No!"

"Why would you do that?"

"Jesse, you can't go!"

After the commotion subsided, Jesse scooted his chair back and stood. "No one can make me change my mind." Without another word, he walked out the front door.

Sarah turned to Hugh, searching his face, but he kept his head down and said nothing, even though he knew his wife was looking to him for an answer about their youngest son's sudden departure.

After the tumultuous breakfast, when Jesse and Tomás were doing their daily chores in the barn, the young boy spoke up nervously. "Jesse, please don't go."

"I have to. Papa and I don't see eye to eye anymore. I've got an idea for breeding more sturdy horses for the West, but Papa won't listen to me. I'll go down the Jackson Military Road all the way to the cutoff and go west to Texas. It's time for me to leave and have my own life and be the man God wants me to be."

"Can I come with you?"

"No, Papa and Mama will need you to take my place in the family."

The next morning, Jesse got up before the rest of his family and walked to the McAlester Cemetery, where he had buried his dogs. Doffing his hat and lowering his head, he looked over the grave markers he had made for Samson, Ike, and Pete.

"Boys, I miss you every day. Wish you were still alive because where I am headed, your protection would be most helpful."

After his family got up, he said his goodbyes to Tomás and to his siblings. Hugh refused to come outside, even though Sarah desperately pleaded with him to do so. Tomás presented one of his plaited ropes to Jesse, and then Jesse went to his mother, who hugged him tightly and whispered, "Be careful, Jesse, and always remember how much I love you."

"I love you too, Mama."

Jesse rode away with saddlebags packed carefully by Sarah for his long journey. Hugh came out of the house and stood on the porch, shaking his head, and then marched, head down, to the barn.

CHAPTER EIGHT
Two Journeys to Texas

February 9, 1836

Filled with youthful fearlessness and elated by his independence, Jesse guided his beautiful black mare, Midnight, to the Jackson Military Road. A thoroughbred sired by Comet's son and foaled at midnight four years earlier, Midnight was eager to run. Her rider held her in check, to conserve her energy for the long trek ahead.

The day promised to be fine. The early morning sun cast dappled shadows across the road, moving as the cool breeze ruffled the glowing, new foliage. Jesse noticed the sunlight glistening on a stream and he reined his horse to a halt, swung out of the saddle, and led her to the water. She drank thirstily while he replenished his canteen with the cool spring water. After the mare had drunk her fill, he fed her oats from his saddlebags.

Curious, he inventoried the saddlebags. "Midnight, by God, Papa gave me his pocket watch. Here's his favorite hunting knife. There's more—a pistol with plenty of ball and powder and a milt. Look, a letter!"

Dear Son,

I know we don't see eye to eye about horses, but please know I love you. Keep your powder dry, the sun in your enemies' eyes, and most importantly, God in your heart.

Papa

Jesse was not a sentimental young man, but the letter and the tokens of his father's love and concern for his welfare brought tears to his eyes. He quickly wiped them away on his sleeve. For a moment, he felt a pang of regret that he had left his family so soon. But he took a deep breath, squared his shoulders, and remounted. He knew he had a purpose, and his destiny lay elsewhere.

With the letter in his left breast pocket, giving him encouragement and strength every day of his journey, Jesse traveled quickly westward on the Jackson Military Road toward his goal, ever mindful of his responsibility to care for his beautiful steed.

In the distance, Jesse could see smoke curling toward the heavens, and before long he came upon a cabin, its chimney the source of the smoke. He headed there to obtain provisions for himself and Midnight, and allow her some time to rest.

As he approached the cabin, he heard boisterous voices and laughter. Upon opening the door, he realized it was not a home but a tavern, teeming with drunken, filthy men, along with a few partially clothed women. He quickly purchased some oats for Midnight and some jerky from the bartender. He figured that was the safest and cleanest bet, refusing the greasy, foul-smelling soup as politely as possible.

As soon as he exited the bar, he found himself in trouble. Midnight was rearing up on her hind legs, snorting and pawing the air as two men attempted to steal her. Jesse pulled out his father's pistol and shot one thief in the arm, the slug burying itself in his flesh clear to the bone.

The wounded man and his co-conspirator hightailed it toward the woods like frightened jackrabbits.

Jesse examined Midnight from head to tail, treating one small cut with ointment from his saddlebags while soothing her with whispered consoling words, along with the milt, a technique he had learned from Hugh to calm and console the high-spirited thoroughbreds.

The tavern patrons were raucous, noisy, and accustomed to gunfire, so no one came outside when the shot was fired.

He stroked the beautiful mare, pressing his forehead against hers. "I promise to be more careful, Midnight, and not let this sort of thing happen again."

For the next few days, the weather remained fine. The azure sky billowed with clouds, the birds chirped, and the squirrels chattered, restoring Jesse's sense of peace as he continued his long journey.

After consuming the jerky, along with many squirrels, rabbits, and a wild turkey, Jesse's face lit up at the sight of a small house with movement in the yard. As he came closer, he saw children playing and laughing. "Midnight, we've come back to civilization," he said excitedly.

Remembering his promise to the horse, he observed the scene intently before coming closer. The children's clothing was clean and neat, the house seemed well-kept, and the yard was free of everything except a few painted wooden toys.

As Jesse halted, a man emerged from the house. "What can I do for you, young man?"

"I'm Jesse McAlester from Tennessee. I'm headed to Texas. Would you be kind enough to tell me where there is a stand around these parts where I could buy some provisions for me and my horse? And may I have permission to dismount?"

The man was impressed with Jesse's demeanor and good manners. "Yes, certainly. I'm Burt Connell," he said, shaking Jesse's hand after he dismounted. "There ain't a store for miles around, but I think we have some extra supplies we can share. You can put your pretty horse back yonder in the barn and then come on in the house."

The Connell children observed Jesse's every move and listened to every word he spoke, and Liza, their mother, pleased by the example the traveler was setting for her children, invited him to stay for dinner. He accepted gratefully.

"Good fried chicken and sweet potatoes, Mrs. Connell—just like my Mama makes back home."

After dinner, as he watched the children play and listened to their father and mother talk about their day and plans for tomorrow, Jesse yearned for his own family, but was pleased that the Connells invited him to sleep in the barn that night. Before dawn, Burt Connell made his way to the barn. "Jesse, I wanted to share a conversation that I had with some strangers last week— out of earshot of my wife."

"Yes, sir, if it pertains to my trip to Bexar, I'd be grateful for any information you might share."

"I was told that the Mexican army is headed toward San Antonio to take back the Alamo, and a lot of the townspeople, especially the Mexicans, are leaving. I'm sure you know what that means."

"Yes, sir. I'd better move quickly if I'm going to a part of the fracas. I'm obliged for the information." He saddled Midnight, packed the supplies the Connells had given him, mounted up, tipped his hat to Connell, and continued on his journey. As Connell had advised him, he left the Jackson Military Road and turned onto the Natchez Trace Road toward the west and his future in Texas.

December 14, 1835
San Luis Potosí, Mexico

Hilario Diaz had been a farmer near San Luis Potosí all his life, as had his father and grandfather. His family had lived in the same place for as long as anyone could remember. The familiarity of the land, his crops, and animals was a comfort to him as he lifted his gnarled hands to grasp the harness traces of his plow. But before he could start down the row, his wife María screamed, alerting him to the presence of the soldiers. He had heard that General Santa Anna was conscripting troops for a punitive expedition against the norteamericanos in the northernmost region of Coahuila. He raced to his wife's side just as a young Lieutenant approached.

"Señor, you are the one that is the *dueño* of the oxen."

"Sí, I am regarded as such."

"Generalísimo Antonio Lopez de Santa Anna has a wish for you to aid your country."

"I am old, and not able to go to war."

"It is not your fighting skills he desires, but your handling of the beasts to pull the cannon."

"Will I be paid for such efforts on my part?"

"Sí, Señor, we promise not to burn down your house and destroy your crops if you are compliant."

"When are we leaving for this war?"

"It would be wise to get your things and say your farewells now."

Hilario made haste, grabbing some spare clothes, some tortillas and dried meat, and followed the Lieutenant out the door while María wailed for her husband.

The groaning of the oxen straining at the traces, struggling to pull the cannon up the steep hill, became a discordant sound to the young conscripts. Most came from the Yucatan region, and were more accustomed to the sounds of the ocean's waves than the wind on a sea of endless scrub brush, cactus, and mesquite trees.

Benito had been silently sobbing. Every step north reminded him of his loneliness and the fear that had so engulfed him. His Sergeant had gathered the young Yucatans to demonstrate the proper way to fire the big muskets. Benito and most of the others from his homeland were unable to fire the muskets from the shoulder, due to the guns' extraordinary length. This ineptness led to beatings and withholding of their already meager rations.

The troops had been ravaged by the Comanche, wolves, and the unusually cold weather for two weeks now. None of the men had ever experienced a climate like this, and none of them had enough clothing to protect them from the frigid January temperatures. More than half the army wore incomplete uniforms, some with only simple work pants. The majority had ill-fitting or worn-out shoes, and some trudged along barefoot. Their commander-in-chief didn't seem to notice or care, so long as they were still on their feet. There were no physicians in the army and precious few medical supplies. Morale had been low even before the Comanche attacks. The Indians had shot sixteen oxen full of arrows and stolen over fifty horses and almost eighty beeves, further threatening their food supply, and had taken a wagon full of Brown Bess muskets, powder, and ball. Their advance scouts, desperately seeking forage for their animals and meat for the army, had either deserted or been killed by the Comanche.

The squeaking of the oxcarts' wheels, a cacophony of noise, became an eerie staccato of sound as the soldados tried everything to soothe their aching ears. Just then, a hawk-eyed Lieutenant wheeled his horse, raced to the scene of the now-shrieking wheels, and shouted in a derisive manner, "Get those wheels repaired *muy pronto*, or I'll see you flayed alive."

Old Hilario tapped the lead oxen with his long stick, imploring the other ox drivers to stop and begin emergency repairs on the wheels. After applying thick layers of grease and allowing the big beasts to feed, the long procession of animals resumed their desultory advance along the narrow road that would eventually lead to San Antonio de Bexar.

Benito, one of the conscripted soldiers, heard an owl hoot at a most incongruous time as he relieved himself behind a juniper bush on a particularly cold and miserable day. He peered around a huisache shrub and behind a mesquite tree and began rapidly making the sign of the cross, backing away from a frightening, terrible apparition.

He frantically screamed, *"El Diablo, El Diablo!"* seeing a fully war-garbed Comanche warrior, replete with red circles around his eyes and yellow stripes on both sides of his face. This heinous figure completed his outfit with a hat made from a wolf's head. The Comanche, as startled as Benito but much quieter, backed away from the scene, mounting his ribbon-bedecked pony with a bloody handprint on the rump, and riding away at a full gallop.

"Socorro! Socorro!" Benito screamed for help to no one in particular.

The closest in command, a burly Sergeant, made his way to the scene and asked an agitated and frightened Benito, "What goes on here, and why are you raising an alarm?"

"Sergeant, I espied a demon in the bushes while I was relieving myself."

"Cómo te llamas?"

"I am Benito Morales from the Yucatan brigade, and I want to report to you what I have witnessed."

"Ven aquí, Benito! Walk with me while I take some air, and you can tell me what you saw."

Benito began speaking rapidly, but his eyes grew wide as the Sergeant slowly removed his pistol from his waist and calmly shot Benito between his eyes.

"This *soldadito idiota* won't be regaling my soldiers with his imaginary visions or lowering their morale anymore," the Sergeant said. As he walked back into the camp, the other soldiers simply scattered, too afraid to ask any questions. After many months, and over six hundred miles, the broken and weary army of General Santa Anna straggled into San Antonio de Bexar in late February of 1836.

March 6, 1836

Accustomed to the north wind blowing, Jesse was surprised by a sudden shift that brought the ominous smell of gunpowder, along with other scents: the smell of death, and an inexplicable odor of burning wood. Midnight snorted and shook her head, and Jesse realized that he must be very close to San Antonio de Bexar. The inhabitants were fleeing the city in droves, and he immediately knew the Alamo was under siege.

"I smell it too, girl. Let's go!" and Midnight quickened her pace.

By the time Jesse arrived at a vantage point that would allow him to survey the scene, he saw a Mexican cannon emplacement hundreds of yards below him, now silent since the battle was over. All was chaos, in the town and in the old, roofless mission and its grounds. Clearly, the Alamo had already fallen. His heart sank, and he berated himself severely for not having arrived a day or two earlier. The scene had a surreal, hellish atmosphere, a vision of chaos and devastation so great that his eyes could scarcely take it in, together with the putrid smells of smoke and sulfur. He then heard a single bugler playing an unfamiliar tune. He later learned that this was the *Degüello*, a bugle call signifying "no quarter," literally translated as "cut throat."

Jesse started coughing, his throat irritated by the heavy smoke and gunpowder permeating the air. But the worst thing that assaulted his senses was the smell of defeat. He could only watch the scene below him and wait for an opportunity to enter the town.

He rode to a brushy ridge east of the Alamo and watched the Mexican soldiers on horseback chasing and killing the retreating Alamo survivors.

He bowed his head and silently prayed. *Yea, though I walk through the valley of the shadow of death, I will fear no evil; for thou art with me; thy rod and thy staff they comfort me.* Then he checked his guns to be certain they were loaded, and only afterward finished his prayer. *Amen.*

Below him, a white-tailed buck leapt from the brush, followed closely by a Mexican Lancer, who lowered his lance and prepared to run it through the deer, but the buck dodged just in time to avoid certain death. Seething with anger over the loss of his prey, the Lancer looked up and saw Jesse and screamed, *"Gringo, voy a matarte!"*

Knowing this was a death threat, Jesse gave Midnight her head and the beautiful black mare raced away at full speed.

The Lancer spurred his own mount, showing no mercy, and in seconds was running stride for stride with Midnight.

CHAPTER NINE
Alamo Letters

T horoughbred blood coursing through her muscular body, Midnight accelerated to an unbelievable speed to provide the advantage Jesse needed in this mortal battle. He dropped to one side of his horse so the Lancer could not see him.

"Where did you go, gringo?"

In answer to the question, gunfire flashed beneath Midnight's neck. A shocked expression appeared on the Lancer's face, as he tumbled to the ground in an awkward sprawl.

Midnight coughed, and Jesse, righting himself on her back, felt droplets strike his face.

Blood! She was coughing up blood! Her speed slackened to a stagger, then her legs suddenly collapsed and she pitched forward and to one side.

Jesse's right leg was caught under her full weight. He had to use all of his strength to pull it free. It was numb and he felt the full length of it, deciding that at worse he was bruised.

His first thought was for Midnight. He pressed an ear to her side, but heard no heartbeat. He limped around the mare and saw the terrible gash between her ribs just behind her left foreleg where the lance, hurled by the dying Mexican, had struck her. He squatted, holding her head and caressing her forelock. Tears rolled down his face as he stroked her. "Midnight, I love you. You saved my life."

He remembered the danger surrounding him and quickly stood and limped to the Lancer's body, removing the blue jacket with brass buttons from the still-warm body and picking up the sword and pistol from the dirt. When he dragged the Lancer's boots off, a paper dropped to the ground. He grabbed it and shoved it into his pocket. He had already noticed the thicket of juniper trees covered in vines that bordered the trail. Still favoring his bruised leg, he dragged the body among the trees, breaking off a number of juniper branches and vine tendrils to further conceal the dead Lancer from any passers-by.

He had not seen what had become of the Mexican's horse, and for a moment worried that he might be stuck traveling on foot, lame as he was, if the animal had returned to the town. He moved out of the juniper thicket and paused, looking sharply around and listening.

The first sign of the horse was a snort and a stomp. The animal was ten yards farther down the trail, nearly hidden by the junipers. He approached slowly, speaking to the horse in a tone he knew would calm him. Jesse reached out, and the horse withdrew one step and then stood still. When he caught the right rein, the horse followed him out into the open, a magnificent Andalusian stallion, white with thick, long gray mane and tail, broad chest, arched neck, and intelligent eyes. Jesse began by stroking him, touching him all over his body. Then he led the horse to Midnight's corpse and began to remove what he would need of her tack.

Amazed at the beautiful hand-tooled leather saddlebag on the stallion, Jesse added his own, primitive in comparison, along with his rifle and the spoils of the battle, including, among other things, the Lanc-er's nearly new black boots. Jesse tried one on. It mostly fit. At last he mounted the stallion to journey to safer ground. Imbued with confidence, but also keenly aware of his surroundings, he rode the majestic stallion away from the Alamo.

When he reached an area thickly covered with ancient live oak trees, he slowed the stallion's pace until he spotted the telltale line of cypress trees that meant the presence of a running stream. He dismounted, uncertain of the horse's loyalty, and hobbled the stallion to allow him to drink. He walked a few paces to stretch his sore leg, and when he turned around, he was astonished again at the majesty of the horse, quite unlike anything he had seen, broader in the chest and more heavily muscled than any thor-oughbred stallion, and yet refined and elegant.

He spoke aloud, "Liberty!" and the beautiful creature raised his head from drinking and turned to look at him as he approached to remove the saddlebags. "You seem to approve of the name."

From his own bag, he removed the salve and gently treated the horse's wounds, caused by the sharp rowels of the Lancer's spurs. Liberty turned his head and nuzzled his new owner.

Wishing to find out more about the man he'd killed, he pulled the letter from his pocket.

Because the text was written in Spanish, he was grateful for Tomás's lessons.

March 6, 1836

San Antonio de Bexar, Mexico

My Darling Alejandra,

Our suffering began on the 28th of November when we marched from Mexico City to San Luis Potosi and from there to Saltillo on January 6. We acquired as many supplies as we could appropriate and continued our march. After we crossed the Rio Grande, the Comanche attacked our troops. They killed many of the stragglers, shot arrows in our oxen, and stole our horses and cattle. We finally arrived in San Antonio de Bexar on the 23th of February.

We have witnessed many horrors from both sides in our siege of the Alamo. General Santa Anna ordered our men to scale the walls of the Alamo and thereby endure withering fire from the enemy.

Hundreds of our brave men have been wounded or killed in that battle. The wounded are suffering terribly because of lack of medical supplies and proper care. This ill-advised campaign is lacking money and provisions for the men and animals.

Without regard for the intense suffering and inadequate supplies, General Santa Anna, intent on pursuing this campaign to its bitter end, ordered the men to continue fighting and track the remaining Texians and Tejanos for as many weeks as it will take to annihilate them.

I portend a disastrous end if we do not get supplies and much needed rest for our neglected troops.

The crude drawing I have rendered shows the proximity to the enemy that our men were exposed to, with disastrous results.

When I return home, you and I will walk hand in hand again to view the Popocatépetl. Although separated by distance, my love, we are united in one soul.

Always, My Love,

Antonio Vargas Delgado

The letter had a crude drawing of Bexar with stick figures representing the troops.

He brushed the caliche dust off the beautiful engraved leather saddlebags, traced with his finger the large engraved "B," and carefully placed the letter inside as he examined the other contents: dried venison, parched corn, gun powder and ball, along with a pearl-and-tortoiseshell-handled brush and matching comb. He ate some of the venison and gave some of the parched corn to the horse, but returned the other items to the saddlebag.

Now nourished, he and Liberty continued the journey.

When the sun was at its highest point, Liberty snorted, alerting Jesse to movement ahead.

It was a family of villagers heading in the same direction he was: away from San Antonio de Bexar. Liberty's long stride easily overtook the dusty, slow-moving wagon, drawn by a team of oxen. As they came abreast, one of the riders in the wagon stood.

"Señor, me no gun," the frightened older man raised his hands into the air.

Jesse made calming gestures with his hands, lowering them slowly from chest height to the saddle. He spoke in Spanish, sensing that their English was rudimentary. "I intend no harm to you or your family. I merely seek news about the Alamo and information to find the Texian army. I'm Jesse McAlester."

The boy who was driving the oxen spoke quickly to the older man, calming him, and introduced himself and his family. "I am Rico López. This is my father José, my mother María, and my brothers and sister. Señor Jesse, everyone inside the Alamo was killed."

"You mean there were no prisoners?"

"Sí, there were a few, but General Santa Anna had them shot. Then he had all the bodies of the defenders burned."

José made the sign of the cross and María cried, pulling her mantilla over her face to hide her tears.

"Señor, we too are trying to find the Texians. We heard they may be in González. It is that way," he said, pointing the direction.

His father whispered to Rico, who then said, "Señor, my father likes the black boots. May we buy them?"

Jesse smiled. "Here are the boots, and I appreciate the information." He tossed the boots to Rico, who said, "Thank you, and God bless and protect you and your family." As Jesse rode away, he turned and shouted over his shoulder, "I will find Santa Anna, and he will pay for his treachery!"

When Jesse camped that night, still far from González, he repeated the venison meal he had eaten before noon and gave the remaining parched corn to Liberty. He picketed the horse in a grassy area so he could graze without needing to wander far, then built a small campfire, not to cook, but to warm himself in the cool spring air. He hoped the light would not attract the prowling Comanche. He then began to examine the Lancer's saddlebag more thoroughly and discovered a pocket with another letter inside. This one was in English. He read by the flickering light of his fire.

March 4, 1836
Rancho Arroyo Verde

My Dearest Martha,

We have been waiting for reinforcements from Colonel Fannin's troops from La Bahía for days. Colonel Crockett and his Tennessee boys have been keeping our spirits up with some lively music.

I remember the first time we danced. You were wearing a beautiful blue dress with a blue ribbon in your hair. I hope with all my heart this letter reaches you so you will know my eternal love for you.

If we are unable to meet again on this earth, do not be distressed, my love, because Death does not erase God's promises.

I love you with all of my heart, and am sending you a lock of my hair. Please give the children my love.

Your Loving Husband,

Angus Burns

Jesse then realized the engraved "B" on the saddlebag meant it belonged to Mr. Burns, not the Lancer. He thought, *I would rather rassle a bear than tell a good woman her husband was killed. I expect many good women will be widows after today.*

He doused the fire, wrapped himself in his blanket and watched the heavens with their skeins of glittering jewels, obscured now and then by thin, high-drifting clouds. He thanked God for saving his life that day, and thought briefly about the men on both sides of the conflict. Both the Lancer and Angus Burns were loving husbands, and he could tell from their letters that they were noble, honorable men, and now both were dead. He asked God's mercy on their souls, then turned over and slept.

He rose the next day at first light, ate the last of the venison, and again salved Liberty's wounded sides. His right leg was stiff and sore, and he massaged it for a while, wishing he had some of his mother's liniment. Just as the sun rose fully above the horizon, he mounted and continued his journey.

As the sun climbed higher, Jesse noticed that the land became gently rolling, with lush, green grass thick alongside the road and plenty of trees for shade. He stopped at a farm that seemed deserted and decided to draw water from the well between the empty house and barn. He lowered the wooden bucket, and when it was full, he cranked it to the surface. He used the gourd to drink all the water he wanted and held the bucket for Liberty to have his fill. He kept a wary eye out for any hostile presence, but the only movement he could see around the farm was the chickens, busily scratching in the grass.

At dusk, Jesse saw a tiny spark caused by an animal striking his hoof on the road. He veered Liberty to the right and moved ahead into the south breeze and halted him in an oak mott, well hidden from the road. As two riders approached, he could hear them speaking English and talking about Sam Houston. Jesse urged Liberty out of the trees and startled the riders. He could tell by the sound rather than by sight that they had drawn their pistols, but so far hadn't cocked them. He halted Liberty a few paces away.

"I'm Jesse McAlester and I'm looking for the Texian army."

The riders were Hamp Wallace and Dob Andrews, who explained they had been lucky to escape the Alamo slaughter and were looking for Sam Houston. "If we don't find him and warn the settlers, all of Texas will be lost."

Jesse smiled at his good fortune in meeting them. "Gentlemen, it would please me to join your search."

CHAPTER TEN
Runaway Scrape

March 7, 1836

Determined to find Sam Houston and the Texian army, Jesse rode eastward toward González, Hamp and Dob following. He was thankful for the company of the two men riding with him, since three would be safer than a lone rider, and they also provided more eyes and ears. The men, keenly aware of their vulnerability to Santa Anna and his army, hoped they would soon find Houston and the troops ready to fight.

The trail was empty, but had obviously been heavily traveled; occasionally they came upon a spot littered with shards of clay pots and old tattered clothing. Birds, oblivious of the drama being played out below them, flitted from one tree branch to another, melodious notes bursting from their tiny bodies, as if they were celebrating the beautiful spring day, the clear blue sky, wisps of clouds above, plowed fields, and forests of ancient live oak trees below.

As they trotted their horses abreast, Hamp told his and his companion's story. "We had family at the Alamo and they perished before we could come to their aid."

Jesse removed his hat for a moment. "I'm so sorry, Hamp." Now he understood his partners' intense interest in fighting in the Texian army.

Hamp nodded, filled his pipe with tobacco, and lighted it while holding the reins at the same time.

Dob asked, "Uncle Hamp, will we ever give those Mexicans a walloping?"

A bit of brogue emerged. "Only time will tell, boy."

Dob shifted impatiently in his saddle. "I didn't come all the way from Tennessee to sit on my horse."

"Nor I, laddiebuck. Fate was not with us at the Alamo, but we've lived to fight another day."

Jesse, sorely missing the language of the lochs and moors, made his origins known. "I'm also from Scotland, by way of Tennessee." As he talked to the men, he realized how lonely he had been. He thought lovingly of his family, hoping they were well and safe.

In the distance, they heard dogs barking frantically, and as they came closer to the sound of the barking, they saw a cabin. "We'll get a hot meal up there," Dob said.

When the three riders dismounted amid the barking dogs, no one exited the cabin to greet them. After knocking on the door to no avail, the trio entered to discover the cabin void of any occupants, but food—ham, fried eggs, grits and bread—lay on the table with only a few flies buzzing around it. Although not hot, the food was abundant, and the trio quickly devoured most of it. Jesse scooped up the few leftovers and delivered them to the hungry dogs.

Jesse and Hamp thought the settlers must have been warned about the defeat of the Alamo and had made a hasty retreat. This conjecture was confirmed as they continued traveling along the road and heard pigs squealing in their stys, chickens clucking and pecking for food, livestock roaming freely in the fields and on the road, but no sign of humans to feed the starving animals. Jesse and the men opened the gates to the stys so the hogs could forage for themselves.

Jesse and Hamp carefully inspected the tracks made by the settlers and discovered they were all headed in the same general direction: east to Louisiana. Obviously, they had been warned that the Mexican army was marching their way. Since the frontier had no protection, they had fled as quickly as possible to find safety in the United States, where soldiers were stationed at the Louisiana-Texas border to prevent Santa Anna from invading their country.

It was late in the day and all three were drooping with exhaustion when Liberty suddenly snorted and picked up the pace. Water! The men dismounted at a sparkling, clear stream and quenched their thirst, and the horses did the same.

Jesse took a quick look around. "This is a good place to camp for the night."

Hamp kneaded his sore thigh muscles. "It's as good as any. We'll not see Houston's army today, and that's a fact."

After feeding the stallion, Jesse applied the salve to his horse's flanks and stroked the beautiful Andalusian. The wounds were already beginning to heal. The horse would show no trace of the gouges.

Meanwhile, Hamp and Dob gathered brush and small pieces of wood for the campfire. Once the fire was going, Dob made the coffee. They drank and ate from their meager store of food, Jesse carefully pulled out the Lancer's letter and read it aloud, translating it from Spanish to English so his partners would have a better understanding of their enemy. When finished, he looked up to see astonished faces.

Hamp whistled. "Tarnation! That Santa Anna has no consideration for his men. They really suffered a heavy blow from our men at the Alamo. Jesse, General Houston will want to set his peepers on that letter. I hear tell he has a favorite scout called 'Deaf,' on accounta' he don't hear too good. By Gawd, if Houston will allow it, I want to throw in with Deaf. That letter you got is just what he'll be a-wantin'.'"

The next morning, they saddled up again and resumed their journey before dawn, hoping to reach Sam Houston and his troops that day. The few people they encountered along the road were disconsolate, their faces and postures making it seem as if they had already been through a war. One old man, tears streaming from his aged eyes and streaking down his leathery face, could only point in the direction where Houston had gone.

"Just follow the horse dung and you'll see where the brave Sam Houston skedaddled," a belligerent, liquored-up fellow shouted. "He's left us behind here, helpless, the bastard." His bedraggled wife and baby wailed all the louder from his shouting.

Jesse urged Liberty forward. "Fellows, the horses went this way, and by God, I'm going to find Houston if it's the last thing I do on this earth!" Hamp and Dob followed him, glad to get away from the misery of the settlers.

What the drunkard had truly meant became clear from the evidence all around them: deserted homes, farms with livestock unfed, and no sign of human life. These scenes were repeated many times as the three men trailed the army. They found extinguished campfires, but no Texian troops.

On March 10, 1836, their luck changed when they saw something moving ahead of them, dodging from bush to bush. As they rode closer, they thought it was an old man with a stooped back.

"Who are you? And what are you doing here?' Jesse shouted.

A youthful voice shouted back, "I'm Grady Thomas, but my friends call me Badger. Got my back broke roping a wild steer. I will not let the Mexicans take me prisoner."

"I'm Jesse McAlester and we're looking for General Houston."

"Erastus Smith—that fellow—came through here yesterday. He told me where General Houston is camped."

Hamp asked, "Who is this Erastus Smith? Can he be counted on?"

Jesse and his friends, exhausted by the ordeal of finding Houston's army, were skeptical of this man. He could be a deserter.

Grady quickly answered. "Why, you fellers might know him as 'Deaf Smith.' He's Sam Houston's main scout."

Hamp nodded. "Oh, yes, I know of Deaf Smith. I never spoke to him, but I've seen him a time or two."

Their spirits lifted by this news, Jesse offered the withered man some pemmican and water.

Hamp pulled out his Meerschaum pipe, put tobacco in it, lighted it, and took a deep draw. "Where will we find the army's camp?"

Eager to join the conversation, Dob exclaimed, "Hallelujah, boys, we're gonna do some fightin'!"

Jesse leaned in and asked, "Grady, how far to Houston's camp?"

"I can show you. You boys gonna let me walk all the way to camp with my bad back?"

"Liberty is still nursing his sore sides, but you ain't nothing but a bag of bones, so he'll hardly notice." Jesse smiled at Grady and pulled him up to ride behind him.

"If we can get to Sam Houston's camp before dark tomorrow, you fellows can meet some real fighting men."

Hamp winced, recalling the panic-stricken settlers headed to Louisiana. "I hope you're right, but all we've seen so far is horse manure on the trails and scared folks a-runnin'."

March 11, 1836

The horses pawed the ground, ears twitching. "We'd better water these horses and get ready for the Mexicans headed our way. We can't chance a fire, not even from the pipe you're smoking, Hamp."

Liberty whinnied, shook his head, and acted like he smelled a mare in heat. His warning provided the time necessary for the men to pull out and cock their guns and rifles. Sure enough, Mexican troops rounded the bend. Without pausing even for a second, Hamp pulled the trigger on his sawed-off shotgun loaded with double 00 buckshot, killing the first three Mexican cavalrymen. They were blown off their horses.

Jesse fired his pistol and the fourth rider fell to the ground, smashing his head against a large tree stump.

Then Dob shot a rifle ball squarely between the eyes of the fifth rider bearing down on him, while deftly dodging the Mexican's lance.

Grady and Dob rushed the sixth rider and brought him to a screeching halt, then grabbed him, yanked him to the ground, pounded him with their fists and began to kick his head and body. Jesse quickly intervened before the cavalryman was beaten to death.

"Men, we need a prisoner to take to Sam Houston. Stop it right now! Search him and the others."

"Come on, men, we've got to get these dead bodies out of sight." He started dragging a dead Mexican into the brush, and the two followed his lead with the other corpses. Meanwhile, Grady kept a close eye on their prisoner, whose mouth he had stuffed with a bandana tied with a second one around his head, secured with a leather strap. They now had a string of spare horses with all their saddles, and Grady chose the best of the lot for himself. Jesse helped him to mount.

After traveling for a few more hours, they were surprised by the intense smell of smoke wafting along the trail. Upon reaching the outskirts of Gonzales, they saw an apocalypse. Every home, shed, store, and barn was burned to the ground, along with livestock, food supplies, even the grasses along the roads. Everything lay in smoking ruins.

Jesse felt a pain in the pit of his stomach, seeing so much waste and suffering. So far, this war had been anything but glorious. They all stood in shock, surveying the scene.

Dob spoke first. "Uncle Hamp, why would someone burn down a perfectly good town?"

"To keep the Mexicans from living off the land. They cannot fight on empty stomachs so when they are weak from hunger, we will attack and beat them."

Jesse shook his head. "Yes, but meantime, these people have lost every last thing they built, raised, and struggled for. What a terrible sacrifice!"

They passed through Gonzales, with small fires still burning, and could see, a short distance away, the tents and campfires of the Texian army. Not wanting to alarm the troops and risk getting shot, Jesse and his men cautiously approached General Houston's camp, leading the Mexican prisoner on his horse. Although he was the youngest, Jesse was clearly their leader.

The sentry challenged them, leveled his rifle and cocked it. "Who goes there, friend or foe?"

Jesse halted his magnificent stallion and straightened his back. "We are friends. We want a private audience with General Sam Houston." Jesse beckoned Hamp, who led the Mexican officer and his horse forward.

The sentry smirked, but when he saw the regally outfitted, bloodied Mexican prisoner, he barked orders to a private standing nearby, "Take this young man and his prisoner to General Houston's private tent, pronto! He may know something valuable."

When Jesse arrived at the tent and dismounted, he took a deep breath and smiled, eager to report his news to the General.

CHAPTER ELEVEN
San Jacinto

A formidable man, six foot four inches tall, with piercing eyes, an authoritative demeanor, and a booming voice, strode out of the tent and demanded, "Who are you?"

"General Houston, I'm Jesse McAlester from Tennessee. I saw the Alamo in ruins and on the way here, my scouts and I captured a Mexican cavalryman."

The two men paused for a second or two, sizing each other up. Jesse saw, despite Houston's impressive size and manner, lines of worry and exhaustion in his face. Houston saw an eager recruit, filled with the strength and energy of youth. The General extended his hand to Jesse, who clasped it, conveying the Masonic symbol of brotherhood.

"So you're from Tennessee. By any chance, do you know Andrew Jackson?"

Jesse nodded. "Yes, sir, General, he buys horses from my father's farm and has told us about you. He said you were raising an army to fight for Texas's independence. I want to join your army fighting for Texas's freedom. That's why I'm here."

"Did Old Hickory send me a message?"

"Yes, sir, he told me to convey this to you." Jesse made a number of Masonic signs to General Houston.

Houston cocked his head to one side, his eyes narrowed as he revised his opinion of Jesse's grasp of the situation. He responded with a ghost of a smile. "So you know Andy Jackson and your father runs a horse farm. Is that your horse by the oak tree?"

"Yes, sir."

"Is your horse from your father's farm?"

"No, sir, I killed a Mexican Lancer who was riding that stallion outside the Alamo. The Lancer killed my horse, so I figured I deserved his. He was carrying a letter." Jesse reached into his pocket and handed the letter to the General.

Houston unfolded the letter and gave it a brief once-over, and then shot a keen glance at an orderly, standing nearby. "Private, find Deaf and bring him here so he can translate this letter and interrogate the prisoner. After you feed the prisoner, bring him here."

"Yes, sir," the private saluted the General and turned about-face to follow the orders.

Jesse spoke in haste. "General, I am well versed in the Spanish language and if you'll allow me to do so, I'll translate the letter, as well as be the interpreter for the interrogation."

A bemused Houston, impressed with the young man's knowledge, skills, and gumption, turned toward his tent. "Step into my humble abode."

The tent was sparsely furnished with a long cot, a large rocking chair, an old, simple, scarred wooden chair with no arms, and a portable desk with a quill pen, ink, and paper on top of it.

Houston sat in the rocking chair, facing the tent opening, and motioned for Jesse to sit in the other chair. Although he knew all too well what had happened at the Alamo, he was always interested in any additional bits of information he could hear. "What did you see at the Alamo?"

"General, I arrived after the fall of the Alamo, but was told by the locals that all the Texian troops were killed, most at the Alamo site, and those that escaped the slaughter were taken prisoner or tracked down and killed as well."

"I told that damn fool Travis to evacuate that roofless church and the surrounding compound, remove the cannon, and wait for another day to fight. That place was never intended to be a fortress and he had too few men to defend it." Houston stopped rocking, propped his cheek on his fist, and stared at the floor, with his brow knit thinking about the loss of Travis and the fallen soldiers.

He gave a start and returned to the letter he had momentarily forgotten. "Let's see what that letter says, and see how well you translate." He handed the paper to the young fellow Mason.

Jesse carefully read the letter aloud, translating it from Spanish to English as he read. When finished, his single-member audience remained silent for several moments, which he thought was probably unusual for the remarkable man.

The silence was interrupted by the private announcing Deaf Smith.

"Deaf, come in. This is Jesse McAlester, who brought me a letter he recovered from a Mexican Lancer slain outside the Alamo."

Jesse handed the Lancer's letter to Erastus "Deaf" Smith, the famous scout. The casual dress of officers in Sam Houston's army surprised Jesse, used to more formality in the soldiers he had seen back in Tennessee. Deaf's dusty buckskins were well-worn, a powder horn hung over one shoulder, a knife in his belt. He wore moccasins rather than boots or shoes. After he read the letter, he looked at Houston, "Sir, this is exactly the information we need to prepare for our victory." He returned the letter to Jesse.

Before Jesse could hear further discussion, two soldiers appeared at the door of the tent and snapped to attention. "Sir, we've brought the prisoner. Do you wish to interrogate him now, sir?"

Houston rose. "Yes. Bring him in."

The prisoner appeared in the opening of the tent between two armed guards. He was clearly the worse for wear, but had at least been given the benefit of a meal before confronting the General. He bore himself with dignity.

He and Deaf continued to interrogate the prisoner, with Jesse translating. After the interrogation, and once the prisoner was escorted out of the tent, Deaf turned to Houston. "General, this young man did a fine job in capturing this prisoner and he sure knows his Spanish."

"Well, then, Deaf, do you think you could use Jesse and his men to do some scouting?"

"Yes, indeed, sir."

"Jesse, round up your men, get them fed and stocked up with provisions, and await orders from Deaf."

"Yes, sir, General Houston!" Jesse saluted and rushed out of the tent to tell Hamp, Dob, and Grady the good news. Grady had already made friends with the camp cooks, who had put him to work. He told Jesse, "The army got a wagonload of food that was headed for Santa Anna so we are cooking up a storm. I'm in heaven!"

On March 25, 1836, the new scouts received their first orders, which were to lead Deaf and his men to the site where they had killed the Mexican cavalrymen, and from there, they were to track the location of the Mexican troops. While on the road, they could still smell the smoldering ruins of Gonzales where the rear guard of Houston's troops had torched the town and surrounding areas to eliminate any food or provisions for the Mexican army. Jesse then knew that the Lancer's letter had assisted with the strategic planning of the war.

On March 27, 1836, outside Goliad, Jesse and his scouts were hidden by some small trees, watching a troop of approximately one hundred Texian soldiers marching down the road as prisoners of a platoon of armed Mexicans.

Dob shook his head and spoke under his breath. "Those look like some of Colonel Fannin's men."

Hamp turned to Jesse. "What in tarnation are they doing?"

"Shush, Hamp, keep your voice down. It looks like the Mexican army is setting them free."

They fell silent as orders barked by the Mexican Sergeant reached their ears. The unarmed prisoners complied; they halted and lined up facing the platoon. A second later, the ear-shattering reports of muskets and pistols were heard, reverberating from the trees, and then the air become heavy with the scent of gunpowder. All of the Texians were lying twisted on the ground, some still moving. Several Mexican soldiers viciously shot the wounded. A second later, they heard another similar volley of gunshots off to their left, and then a third volley farther away. Jesse turned to Dob. "How many men did Colonel Fannin have?"

"About three hundred or so, I think."

"Then General Houston has lost a large troop of soldiers, and Texas far too many brave men."

"Jesse, let's get the hell out of here."

Jesse shook his head at Dob and gave the hand signal for his men to keep still and be quiet.

Jesse had observed movement in the brush and gave the hand signal for the men to draw their weapons. Gradually, a man with no pants and no boots, with a shock of red hair came into focus.

Jesse asked the half-naked man, "What happened down there?"

"That damn fool Fannin offered armistice to the Mexicans, then they marched us out of town and shot us to hell. Shot the colonel, too, I think. At least, I heard guns firing as my platoon was marched away from the fort. The firing distracted our guards long enough for me to dive into the bushes and then run like hell."

"What's your name?'

"Walter Riley."

"I'm Jesse McAlester, you can join us. We're on our way to report this tragedy to General Sam Houston." He produced a spare pair of pants from his blanket roll for the man to cover himself and then pulled him up onto Liberty.

Jesse decided to remain hidden, to see if the Colonel or any other officer had been spared.

Another movement caught Hamp's eye: a dark shape moving silently through the trees.

"Jesse! I saw what looked like a man behind those trees. Just a shadow. It disappeared right away. Want me to investigate?"

"All right. We'll cover you. But you'd better keep low. Dob, move behind that brush to see if it is human and if it is, stop him if he tries to run."

Hamp took his time, moving furtively through the trees.

Dob shouted from a distance away, "*I've got you covered, Mexicano.* Stand up with your hands raised!"

A small man in uniform stood, shaking, his arms in the air. "*No me mates! No me mates!*"

Jesse called from where he stood next to Liberty and Riley, "He says, 'Don't kill me.' Well, we won't. We need information from him."

Jesse ordered the man to stand clear of the trees and to approach. Jesse spoke in Spanish, "What possessed you and your men to murder unarmed prisoners in cold blood?"

The Mexican soldier replied in Spanish, "Those were General Santa Anna's orders, sir. But I could not take part in anything so despicable. I deserted."

"Were any of Colonel Fannin's men spared?"

"I'm not sure. With the confusion of the firing and the smell of gun powder, it was hard to tell."

On March 31, 1836, Jesse and his men arrived at Houston's camp, across the river from the Bernardo plantation, and reported the Goliad massacre. Although Houston was already aware of Fannin's defeat, Jesse, Riley, and the Mexican deserter provided firsthand knowledge of the tragedy, along with the important information that Santa Anna had ordered the execution of Fannin and his men.

The news of the massacre at Goliad spread through the troops like wildfire. At least a hundred and fifty men packed their belongings and left to join their families on the trail to Louisiana. It was clear to everyone that Santa Anna was determined to murder every last Texian, and all feared defeat by an army with superior numbers, training, and equipment.

Knowing a battle was imminent and his troops were in poor condition, Houston ordered Jesse and his scouts to remain in camp to assist with training and drills.

To motivate the weary, depressed men, Jesse, Hamp, and Dob demonstrated their riding and shooting skills. Riding the majestic stallion at full speed, Jesse dropped out of the saddle and touched the ground with his feet, and then he repeated the maneuver on the other side of Liberty.

Then, while mounted, with his horse at full gallop, Hamp fired his sawed-off shotgun at one of the targets, which totally disappeared, with only miniscule pieces of wood splinters fluttering in the air.

Dob was next in line to perform. While on horseback, he fired his rifle and hit the center of a target from thirty yards away.

For the finale, Jesse gave Liberty full rein, dropped under the horse's neck, and fired his pistol at a target, hitting another bull's-eye for his scout team. Then he maneuvered his horse to the edge of the field and rode full speed ahead toward one of the targets, and at the last possible moment, Liberty jumped into the air, as if he could fly, all four legs easily clearing a target and landed on the other side.

After this demonstration, the soldiers were shouting, boisterously laughing, and totally invigorated; they were now ready to learn to ride and shoot like Jesse and his scouts. Sam Houston smiled as he saw the positive effect of the performance on his men's morale. The men were trained there for nearly a fortnight.

One hothead, Colonel Sidney Sherman, chafed at the delay. He had considered General Houston a coward from the beginning of the march east. It seemed to him that Houston was fleeing from Santa Anna's army. At the Colorado River, he had requested permission to re-cross the river to fight a contingent of the Mexican Army under the command of General Joaquín Ramirez y Sesma. Houston had refused the request, which heightened Sherman's resentment and suspicion of the commander. He had convinced a small group of friends that he, not Houston, should command the Revolutionary Army, and he vowed to engage the enemy at the earliest opportunity.

On April 11, 1836, two cannons called the "Twin Sisters" arrived at the Bernardo camp, sent by the generous citizens of Cincinnati, Ohio. The soldiers cheered the arrival of the weapons, and Houston, now that he had an army with cannons and troops in greatly improved condition and morale, thanks to Jesse and his men, gave orders for his army to move forward. He arranged for most of the troops to board a steamboat, the *Yellow Stone*, to cross the Brazos River. A few of them had to cross on a barge.

Jesse and his men returned to scouting and discovered that Santa Anna and a large number of his troops were nearby, but moving more slowly than the Texian troops because they had furniture and many accouterments to carry. There were a number of Mexican women—wives and concubines—and even children riding in the wagons. Many also followed the army on foot.

For several days, the two armies approached each other. By April 17, Houston's forces had reached White Oak Bayou, and Jesse's scouts reported that Santa Anna's army had gone down the west side of the same bayou, crossing over a bridge to Vince's Bayou. General Houston was pleased that the Mexicans had surrounded themselves with water and marshes, their only escape route being that same bridge.

On April 19, Houston crossed Buffalo Bayou below Harrisburg with his fittest men, leaving behind hundreds of others who were sick or unfit to fight. He continued the march down the Bayou on April 20 and had the good fortune of capturing a boat at Lynch's Ferry loaded with supplies meant for Santa Anna. Jesse and his men helped capture the boat. This bit of luck cheered them all. That evening they marched until midnight. They camped along the Bayou on the high ground and among trees that hid them from a large, open field that sloped down toward Peggy's Lake and its surrounding marsh.

On April 20, Santa Anna set up his camp only three quarters of a mile from Houston's forces, on the opposite side of the open field. Their backs were to the marsh and the lake, on their right was more marshland and the San Jacinto River. On their left, lay still more swampy ground with the only exit possible via Vince's Bridge.

Jesse and his fellow scouts observed a few enemy troops gathering rusty wagon wheels, parts of saddles, broken furniture, tree branches, and all manner of brush. The Texian scouts rode quickly back to the camp to report their observations. On their arrival, Jesse dismounted and walked to Houston who was standing outside his tent.

"Jesse, what news do you have for me?"

"If I may have a pen and paper, I will draw the location of the enemy." A private immediately retrieved the requested items and gave them to Jesse, who started drawing.

"General, we are here and the Mexican army of possibly a thousand men is located here. Santa Anna's tent is here. About twenty men are building a breastwork of tree limbs, broken furniture, and anything else they can scrape together."

Their discussion was interrupted by shouting coming from the direction of the open field, and a bugle call signaling attack. They could hear the thunder of hooves and felt the ground shaking under their feet. Houston led Jesse and many other troops to the edge of the woods overlooking the field.

Jesse was shocked to see Colonel Sidney Sherman commanding a group of twenty horsemen, galloping to engage a contingent of Mexican infantry drilling outside the freshly completed barrier.

Jesse pointed toward the center of the barrier. "General Houston, sir, they have a cannon set up there. I think Sherman is trying to confiscate it."

"Damn! That fool has undermined me for weeks already. He has no regards for any plans his commanding officer may have, and might very well lose the battle for us if Santa Anna decides to attack in force."

The Mexican infantrymen held their ground. They fired back, killing several much-needed horses, and wounding two of the attackers. Realizing that the Texians were after their one cannon, they shouted orders and the weapon was hastily withdrawn.

Then Texians Thomas Rusk and Walter Lane were surrounded by the enemy, but suddenly a young Lieutenant Mirabeau Lamar emerged to rescue them from certain death. The Mexican Infantry was overwhelmed with the boldness of Lamar and allowed him to lead Rusk and Lane to safety.

"Gentlemen," he screamed, "This adventure is madness. The cannon is lost to us today. We need to save ourselves and our mounts. Follow me!" Jesse watched him skillfully guide and goad the remaining cavalry up the slope and back to the cover of the trees. The Mexicans, who had been preparing to counterattack, stood down, apparently realizing that the engagement had been a mere skirmish.

With Jesse nearby, Houston, in a rage, reached toward Sherman to pull him off his horse.

At the last moment, he restrained himself. "God damn you to hell, Sidney Sherman! What in the name of hell did you think you were doing? You could have started a full-out engagement before we were ready. I should have you shot for insubordination, but for now, get out of my sight. We will fight when I am ready, and I'm wondering if I can trust an officer who has so little regard for military discipline and plain common sense!"

Sherman, for once impressed with his commanding General, and heeding his words for a change, dismounted and disappeared among the trees, head down.

Houston turned to the young private who had saved the lives of Rusk and Lane. "Son, what's your name?"

"Mirabeau B. Lamar, sir."

"You saved those two men under Sherman's command. I'm promoting you to Colonel and you will share command with Colonel Sherman."

Lamar beamed. "Yes, sir!" He saluted.

"Who are the wounded?" Houston walked over to the injured men being taken down from their horses. One, Olwyn J. Trask, was mortally wounded, and died that night. The other man would survive, but would not be in the battle line the next day.

Later that night, Sam Houston consulted with the six other officers. Four were in favor of waiting for Santa Anna to attack. But their General had other ideas.

The following day, April 21, Jesse interrupted Houston's preparations with an urgent message. "Sir, my spies identified General Martín Perfecto de Cos and about five hundred men crossing Vince's Bridge. That brings Santa Anna's strength up to over twelve hundred, sir."

"Hell! That means they outnumber us again. Well, go get Deaf. I want him to take his men and burn down that damned bridge. That needs to be done immediately to prevent any more reinforcements from crossing— or Santa Anna from re-crossing."

"Yes, sir. That means we can't re-cross either."

"You're right, son. The die is cast."

The hours crept by. Jesse and his men were in camp, knowing the fight was imminent.

They and the other Texians cleaned and oiled their muskets and pistols, and sharpened their knives and bayonets. And waited.

The men were assigned their places in the battle order.

Finally, at about three-fifteen in the afternoon, Houston asked Jesse, "What are the Mexican troops doing?"

"Sitting around, singing, dancing, and taking siestas, some with their señoritas. General, if those men are ready to fight, I would be greatly surprised."

Although it was late in the day, at approximately three-thirty, General Houston ordered his troops, about nine hundred men, to get in position for the battle. Meanwhile, the enemy troops were quiet, and Santa Anna apparently had posted no sentries.

At four, Sam Houston commanded, "Advance!" and a wide swath of men appeared from behind the trees, ready to head for the rise of land beyond where the Mexican army was encamped. Sherman commanded cavalry on the far left, Lamar an equal number of horsemen on the far right, with three squadrons of infantry in between: Burleson's Volunteers to the right of Sherman, Hockley's artillery in the middle with the Twin Sister cannons dead center, and Millard's Regulars on the right, next to Lamar.

Houston rode his horse Saracen in front of the line of Texians, ordering them to wait before firing. Then Deaf Smith rode in to advise Houston of the destruction of Vince's Bridge, and Houston passed on the good news to his troops, giving them last-minute encouragement.

The Twin Sisters started firing at approximately four-thirty, hurling cannon balls into the ranks of the Mexican troops, followed by the line of men who charged forward, crying repeatedly, "Remember the Alamo" and "Remember Goliad." They easily climbed over the makeshift Mexican breastworks, firing their weapons as they ran.

Jesse shouted the fighting words and added, "Remember Angus Burns!" He heard a fife playing "Come to the Bower" and realized that the song further invigorated the Texians. Although they had fewer men, the Texians fought harder, remembering their battle cry, fighting for their friends and family members.

Santa Anna's sleepy, surprised troops were blinded by the sun shining in their eyes, and the glint of rifles, pistols, and knives made it even harder for his men to focus on the enemy. Santa Anna's troops fired shots and killed or wounded some of the first group of Texians coming over the rise, but when they kept coming, on foot and horseback, the Mexican troops panicked.

Jesse noticed a Mexican officer in a brightly colored uniform, trying desperately to rally his troops. Jesse fired and the officer was killed instantly. Later, upon examination, the officer was identified as General Castrillon.

Pursued by the Texians, the Mexican troops ran pell-mell, abandoning their artillery and weapons, retreating as quickly as they could.

Jesse, slashing his sword, killed five Mexican soldiers as they fled away from the battle.

Out of the corner of his eye, he spotted a diminutive Mexican soldier scrambling to get away. Raising his pistol, he blew the back of the soldier's head off.

The Texians continued to fight, and captured the fleeing Mexicans soldiers, killing them with their pistols, musket butts, or knives. Some of Santa Anna's troops fled to the swamps, where they were mired in mud; others ran to Vince's bridge, only to discover that it no longer existed.

Sam Houston ordered, "Hold your fire," but the enraged Texians could not stop fighting. Jesse and his men attempted to subdue the Texian warriors, but to little effect. The men were intent on taking revenge for the merciless killings at the Alamo and Goliad—the deaths of fathers, brothers, and sons.

The main battle was over in eighteen minutes, but the Texians continued the slaughter for hours. And though they did not know it yet, Texas had gained its independence.

CHAPTER TWELVE
Rancho Arroyo Verde

April 22, 1836

Jesse rode the perimeter of the bloody battlefield, stroking Liberty and thinking about the strategic planning of yesterday's decisive attack. His thoughts were interrupted as he reached the top of the field where the Twin Sisters, the two cannons whose blasts had opened the assault the day before, still pointed toward the now-vacant enemy position. General Houston seemed also to be reliving the battle. Seated on the ground, he rested his back against the trunk of a large oak tree, one foot bandaged.

Jesse dismounted and saluted. "Morning, General Houston, sir."

"Morning, Jesse." Houston shifted slightly, and a grimace of pain crossed his face. "Sorry not to be standing to thank you for your part in the battle yesterday. Grape-shot shattered my ankle."

"It must be pretty bad, sir, to keep a man like you off his feet."

"I fear it is. They dug bone fragments out of the wounds yesterday." Houston paused briefly to draw a breath through clenched teeth. "Reckon they'll have to haul me to New Orleans to see a real surgeon and try to save the foot, but not before I know what those other Mexican soldiers are up to. But tell me, how are you and your men?"

"None the worse for wear. We came through the battle with only a few bruises and scratches, sir."

Their conversation was interrupted by a group of riders approaching along the line of trees. As they got closer, Jesse saw they had captured a Mexican soldier. He was wearing shabby clothing, and his hands were tied behind his back, his legs secured to the horse's girth on both sides. He wondered why they were bothering General Houston with such a trivial matter. There must be hundreds of such prisoners.

The Sergeant in charge of the group halted his horse and saluted. Houston beckoned, and two corporals led the horse bearing the prisoner forward. The man hung his head for a moment, but then took a deep breath, straightened his body, and met Houston's eyes with a defiant gaze.

The Sergeant explained.

"Sir, this here is General Santa Anna. This sorry-looking peasant is the president of Mexico, believe it or not! The murdering coward was hiding in a field of tall grass and had traded his fancy uniform for these rags. As we were bringing him here, the Mexican prisoners were bowing to him and calling him 'Señor Presidente.'"

Houston nodded to Jesse and the Sergeant. "Get me up!"

They lifted their General to an upright position, standing on one foot, and supported him as he inspected the prisoner. Santa Anna immediately gave General Houston the Masonic sign of distress, which Jesse recognized. He could tell by the sweat on Houston's brow and upper lip that he was in great pain, but his mental acuity and concentration were obviously good as he interrogated Santa Anna.

"We have you in our power, Señor Presidente. You must order your other Generals to withdraw to Mexico without further hostilities."

A son of Lorenzo de Zavala translated the interrogation. Santa Anna's face reflected anger, then fear, then resignation.

"I will consider the matter, General Houston."

"Perhaps I should remind you of the fate of your soldiers in yesterday's battle. Half of them were killed without mercy by my men, just as you showed no mercy to our people."

Santa Anna began to tremble, and his reply was suddenly obsequious. "*Naturalmente*, we will parley. Of course, General Houston. I will send orders at once to my Generals to stand down."

Houston's lips tightened in a grim smile. "Good. You will pick your couriers from the prisoners, and we will escort them to the two Generals. Afterwards, we will discuss the matter of Texan independence."

He turned to the Sergeant. "Place this man under full-time guard, and keep him separated from the other prisoners until further orders."

When the men and their famous prisoner rode off, Houston's attention returned to Jesse. "Well, I guess we won't have to fear attacks from their other Generals, now that this battle is won. Would you and your men be interested in Rangering? While we fought the Mexicans, we neglected to protect the civilians from attacks by the Comanche and other hostile tribes. They've been murdering folks who are peacefully trying to tame the land, planting fields, and raising livestock."

"Yes, General, we would be most interested."

"Bring your men to my tent this afternoon and I will swear you all in, and give you detailed instructions, including possible land grants you should receive for waging this war." Houston instructed Jesse and his men to protect the areas north and west of San Antonio.

He advised them to go to Captain Murray's tent to learn about the land awards.

Jesse followed Houston's orders. As soon as he and his men had been sworn in, Jesse asked, "General, how are we to be identified as Texas Rangers?"

"Some of the men are making their own badges out of Mexican cinco pesos, and some of them are wearing white dusters."

Jesse, Hamp, and Dob made plans to head out for Rancho Arroyo Verde at morning's first light, so Jesse could deliver Angus Burns' letter to his widow.

During the trek to the ranch, the three men talked about the land they had been awarded, and keenly assessed the features of their surroundings to decide where they might settle. They saw thick, green, piney woods with abundant water, rolling plains—some arid, only fit to support cactus, with no water in sight—and some with spring grasses and other vegetation popping up in tufts, with a line of trees nearby where the waters of creeks or rivers flowed. Jesse talked about his dream of having his own homestead and horse ranch, now closer to reality than when he had left Tennessee.

Suddenly, Liberty snorted and swung his head back and forth to alert Jesse and his men to danger ahead. Then they saw the smoke and flames filling the horizon north of San Antonio. The newly designated Rangers rode straight toward the fire, discovering a cabin engulfed in flames, with heavy smoke drifting in their direction. They coughed violently until they poured canteen water on their bandanas and wrapped them around their noses and mouths.

Jesse backed Liberty away from the intense heat. "Boys, let's get moving before our horses get away from us."

When the cabin collapsed, the Rangers noticed a surreal scene: A human leg protruded from a pile of feathers. Then the heat caused the feathers to swirl around and lift toward the sky. After a few minutes, the feathers fell like snowflakes on the grisly scene.

Books littered the ground, their pages ripped out in senseless violence and decorating the trees and ground, far from the roaring flames.

"Jesse, look!" The feathers released their hold on the body of a woman who had been scalped, raped, and mutilated beyond recognition. Hamp violently retched at the sight.

"This is worse than anything we witnessed at San Jacinto." Dob, who was in shock, sat in stoic silence.

"Jesse, I believe that was her husband," Hamp pointing to the ground, where a body was prostrate, his arms reaching out for his wife. He had been brutally seized and murdered. His privates had been cut off and his eyes gouged out.

"What a horrible death!"

Then Jesse bent down and retrieved a book, discovering it was the family Bible with very few pages remaining. As he examined it, he found the hand written entries with the names of the family and their births duly recorded.

Dob came to his senses, realizing he needed to help secure the bodies. "Uncle Hamp, I've never seen the evil the Comanche are capable of doing up close."

"The Comanche are sure enough cold-blooded savages."

"Boys, it says this Bible belongs to Otto, Olga, Rudy, Greta, Bertie, and baby Hannah Schwartz. So all four of the children are missing."

The family's cow was dead, with arrows lodged throughout her carcass, and their mare, obviously too old to travel, was quivering and helpless because her loins had been hacked open with a tomahawk. Jesse ran to the mare and compassionately put her down, so she would no longer be in misery. There were no other animals, so he assumed that the Comanche had taken the children and horses after killing the parents, their cow, and leaving the old mare to die a slow, horrible death. The men buried Otto and Olga, and Jesse said the Lord's Prayer over their graves.

Realizing there was nothing else he could do for the family at their home, he set out with his men to find the children and the murdering Comanche. On the trail, he noticed overturned rocks and fresh horse manure, which told him they were getting close to the Indians.

Gray Wolf was pleased with the raid, having captured two girls along with a boy and a baby. He planned to give the baby to his squaw No Tah Wah, who had been unable to have her own children. But when the little one started crying from hunger, One Who Dances, a Comanche with a face horribly distorted by a scar, grabbed the baby, slit her throat, and threw her into a patch of prickly pear. Gray Wolf wanted to kill One Who Dances, but restrained himself, knowing that the culprit was a good horse thief. The other braves were violating the young girls, who were screaming while the Indians howled like wolves. When their older brother tried to rescue his sisters, he was run through with a lance by the youngest Comanche, who gleefully pulled out his knife and cut off the boy's scalp, yelping with delight as he danced around holding the bloody flap of skin and hair high over his head. Gray Wolf was angry at that killer, too. That half-grown boy might have made a fine warrior, just as the baby would have been useful to the Comanche women. *A glorious raid, but two stupid raiders.*

The new Rangers tracked the Indians, and found the bodies of the baby and Rudy. They strapped them to one of the packhorses, up to then carrying a light load of supplies. They feared that the traces of the fleeing savages would be impossible to track any farther, since there was very little soil ahead. There were limestone table rocks everywhere, but Hamp jumped off his horse when he saw some broken brambles and found a hoof print underneath. They rode in the direction Hamp indicated, checking the path all along the way for signs of the Comanche. When they saw smoke drifting toward the heavens, buzzards circling in the sky, and smelled meat roasting, they knew they were very close.

Dob tied the packhorse with its precious cargo to a sage bush, then remounted and followed the other men, moving slowly and carefully to avoid being discovered until the right moment arrived.

While the Comanche were busy eating the roasted meat, Jesse threw a rock over the campsite. It hit a limestone boulder. The startled Indians sprang up and turned toward the source of the noise, to see what was happening behind them. Jesse then gave the signal, and he and his men started firing. Hamp ran to the girls, tied up in a separate area near the horses. He quickly cut the ropes, grabbed them, and sprinted them to safety.

Jesse and Dob killed two Comanche, the warrior with a horribly scarred face and the youngest in the war party. They seriously wounded another.

Jesse interrogated him, and although he understood little of what the Indian murmured, he recognized the name Gray Wolf, who had fled with another Comanche. Jesse raised his pistol and fired a bullet through the Indian's head. Meanwhile, as the two other Indians were fleeing, one turned around on his horse and released his arrow as a Parthian shot, hitting Hamp in the leg.

Hamp did not cry out, but he was in severe pain. The arrow had pierced the back of his leg and was embedded in the bone.

Jesse started to push the arrow through Hamp's leg, but realized that the arrowhead was lodged in the bone. All he could do was pour turpentine on the entry wound and cut off some of the arrow. "Hamp, I wish I could do more about the pain. When we find a shelter, I'll sterilize a knife and cut that arrow out."

"Just get me back on my horse. The pain isn't so bad that I'll faint or anything, so let's get back on the trail."

Meanwhile, Dob had recovered six horses—three belonging to the Schwartz family, and three Indian mustangs.

Jesse and Dob quickly dug a shallow grave for Rudy and the baby and covered the bodies with rocks. The girls sobbed and wanted Rudy and the baby to be buried with their parents. Jesse explained, "We need to get out of here quickly. There may be more Comanche around here."

On the trail, he and his men talked of finding a place where the girls could stay, or better yet, a new safe home, but their conversations always ended in an unsatisfactory resolution of the problem. The nearest ranch they knew of was the Burns place, so they took the girls there.

Rachel Burns looked up from her sewing when she heard the dogs barking. Through the cabin's window, she saw the dogs running excitedly toward several figures in the distance. Her heart pounded and she raced to the door, grabbing the shotgun. Since she had learned of her father Angus's death at the Alamo, she had become the self-appointed protector of her mother, her younger brother Isaac, their ranch hand Tobe, and the ranch.

When the dogs stopped barking, she was puzzled and walked out of the house. She stopped on the porch with the cocked shotgun pointed toward the three men, but she now saw that two young girls were riding with them. One of the men was unsteady in his saddle with his head bent low.

On the porch, Jesse saw a slender young woman who looked like an angel with long golden hair, wearing a simple dress, and pointing a shotgun straight at him. He liked her looks, and liked her even more for her courage. The dogs continued to lick his hand after devouring the dried liver he carried in his pocket. He held up his hands and Hamp and Dob followed suit.

Being so mesmerized by the beauty of the young woman, he failed to notice an older woman standing beside the house. He noticed her presence when she said, "Come on in and rest yourselves for a spell. Rachel, get the men some coffee and milk for the girls. Isaac, take their horses to the barn so you and Tobe can feed and water them."

Jesse and Dob helped Hamp and the girls dismount. Hamp, whose face was strained and his shirt was wet with perspiration, needed assistance in hobbling into the house.

Jesse turned to the older woman. "Ma'am, may we use your table to cut this arrow out of Sergeant Wallace's leg?"

"Of course. My name's Martha Burns. Just let me get some candles and take the tablecloth off." She quickly retrieved the items. "You'll need something to deaden his pain. Just a second. I've got some whisky in the cabinet." After a second or two of rummaging, she produced a bottle and removed the cork.

Hamp opened his clenched teeth. "Thank you, Mrs. Burns!"

His fellow Rangers carefully lifted him onto the table, and handed him the bottle of whiskey and a small, rolled-up piece of clean cotton cloth provided by Rachel. Martha heated the knife in the fireplace to sterilize it. Hamp drank two deep gulps of the whiskey, placed the cloth between his teeth, and managed to mumble, "Get to cutting."

After the arrow with its barbed head was successfully removed, Jesse walked to the fireplace, took the poker, and held it in the blazing fire, then walked back to the patient and pressed the red hot poker against the wound to seal it.

Hamp, having been silent during this ordeal, passed out while Martha dressed the wound. When she completed her task, she told the men to carry the patient to her son Isaac's bed. When he was settled in, she gently covered him with quilts.

Once Jesse was outside the hearing range of the girls, he told Martha their tragic story, and how Hamp had been struck by the arrow while rescuing them.

Meanwhile, Rachel had cleaned the table, replaced the tablecloth, poured fresh coffee into various types of cups and placed them on the table. She then poured milk into two small cups and placed two biscuits left over from breakfast on plates and set them beside the milk. Everyone except Hamp gathered at the table and Jesse bowed his head and said, "Lord, thank you for the kindness and generosity of the Burns family. Please, God, watch over Hamp," and the group said "Amen" in unison.

Martha told the girls, "You are welcome to live here with us."

The girls hung their heads, but nodded. "That's very kind of you, Mrs. Burns," Greta, the older one said.

Rachel poured them more milk and picked up the plates, which were licked clean.

Jesse stood and turned to Martha. "Thank you, Mrs. Burns; we came here to deliver something from your husband. If you'll excuse me, I will get it." He went out the back door to the barn to get Angus's saddlebags. He stroked Liberty and whispered kind, soothing words to him. After removing the saddlebags from his horse, he returned to the house and gently placed them on the table in front of Martha, who rubbed her hands over them, one finger tracing the initial B tooled into the beautiful leather.

"Angus must have had these made while he was in San Antonio."

Jesse spoke softly. "There's something inside for you."

She opened the compartment, pulled out the letter, and read it. With tears rolling down her cheeks, she handed it to her daughter, who read it and, with tears also welling up in her eyes, returned it to her mother.

Gently stroking the lock of her husband's hair, Martha said, "Jesse, the saddlebags are yours. You brought me the most important things."

She held the letter close to her heart, while her daughter nodded her head in agreement.

"Girls, Rachel will get you settled in and give you men some blankets so you can be more comfortable in the stable where our worker Tobe sleeps."

Rachel took the girls' hands and walked them to her bedroom, saying, "I've wanted a sister and now I have two!"

After the chores were completed, everyone except Hamp, and Martha, who compassionately attended to the patient through the night, slept soundly at the Burns' Rancho Arroyo Verde.

The next morning at dawn, Rachel prepared breakfast, then went out the back door and saw Jesse sitting on the grassy, green bank above Verde Creek, where he could hear the calming sound of water tumbling over the rocks and bubbling over the cypress tree roots. The trees lined the banks of the creek like silent sentinels. As dawn quietly receded into the shadows, a solitary deer drank from the crystal clear water. She had enjoyed this scene many times before, but this morning was different from the others. She sat beside him and they absorbed the quiet around them, disturbed only by the voices of nature.

She broke the silence. "Come inside, Mr. McAlester. I've cooked a big breakfast for you and your men."

"Please, ma'am, don't call me Mr. McAlester. When I hear that name, I look around for my father."

"I will stop, if you won't call me 'ma'am.'"

"I promise, ma'am—I mean Rachel."

She grinned at him. They walked to the house, and he opened the back door for her and once inside, pulled out the chair she had sat in yesterday.

"You are quite the gentleman."

The breakfast was on the table and everyone except Hamp squeezed in and ate a hearty breakfast.

Jesse looked at Martha. "Do you have chores that Dob and I could do today?"

"Well, we do have a fence that needs mending, and the horses need to be worked."

Jesse turned to Rachel. "I grew up on a horse farm and would enjoy helping."

Dob said, "I'll take care of the fence if you show me where it is." Isaac led him to the barn, gathered tools and supplies, and then took him to the broken fence, while Jesse helped Rachel wash, dry, and put up the dishes. Then he followed her to the barn.

She looked him up and down a bit doubtfully. "We have a wild stallion that needs to be broken."

"I love training wild horses." He smiled at her.

Tobe was already bringing the stallion from the barn on a rope, carrying a horse blanket and saddle, which he laid across the corral fence.

"Tobe, get that rope around his leg and tie him off on the post," Rachel shouted, as the wild horse fought Tobe and the rope every step of the way.

Jesse stepped forward. "That's all right, Tobe. I have my own way." He loosened the rope and handed it to Tobe.

Rachel protested. "Jesse, are you crazy? That horse is going to kick you and Tobe to death, and I'll have to bury the both of you!"

"Whoa, boy. I'm not going to hurt you." Jesse's gentle voice began to soothe the wild-eyed, snorting stallion. He pulled out the milt from his pocket, and using the training that he had mastered from Hugh, let the horse smell it as he kept whispering to it.

Rachel stood with her hands on her hips. "I suppose you think you can just talk to a wild horse and he will mind you."

Then it happened: Jesse gently slid the blanket over the stallion's back.

"Well, I never," Rachel gasped.

Jesse instructed, "Tobe, slowly ease your weight on his back and stroke his neck."

"Mr. Jesse, that horse doesn't like me."

Rachel, stunned by the transformation in the wild horse, made an offer. "I'll do it if you're sure it's all right." After Jesse's affirmative nod, she gently eased onto the horse's back and stroked his neck. Soon the beautiful, powerful horse started to trot around the corral.

Martha watched the scene from a window and saw the miracle occur, while Jesse admired how comfortably her daughter sat on the horse.

After the stallion had trotted around the corral several times, he slowed to a walk and then came to stand before Jesse. He pushed his face against Jesse's chest and was rewarded with kind words, stroking, and another sniff of the milt.

Rachel dismounted and added her own caresses to Jesse's. "I never would have believed it in a million years. You performed a miracle!"

"It's all in knowing horses, Rachel. I grew up with them."

Martha came outside, walked to Rachel, and spoke softly in Gaelic, "He sure is a good-looking boy."

"Mama, you mean a good-looking man," she replied in Gaelic. Jesse, being born in a Gaelic-speaking house, smiled at the pair.

After several weeks, Jesse and Dob had repaired every broken thing at Rancho Arroyo Verde. Jesse had trained four horses and broken another one, and Hamp's leg was healing but not yet whole.

The next evening, Rachel and Jesse were strolling hand in hand on the banks of Verde Creek.

"I know we've had this conversation several times before, and you know that I really don't want to leave," Jesse said. "But I'm determined to be a Ranger so I can make Texas a safe place for families and prevent the kinds of things that happened to the girls and their family. By the way, you and your mother are doing a great job with them."

"Oh, you are a stubborn man. I've already lost Papa and now I fear I'll lose you, too."

"Don't worry, because I have right on my side." He stopped and whispered into her ear, "Tha gaol agam ort." *"I love you."*

Without thinking she replied, "Tha gaol agam ort-fhein." *"I love you too."*

Then she realized what had happened and berated him, "Jesse McAlester, you understood everything my mother and I have said to each other!"

"I'm sorry, I thought you knew my family spoke Gaelic. Au toir thu dhomh pog?" *"Will you give me a kiss?"*

"Cha toir, ach bheir mi dhut sgailc!" *"No, but I'll slap you!"*

"I'm sorry, Rachel," he said as he gently nuzzled her neck. "I love you. Please don't be angry with me."

"I love you too. Please don't go."

They heard hoof beats and the dogs barking, as a sole rider approached the house.

He was a courier sent by Sam Houston, bringing orders for Jesse, Hamp, and Dob to report to Major William Patton's home in Columbia.

Jesse told the courier, "Sergeant Hamp Wallace will not be able to travel because he was severely wounded by a Comanche arrow. Dob and I will leave at dawn tomorrow." He found himself unable to look at Rachel when he spoke the last words.

Rachel ran into the house, and Jesse gave her a few minutes to deal with the sudden news of his departure. Then he went inside and held her in his arms. "Rachel, I have to follow orders, but someday we can spend as many days together as you want."

She longed for the day when she could be with Jesse all the time.

CHAPTER THIRTEEN
Orozimbo

S anta Anna was being held at Major William Patton's home in Columbia. On June 27, 1836, a drunkard fired a pistol through a window in an unsuccessful attempt to murder the prisoner. Concerned for his safety, Houston planned to move him to a safer location.

When Houston received an affirmative response from Dr. James Phelps to his request to house Santa Anna at his Orozimbo Plantation, he was greatly relieved. Old Sam summoned Jesse McAlester and his men, ordering them to assist Major Patton for the short trek to Orozimbo.

Houston had received reports from his spies that some locals might try to capture Santa Anna and Juan Almonte, his friend and translator, and administer frontier justice.

On the trail to Columbia, Jesse's and Dob's spirits soared like eagles in flight, and their horses, feeling their riders' exultation, galloped at full speed, until Jesse reined Liberty to a slower pace, to conserve the animals' energy for the long ride ahead. Moving at a ground-eating trot, they had time to look around and enjoy the beauty of the hills, as the sun began to rise above the horizon. It cast a coral and pink glow over the precipices and massive live oak trees, with their tiny but abundant emerald leaves. Their branches grew in various and unusual directions.

At dusk, tired after riding many miles, they stopped and set up camp. While Jesse fed and watered the horses, removed their saddles and bridles, and brushed them, always whispering soothing words to them, Dob started a fire, brewed coffee, and made a hearty soup with dried beef jerky, carrots, and onions.

When their stomachs were full, Jesse looked up at the stars overhead and told Dob the direction they needed to take on the following day.

Jesse loved adventure and knew Rachel loathed his sudden departure. He silently said a prayer. *Lord, thank you for this beautiful world. Please watch over us on this mission and keep Rachel safe.*

They slept well that night.

At Rancho Arroyo Verde, the moon was full, with no clouds in the sky, and the only sound was an owl hooting, answered by a growl from Buck, Rachel's dog, who had been lying on the porch. The growling became louder. He ran off the porch barking a fierce alert, but suddenly stopped, emitting a loud whimper.

The adults in the cabin immediately doused the lights. In the barn, Tobe heard the commotion and ran to the house with the other two dogs.

As she picked up the shotgun, Martha told Rachel, "Take the girls to the cellar."

Rachel carried the youngest girl, Bertie, who was sound asleep, to the cellar, with the older girl, Greta, following behind them.

After the girls were settled in the cellar, Rachel ran back up the steps, grabbing a loaded rifle from the two pegs above the front door, and waited. The bright moonlight offered ample illumination for those inside the Burns' cabin to see the Comanche. She saw two Indians running toward the cabin with weapons in their hands. She placed her cocked rifle in one of the shooting holes in the cabin, fired once and hit one of the raiders in his chest. He fell to the ground, writhing in pain, and began his death chant. Rachel grabbed her father's rifle, which she had also loaded, cocked it, set it in the shooting hole, fired, and killed the second Indian.

Gray Wolf, determined to gain entry into the cabin, had three remaining braves pick up a large log and ram the front door. The Indians kept battering until Hamp thumbed aside the shooting hole in the door and blasted all three with his sawed-off shotgun.

Gray Wolf sneaked around to the back door and tried to dislodge it, while Tobe and Isaac were straining to keep the Indian out of the house.

Hamp said, "When I say 'Now,' yank the door open."

The boys, uncertain of their fate, yanked the door open on command, leaving Martha face-to-face with Gray Wolf. She did not hesitate, and blasted him with both barrels of her shotgun, the recoil driving her backwards and the force of the shot splitting the Indian in two.

Hamp told Martha, "That's the Indian that shot the arrow in my leg. His name is Gray Wolf."

With Gray Wolf dead, Hamp took a risk, went to the front door, opened it, stepped over the three dead Comanche, and hobbled to Buck, relieved to find him still breathing, with an arrow in his side.

He shouted, "Tobe! Isaac! Get Buck inside the house!"

They followed his instructions and placed the severely wounded dog on the table. The arrow had almost completely penetrated Buck's body.

"Boys, I need you to stand Buck up and hold him as best you can. I'm going to push the arrow through."

Hamp broke off the barbed end of the arrow and told Martha, "Pull the shaft out. If we're lucky the arrow missed his vitals."

Martha successfully completed her part of the procedure, and then Hamp poured whiskey into the gaping wound. Martha retrieved her sewing box and selected a large needle and heavy thread to suture the skin together. Afterward she applied a special salve to aid in the healing.

The girls came up from the cellar and stood nearby, praying for Buck. Then they gathered quilts and placed them on the floor beside Rachel's bed and asked Isaac to carry the dog to the middle of the pallet they had made. They cuddled on each side of Buck and petted him until they all fell fast asleep.

The next morning, the girls woke up when Buck began licking their faces and saw him wagging his tail. Rachel brought him water and leftover soup. After having his fill of water and soup, he licked his lips and reclined on the blanket to take his morning nap, enjoying more petting from the girls.

That morning, Hamp, Isaac, and Tobe gathered the Indians' six mustangs that had been grazing in the field nearby, and herded them into the corral. Among them, three were well proportioned, large mares with refined features. Hamp drew the boys' attention to their arched necks, sloping shoulders, fine but strong legs, and well-formed hooves.

"I know that Jesse wants to start a horse ranch one of these days. These mares look like almost pure Spanish mustangs. Maybe he can breed them with Liberty and start a herd."

"Darn!" Isaac exclaimed. "I was hoping to keep that pale yellow one with the black mane and tail for myself."

Hamp squeezed his shoulder. "We'll see when Jesse gets back, son."

They collected the Comanche weapons and put them in the barn and removed the Indians' moccasins, leggings, and anything else that could be reused, along with necklaces, other jewelry, and Gray Wolf's war bonnet. Then they loaded the Indians' bodies into a wagon and took them to a remote field, where they burned them.

Martha and Rachel picked up the Indians' clothing, the war bonnet and jewelry, and placed them in the toolshed. Then they carried buckets of water from the well and scrubbed the porches to remove the blood from the raid.

Jesse and Dob rode as fast as they considered safe for the horses down the trail to Columbia. Fortunately, they had no problems on the journey, arriving several days later.

Major William Patton was in charge of the escort of Santa Anna, along with Juan Almonte, to Orozimbo.

Jesse and Dob hoisted Santa Anna and Almonte, whose wrists were tied, helping them mount the horses brought by Major Patton for them.

Once they left Columbia, Jesse asked the Major's permission to remove the rawhide bands from the prisoners' wrists, promising he would be responsible if any attempt to escape were made as a result. When he received the go-ahead, Jesse removed the rawhide bands, and while he was doing so, both prisoners smiled slightly at him and rubbed their sore wrists.

After a few miles, the traveling became harder as they entered a thick forest by the Brazos River, where huge trees clustered together and surrounded them. Bristly vines draped over their branches, looped down to claw at their faces, and crept across the spongy trail, tangling the horses' feet. The air, thick with moisture, made it hard to breathe.

Jesse looked at Dob. "Hamp will sure be sorry he missed this." Then he and Dob had a good laugh.

They followed the Brazos River until they reached the Orozimbo Plantation. Although Jesse and Dob thought their mission was over, Major Patton had not yet revealed all of the General's plans.

"Jesse, General Houston has ordered you and Dob to safeguard the prisoners until a relief detachment arrives to assume your responsibilities."

"Yes, Major. But I will need to write a letter to my friends explaining the extended duty."

After he completed his letter and gave it to the Major, Jesse walked to Santa Anna.

Speaking in Spanish, he said, "It seems we'll be here for a while, yet, General. We'll wait until a squad of soldiers arrives to protect you. Meanwhile, Dob and I will see that you remain safe."

Santa Anna nodded at Jesse, with a smile of gratitude. "I will never forget your kindness. I hope to repay you someday." He pulled off his gold Masonic ring and extended his hand to Jesse, who admired it.

"Please accept this ring as a token of our friendship."

"It's a beautiful ring, General." He slipped it on his finger, as they clasped hands in a Masonic embrace.

Several weeks later, Texian soldiers rode into Orozimbo to relieve Jesse and Dob, who immediately packed up their blankets and saddles, and said their goodbyes to Dr. Phelps and his wife.

Mrs. Phelps embraced both men. "You men have been exemplary. Here's some food for your journey." She handed them fresh-baked bread, salt pork, and six fresh eggs packed in straw. "Mind you—be careful with those eggs. I hate to see you two boys go. You've been like sons to us."

"Thank you, Ma'am," Dob smiled as he took the food and carefully placed it in his saddlebags.

Dr. Phelps brought a bag of oats for the horses and handed it to Jesse, who strapped it on the back of his saddle. He and his wife bid Jesse and Dob a tearful goodbye as they rode off toward Rancho Arroyo Verde, which they now considered their home.

Later, Jesse was advised by Sam Houston that on August 17, a plot to rescue the prisoners and send them on a ship to Mexico was discovered. This report made it necessary to shackle Santa Anna with a ball and chain on his ankle, and the following day, Almonte was chained in the same manner. The prisoners remained chained there for 53 and 52 days, respectively.

Jesse felt bad for Santa Anna. Although the Mexican was his enemy, he had observed a vulnerable and lonely man, who yearned to return to his home near Vera Cruz.

Jesse later received word that Santa Anna had attempted suicide twice at Orozimbo. Dr. Phelps, who remained respectful of the prisoners, gave him a medical antidote to counteract the poison on both occasions.

Jesse found out that Major Patton and two other men left Orozimbo in the early morning of November 25th, taking the prisoners in a horse-drawn coach through East Texas, crossing the San Jacinto battlefield, and then traveling through northern Louisiana. They avoided New Orleans, where many people wanted Santa Anna to be executed. Finally, they reached the Mississippi River, where they boarded a steamboat sailing upstream to the Ohio River, where they changed steamboats, with a final destination of Washington, D.C. After they arrived there, they met with President Andrew Jackson and his cabinet, who found Santa Anna of no political use to them. He and Almonte were then sent on a U.S. Navy ship to Vera Cruz.

CHAPTER FOURTEEN
Rangering

August 1836

As Jesse and Dob trotted their horses down the lane to the Burns ranch, Buck limped toward the pair, while Lucky, the small terrier, ran in circles around them. Maggie, Isaac's hunting dog, ran from the barn to investigate the disturbance. Jesse dismounted, felt Buck's side and realized he had suffered a serious injury. He pulled out dried venison as a treat for the three dogs.

Martha and Rachel, alerted by the excited barking, waited on the front porch while Isaac, Tobe, Greta, and Bertie ran to greet the two Rangers, followed by a limping Hamp.

As usual, Martha took charge. "Jesse, Dob, get yourselves off your horses. Isaac, you and Tobe take the horses around back and feed and water them. Rachel, you and the girls start setting out some food, and Hamp, please don't strain that bad leg if you ever expect it to heal."

Jesse and Dob poured water from a bucket hanging on a nail beside the porch into a battered tin pan and sloshed their faces and hair, dried off with a rag towel, and slapped their clothes, removing as much of the road dust as possible.

Hamp cleared his throat and said, "Jesse, I need you and Dob to sit at the table and listen to our story about our battle with the Comanche." Jesse grew pale while hearing the story and the danger the Burns family had experienced, especially Rachel.

Dob, usually the less talkative of the two, spoke up. "I'm glad you finally got that murdering Gray Wolf. He won't be lifting any more scalps around here."

Jesse reached over and clasped Hamp's hand. "Hamp, I'm grateful to you for protecting the family."

"Jesse, it wasn't just me. Martha, Rachel, and the boys did their share of the fighting. Even Buck did his part in alerting us to the Indians."

"Yes, and I see he paid the price!"

After a late dinner, Jesse excused himself and asked Rachel to take a walk with him down to the large cypress trees, along the banks of Verde Creek. With dusk approaching, they walked in silence for a while, enjoying the beauty of the grass interwoven with wild flowers and the pure fast-running creek. Even as the sun went down, they could see clear to the bottom, the water sparkling over cypress roots and rocks.

"Jesse, why the secrecy and urgency to talk right now?"

"Rachel, my love," he said, now on bended knee, "I am asking you to marry me."

She started crying. "While you were gone, I was so worried that you might not come back."

"Does that mean yes?"

"Of course, I will!"

Jesse's face lit up like the full moon.

"But I want you to come with me so that we can tell Mama."

"Will she approve?"

"Mama loves you and thinks of you as a son."

Martha had been watching out the window, with a clear view of Verde Creek, and had seen Jesse kneel and clasp her daughter's hands.

Martha had been expecting this, and upon gaining her composure at the loss of her daughter, she reminded herself of the new son she was getting.

Jesse and Rachel entered the house, but before he could explain that he'd asked for her daughter's hand in marriage, Martha wrapped her arms around the couple, crying tears of happiness, and proclaimed, "Jesse, I am so proud for you to become a member of our family."

"Mrs. Burns, I will always protect and honor Rachel until my dying day."

"Mama, how did you know he had asked me to marry him?"

Martha winked at her daughter and future son-in-law. "Mothers know these things."

The whole family assembled in the cabin, and Martha shared the joyous news with them.

Afterwards, they became quite loud, some cheering, some laughing, but all congratulated the happy couple.

"I want to get married on Papa's birthday, October 15."

Jesse, obviously pleased, agreed. "October the 15th it is, and every year we will celebrate your Papa's birthday and our anniversary."

While Jesse and Dob were gone on their mission to escort Santa Anna, Martha and Hamp had grown closer. He had told her about his family, including his deceased wife, along with Jesse's bravery at San Jacinto and his resourcefulness in the fight with Gray Wolf. A spark of friendship had developed between them. Martha started wondering how long she should remain in mourning to honor her late husband.

The grim reality of the frontier life meant that Martha needed Hamp as much as he needed her, so she decided to discuss the matter with Rachel in due time and, certainly, after her daughter's wedding.

On October 15, Jesse was nervous, standing on the banks of Verde Creek, wearing his best clothes. His nervousness quickly disappeared when Rachel walked out the front door of the cabin, wearing a beautiful white gown she had made, with embroidered flowers on the bodice, a skirt that moved with her graceful walk, and on her head a crown of wild flowers.

He thought, "She's even more beautiful than the first time I saw her with the shotgun aimed at me. She truly is my angel."

The wedding began with Isaac singing a romantic song in a beautiful tenor voice. Everyone, except his mother and his sister, was astonished at the quality of his voice.

The circuit preacher performed a short ceremony, and after they both said, "I do," he recited the Lord's Prayer, as the groom had requested. Jesse kissed his bride and everyone shouted, "Cheers!" "Kiss her again!" and "What a beautiful bride!"

After the wedding, Martha invited everyone to the house and served a beautiful cake while Hamp poured liberal portions of whisky. He then played his harmonica as Isaac sang lively tunes and the dancing commenced.

When Tobe walked in the back door with his guitar, Hamp put his harmonica down and asked Martha to dance, and this time she didn't say, or even think, "Hamp, you shouldn't exert your bad leg."

Jesse had eyes only for Rachel. "Rachel, my beautiful wife, I have loved you since the first time I saw you on the front porch and I love you even more today." Then he kissed her, with more cheering erupting in the cabin.

The preacher drank so much liquor that Dob had to hitch the wagon and take him home with his horse tied to the back of the wagon.

Martha moved Greta and Bertie into her room to give the newlyweds privacy. Rachel and Jesse were embracing when Jesse whispered in her ear.

Rachel blushed, "Jesse McAlester, you ought to be ashamed of yourself." Then she smiled and kissed him.

While Jesse and Dob had been on their mission, Hamp had grown stronger. He rode the land beyond the Burns ranch for hours each day, determining the best sites for the three men to claim with their land grants.

He now discussed his findings with Jesse and Dob, who whole-heartedly agreed with him.

After his marriage, Jesse claimed his grant of 1280 acres, and Dob claimed his 640 acres, and then Hamp surveyed both ranches. For some reason he did not disclose, Hamp did not claim his own land grant.

Rachel teased, "Is the extra land the reason you wanted to marry me?"

Laughing, Jesse picked up his new bride and twirled her around until she yelled, "Stop!"

"Rachel, I would like to breed and train horses for the Republic of Texas. What do you think about that?"

"That's something I can help with, and I love the idea."

In late October, Jesse put out word to friends and neighbors that there would be a house-raising to build a home for him and his new bride.

With all the folks coming with the needed tools and an abundance of food, the cabin was completed very quickly, and ready for the newlyweds to move in. Rachel had so much fun placing the furniture and adding her final touches to the cabin that she made Jesse smile, realizing how lucky he was to have her as his wife.

In December 1836, Jesse's new commander, Captain Hawkins in San Antonio, sent him a message, ordering him to build a permanent Ranger station, with corrals and bunks for up to ten men. The Captain also authorized Jesse to hire and train seven new Rangers.

"Hamp, I need you and Dob to help me find seven good men interested in becoming Rangers."

While Hamp figured where to situate the new home for the Rangers, Jesse asked him, "What accommodations do they need?"

"I figure we need to be close to water and have a clear open field for training," Dob unrolled a map and pointed to a plot of land a half mile from Rancho Arroyo Verde, but Jesse said, "We need to check with Mrs. Burns and get her agreement."

"Martha won't object." Hamp's face reddened, realizing he had called her by her familiar name.

"Martha? Is that what you call her when we're not around? Sounds serious, Hamp. Does this mean you're going to be my new father-in-law?"

"Jesse, we talked about it when you and Dob were gone, and we're just waiting for the right time to tell Rachel and Isaac."

"Well, guess what? Rachel and Isaac know that you and Martha have become quite friendly, and they are surprised that you're not already married."

"That's a burden lifted off of my shoulders. I've been praying that they wouldn't object."

"Uncle Hamp, it's about time you got married," Dob interjected. "You've been a widower a long time now."

But before Hamp had time to propose to Martha, Jesse sent him south toward San Antonio, Dob to the east, and he went north to find new recruits. They posted notices in saloons, dry goods stores, and everywhere they could think of to draw the attention of potential new recruits. The notice included details on where to meet, required qualifications, supplies they needed to bring, and lastly the monthly pay.

By the end of December, nineteen recruits had showed up at the location of the new Ranger station. But in those early days, the only shelter they had was a tent.

Jesse, pleasantly surprised at the turnout, decided to test the candidates' skills in shooting and riding.

"Men, I want you to line up on your horses, and then one by one, you will race your horses within thirty yards of the target log and shoot your pistol into the circle drawn around the log."

The men did their best to comply with Jesse's instructions, but twelve of the men were dismissed immediately because of their inaccuracy. The remaining seven passed the test with flying colors.

They were twins Cager and Cuddy Holley, Rube Reynolds, Quill Parker, Charlie "Choc" Wilson, Bonner Pickens, and Chato Obregón.

The next step was to test their ability with a rifle. The men, all experienced frontiersmen, easily passed this test too.

Jesse set up a schedule for their training: they would work on riding and shooting in the morning, and help build their future quarters in the afternoon.

Under the seasoned Rangers' supervision, and with the weather getting colder every day, all the men worked hard to be able to sleep in a building rather than a tent.

Jesse told Hamp, "The hard labor will toughen up the men."

They trained the men in riding, shooting, and tracking through demonstration and repetition, as they had trained Houston's soldiers.

After several months, they thought the men were ready to become Rangers, but first they had to pass a final riding test.

The first to be tested were Cager and Cuddy, who ran to their horses and with one leap mounted them from behind, then raced down the field. They turned their horses around and raced back, both reaching down at the same time to pick up a small log from the ground, without losing any speed. This was a well-known Comanche maneuver to rescue their dead and wounded on the battlefield. Everyone was whooping and hollering.

"Choc" was next; he raced across the open field with his hands in the air, controlling his mount with only his knees and legs. He raced back, dipped down to pluck a flower and set the flower at Jesse's feet.

Then Bonner Pickens, at full gallop, uncoiled his lariat, swung it deftly over the target log and dragged it fifty feet before recovering his rope.

Jesse relished his memories of the fancy riding he and his brothers had performed in Ayr and Nashville.

Rube Reynolds was next. At a gallop, his horse jumped across a brook with man and beast still intact, resulting in "huzzahs" from the Rangers, and upon his return, he had his horse rear up. At his command, it lay down, and Rube slid off its back.

Quill Parker, never afraid of a challenge, ran and mounted his horse, and at a full gallop, reclined flat on its back. He sat up in the saddle, then reined his horse back toward the others, dropped to the ground to the left, swung back in the saddle, dropped to the ground on the right side, and came to an abrupt halt in front of the men, who were cheering, whistling, and clapping.

Jesse shouted, "Chato, you better be good, if you expect to outride these boys!"

Chato rode his horse in small circles, and then raced down the field. He turned around backwards, while still controlling his mount, swiveled in his saddle, then dropped his whole body to the left side of his mount, and then repeated the maneuver on the right side, a maneuver that would completely shield his body from an adversary.

Hamp and Dob declined to enter the riding contest, and the new Rangers implored Jesse to display his riding ability.

"I don't know how I can best your riding, but I will try."

Liberty bolted down the field, and Jesse stood up on his back to the shouts and cries of all the men. Back in the saddle, he raced back toward the men, came to a sudden stop and shouted, "Up!" In response to the command, the beautiful Andalusian jumped and held all of his legs off the ground for a frozen moment, kicking his rear legs backward once he landed again. "This movement is called the Capriole and is used as a tactic for clearing the area behind you in a battle."

The men surrounded Liberty, admiring him, and praising Jesse for owning such a magnificent animal, and complimenting Jesse for his incredible riding.

The seven men were sworn in as Texas Rangers by Jesse, who presented each man with his badge. They then waited for their first mission.

CHAPTER FIFTEEN
Battles

January 1837

Before he received his orders from Major Hawkins, Jesse thought about how he would deploy his men. He decided to divide the ten Rangers, including himself, into two groups. He would have Cager and Cuddy Holley, Quill Parker, and Chato Obregón under his command. Jesse reasoned that he and Chato could communicate in Spanish, and Chato had a deep understanding of both sides of the Rio Grande.

Sergeant Hamp Wallace would lead Dob Andrews, Charlie "Choc" Wilson, Rube Reynolds, and Bonner Pickens in the second group. Hamp would have the benefit of the mixed-race Choc, whose name, Charlie, had been picked by his Scottish father; his nickname derived from his Choctaw mother. Born into both worlds, he was an expert tracker and hated the Comanche.

Once he discussed the structure of the two groups of Rangers with Hamp and received his approval, Jesse sent a message to Major Hawkins in San Antonio, advising him of his plan.

Hawkins, the commander of the Rangers in San Antonio, had set up a network of spies throughout the city, who advised him about illegal trading going on between Comancheros and the Comanche on the Pinta Trail. One of his spies had told the Major, "There is suspicious activity at the livery stable, the mercantile store, and Jacob Wheeler's fur trading place. I'm certain there are stolen horses at the livery stable, large quantities of whiskey being sold at the mercantile, and a lot of buffalo hides coming into Wheeler's. Do you want us to arrest them?"

"Not yet."

Hawkins sent a message to Lieutenant McAlester at the Ranger camp near Verde Creek:

January 17, 1837
San Antonio

Lieutenant McAlester:

I have been made aware by my associates that Comancheros and horse thieves are operating freely in this city. Have Sergeant Wallace head up the Pinta Trail and make contact with these Comancheros. He should be able to track them by the heavy loads they are carrying. After he finds the Comancheros, I want him to bring the wagon and its contents back to San Antonio, and, Lieutenant, tell him to bring the criminals back alive so I may interrogate them.

Lieutenant McAlester, I want you to cut the horse thieves' trail and find out where they are taking the stolen stock, recover the horses, and punish the thieves with impunity.

Respectfully yours,

Major Henry Hawkins

Hamp, reading the letter over Jesse's shoulder, asked, "What does 'impunity' mean?"

"No prisoners." Jesse laughed. "Hamp, the Major has a plan he would utilize as soon as you return the prisoners to the Ranger headquarters in San Antonio."

"Can we at least have a little fun in interrogating them?"

"As long as they arrive in San Antonio in one piece."

Sergeant Wallace and his unit started out immediately on the Pinta, and soon spotted deep ruts in the ground, caused by a wagon. Choc was sent ahead to scout for the Comancheros, and then returned to Wallace.

"Sergeant Wallace, sir, I've found them!"

"What are their movements now?"

"They still have their wagon, and when I left them, they were making camp for the night."

"How many men were there?"

"Just two, Sergeant."

"We'll surprise them at sundown, just when they are settling in. I want you, Dob, Bonner, and Rube to surround them. But don't shoot unless you have to."

At dusk, the Rangers surrounded the wagon, noticing that it was sagging in the middle, which meant they were carrying heavy cargo.

"You men get up from that campfire! I'm Sergeant Wallace with the Texas Rangers and I want to inspect that wagon." Hamp cocked his pistol. "Who are you, and what's your business?"

"I'm Cam Howard, and this little fellow is Bob Rawlings."

"We have reports that you men are Comancheros, trading illegally with the Comanche. We need to inspect your wagon."

The little fellow began to whine. "I told you, Cam, we were headed in the wrong direction."

"Shut up Bob, don't you say another word, or…"

Hamp interrupted. "Mr. Howard, what's in the wagon?"

"Nothing, Sergeant, we trade with friendly Indians and provide them with beads, pots, pans, some fabric, and bits of metal for starting fires."

"Dob, you and Choc roll back that canvas tarp and see if these boys are the liars I believe they are."

They examined the trade goods and discovered exactly what Cam had said.

"I told you, Sergeant, we're just innocent traders trying to make a little money."

Bob began to snivel, pointing at a metal rod, curved at the end, in Choc's fist. "What do you need a pry bar for?"

"Rube, bring that torch over here so we can see what these boys are really carrying."

Cam and Bob, sweating profusely and nervously fidgeting, had looks of resignation on their faces. "Okay, Sergeant, you got us, but please move that torch away, or we'll all be blown to hell."

Upon further investigation and with the use of the pry bar, the Rangers found a false bottom in the wagon stuffed with whiskey, metal for Comanche arrowheads, rifles, pistols, ball, shot, and a massive amount of black powder.

Hamp turned to the two culprits with a bleak smile. "You're just the fellows we've been looking for. This answers my question about who is supplying weapons to the Comanche. Dob, get a rope, I believe this tree will suit our purpose."

"You're not going to give us a fair trial?" Bob began to weep again.

Cam barked at him. "Shut up, you sniveling rat!"

Choc tied the Comancheros' hands behind their backs while Dob threw the rope over the tree branch, made a noose and coiled it around Cam's neck. The two hoisted Cam on a horse, but then he began to struggle.

"To hell with you Rangers!" Cam kicked his horse violently, and the horse lurched forward at a run before anyone could stop him, causing the rope to tighten with a jerk and the massive knot twisted Cam's head and broke his neck with a snap like a dry twig. The horse ran on, leaving Cam swinging wildly under the tree branch.

Bob, seeing Cam's eyes popped out of their sockets and his soiled pants, threw his hands up, begging, "Sergeant, please don't hang me."

"Bob, we never intended to hang either of you. Your partner caused his own death. Our orders are to take the freight to Ranger headquarters, and bring any prisoners there for questioning."

Hamp waved a dismissive hand at the ground. "We won't waste time digging a grave," he said. "Put some rocks over the body. Choc, Dob, take the prisoner and put him in the back of his wagon. Bonner, you and Rube tie your horses to the back of the wagon and drive it to San Antonio."

Once they had arrived in San Antonio, the Major advised Bob, "You either agree to my plan, or we'll invite any friends and family you have to the square and hang you publicly."

"What do I have to do, Major?"

"We'll find you another partner so you can deliver the goods to the Comanche, but with a change of plans."

"What do you mean?"

"We're going to dilute the black powder and disable the firearms, but I suggest you get the Comanche drunk quickly before they figure out what you've done."

"That sounds like a death sentence."

"If you act quickly, you can complete the trade."

"How do you expect me and my new partner to escape, driving a wagon?"

"After you make the trade, drive your team back on the same trail and make sure you drive slowly so you won't arouse suspicion. About a mile from your rendezvous with the Comanche, our Rangers will be waiting to lead you to San Antonio under their protection. Upon completion of your mission, I have the power to pardon you. Obviously, you can't be a Comanchero anymore, because the Indians will kill you for sure."

"And what if I don't come back?"

"Either the Comanche will kill you, or we will hunt you down and hang you."

January 26, 1838

The mesquite was thick on the trail above the Nueces River. Chato had scouted ahead to locate the horse thieves and the stolen herd. He reported to Lieutenant McAlester.

"Lieutenant, I've found the rustlers. They're bedded down in a grove of mesquite trees just above the river. It appears from their tracks they're headed toward Mexico."

"Good job, Chato. How many men are there?"

"I counted seven men, including a guard."

"It's too late tonight to make a move against them. Here's our plan. At daybreak, I will signal like an owl for the hostilities to commence."

"Cager, you and Cuddy round up the stolen horses, cut the thieves' horses loose, and drive them a distance from the campsite, with the stolen herd, so they'll be afoot."

"Quill, I want you to soak a saddle blanket in the creek."

"What are you going to do with it?"

"Not me, Quill—you are going to put that wet blanket over their campfire to give us an edge. The smoke will temporarily blind them. Chato, I'm going to get the guard first, and then I want you and Quill to shoot anyone trying to escape."

At dawn the next morning, Jesse hooted like an owl, and immediately his men got into position. Quill soaked the blanket and ran to throw it on the campfire, while Jesse simultaneously drove a knife into the guard's back.

Quill and Chato, their rifles and pistols blazing, cut down two of the horse thieves immediately. Two more bandits reached for their weapons and were cut in two by Jesse's double-barreled shotgun.

The two remaining bandits, lucky to be alive and blinded by the smoke, were cursing in Spanish and writhing on the ground.

"¡No más! ¡no más! ¡Sois Diablos!" moaned one of the remaining bandits.

"Son, we aren't devils. I'm Lieutenant McAlester of the Texas Rangers, and we are trying to protect people's stock from the likes of you."

The first bandit spoke to Chato in Spanish, "¿Van a darnos un juicio justo?" "Are we going to get a fair trial?"

Chato replied, "Sí, y entonces vamos a estirarles el cuello." "Yes, then we're going to stretch your necks."

Quill began forming a noose, and the younger bandit began crying and begging for mercy.

Nature brightened the scene as the sun started to rise, and birds sang as if nothing had happened.

Cuddy and Cager rode up to a grisly scene of bloody men on the ground, their faces like death masks staring into the air as dawn broke over the camp.

"Men, let's get this business over with," McAlester ordered. "Boys, if you want to get your amigos buried, I suggest you start gathering rocks before the buzzards start circling and giving our position away! Cuddy, you and Cager, pile everything we can use next to our horses. Quill, you and Chato get two horses and put them under that tree."

The youngest bandit, suddenly fluent in English, said, "Señor McAlester, I'm but a boy of sixteen, and these men forced me to rob and steal with them—they said they would kill my family."

While Chato held the horses under a large oak tree, Quill threw the nooses over a large branch about ten feet off the ground. The bandits were forced to mount the horses, and a noose was secured around each of the bandits' necks.

Jesse began questioning the short bandit with the missing teeth. *"¿Dónde están los hombres que compran estos caballos?"* "Where are the men who buy these horses?"

The short man growled, *"¡Vaya al infierno."* "Go to hell."

Jesse and Chato whacked the horse's rump as Chato shouted, *"¡Vaya con Dios!"* "Go with God!"

The horse thief's neck popped with a crack. Eyes bulging, his body swung to and fro in the air like a pendulum. All of the Rangers were silent for a moment, giving the young horse thief some hope.

"How about you? You want to tell us where you were headed with the stolen horses?"

"Lieutenant McAlester, sir, I heard someone say something about Piedras Negras, but I don't know for sure."

"Do you know the name of the ranch where you were going?"

"No, Señor!"

Chato looked at Jesse with a knowing glance because he knew what would happen next. "Do you mind if I read a prayer?" Jesse opened a small Bible.

The bandit looked hopeful. *"Sí, Señor, muy bien."* "Yes, sir, very good."

"God, receive this poor man's soul," were the last words he heard, as Chato slapped the horse on the rump.

"Chato, do you have an idea where they were taking the horses?"

"Lieutenant, I'm afraid they are taking the stolen horses to the Rancho Ventana for El Malo."

"The Evil One? Who in blazes is that?"

"His real name is Santos Barbosa, and he is a murdering cutthroat! Legend has it that when the Spanish Cavalry came to the Rancho Ventana in 1812, demanding horses, they killed his father. Santos was but a boy then, but he managed to plunge a knife into the chest of the Lieutenant responsible for his father's death. Santos has been murdering and stealing ever since."

"Do you think we could cross the Rio Grande into Piedras Negras and take him by surprise?"

Chato made the sign of the cross. "Many have tried and failed, including the Mexican army."

"All right. We will tell Major Hawkins what we've found, deliver the stolen horses, and await his decision."

After hearing Jesse's report, Hawkins alerted Jesse to the number of persons who were arriving in Texas from Ireland. "We need to protect these people. We do not have funds to add new Rangers."

Jesse replied, "Major, my men are very capable and we will do everything necessary to protect them."

CHAPTER SIXTEEN
Santos Barbosa

November 1812

Santos Barbosa was born in 1801 in the sleepy village of Piedras Negras in New Spain. The stoutly built Rancho Ventana utilized irrigation from the Rio Grande for the ranch's crops, water for the stock, and for the family's use. His father, Santiago, a Castilian immigrant of bold stature with green eyes, was a devout follower of the Catholic Church. Santiago had a keen eye for judging livestock and sizing up people.

There was an insurrection in New Spain in 1810. Initially, the major fighting was concentrated in the large cities with dense populations, such as Guadalajara and Mexico City.

Because of the geographical distance, and the seeming indifference of the Spanish government, Santiago's interest in the brewing storm of politics was tempered by his relative ignorance of the peril his family was facing.

Believing that he, his family, and his rancho were in an area outside the interest of the government, Santiago was shocked to see a cloud of caliche dust following a long column of mounted Spanish cavalry, with lances shimmering in the sun and guidons flapping in the wind.

Santiago knew this much: there was a conflict between the Spanish Royalists and Father Miguel Hidalgo and Ignacio Allende and the army of the desperate poor they had raised. Although the leaders had been killed, the rebellion continued. He shuddered when citizens of Piedras Negras told stories of Father Miguel Hidalgo's, Ignacio Allende's, and two other insurgents' heads being placed on display on the four corners of the Alhóndiga de Granaditas in Guanajuato as a warning to others that revolt against the Spanish crown would not be tolerated.

However, a new leader had taken the place of Father Hidalgo and Ignacio Allende, and the cry for independence, the *"Grito de Dolores!"* became a refrain that even the mighty Spanish government could not ignore in liberating Mexico from Spain. But not just yet!

A gaunt Spanish Lieutenant, wild-eyed and obviously agitated, barked orders to the eleven-year-old Santos, orders to be conveyed to the boss of the rancho. Santos simply shook his head.

"No, Señor Teniente, usted no tiene ningún autoridad aquí. Este rancho pertenece a mi padre. El solo manda aquí." "No, Lieutenant, sir, you have no authority here. This is my father's ranch. He alone gives orders here."

Santos, a lithe little *vaquero* accustomed to dodging horse hooves, adroitly moved when the Lieutenant attempted to quirt him, which further incensed the Spaniard.

His father, Santiago, appeared then and, speaking gently, asked the young Lieutenant, "What may I do to be of service?"

"We don't need your insolence, or your service, old man. We need, and we're going to take, your best horses."

Santiago, remaining calm, asked how much they would be paying for the mounts. "Paying? You fool, we're not paying you anything, and you'll also be providing us food, drink, and any spare señoritas."

"Lieutenant, what you propose is not possible. I am but a modest, Christian man, and what you are asking would be a sin before God."

"Are you disobeying me, old man?"

Santos edged closer to the young Lieutenant's horse.

The Lieutenant, unaware of the boy's presence, removed a pistol, leveled it at Santiago, and blew his brains out.

Santos sprang into action. Unsheathing his calving knife, he plunged it into the young Lieutenant's chest to the hilt. The officer clutched at the weapon, mouthed something that sounded like *"¡Válgame Dios!"* "Oh, my God!" and slowly tumbled from his horse. And then utter pandemonium broke out.

An instant was all Santos required to make his escape.

The startled cavalry, in total disarray, searched the scrub in vain for the boy.

After avenging his father's death, Santos killed dozens more Spanish soldiers, always hiding, always appearing when least expected. He became known as *El Malo*, "The Evil One."

In 1821, the Spaniards agreed to grant Mexico its independence and to allow it to create its own government. Now, however, the Mexican authorities were imitating their former overlords, continuing to raid Rancho Ventana, confiscating cattle, horses, supplies, even raping some of the women.

In 1823, Santos decided to design a new ranch, configured as a square, impregnable fortress. The only windows in the fort faced the interior courtyard, in order to invite natural light, but prevent exposure to enemy fire. His workers completed a stable for seventy-five horses. They built a bakery and a smithy. His men doubled the thickness of the walls, erected four guard towers, and even dug a twenty-foot-wide moat—ten feet deep, complete with a drawbridge.

Cannons were positioned on each of the four corners of the guard towers. His men also dug a well inside the grounds of the fort, ensuring they would always have fresh water when besieged by their enemies, an eventuality they expected and prepared for.

There were accommodations for one hundred people including men, women, and children. In order to keep the people fed, Santos sent out groups of men to steal and plunder on both sides of the border. He himself became an apparition, and many crimes were blamed on him, even ones he did not commit. He had a simple plan in life: he did not discriminate; he would kill anyone who got in his way. He became a human destroyer, and a person with no conscience.

November, 28 1827

A strong cold autumn wind blew in that morning, and the winds had shifted, southerly to northerly. The animals instinctively sought refuge.

Twenty miles north of the Rio Grande, four Mexican soldiers had started a small campfire to warm themselves and prepare breakfast. Concealed in the juniper, Santos watched the four preparing coffee and roasting strips of venison. Even at this time of day, the soldiers took swigs from a large jug of mescal.

Taking advantage of their drunkenness and incoherent state, Santos took aim with his dagger at the back of a soldier and with a silent throw, lodged it between his shoulders, instantly killing him.

Breaking the neck off the mescal bottle, he doused the remaining three soldiers with the alcohol and lit them on fire with a stick from the campfire. They panicked and wildly flailed their arms until they were totally engulfed in flame.

Santos calmly sat by the campfire after rolling the soldier whom he had knifed out of the way, poured a cup of coffee, and had just reached for the venison when he heard a wagon approaching.

The muleteer was on his way to San Antonio with a wagon full of goods when he had the misfortune of appearing on the scene. The horrendous odor of burning flesh, and the sight of Santos sitting there, calmly drinking a cup of coffee, was more than he could endure.

"What's your name?"

"I am called Santos Barbosa."

The muleteer barely had time to begin shaking when Santos leveled his pistol at his heart and took his life. He saw a sudden movement in the back of the wagon, but before he could react, a boy leapt out of the wagon and took to the brush. Santos, familiar with the terrain and his bloodlust momentarily quenched, did not pursue, thinking that the forces of nature would overcome the escapee.

The boy cowered under a huisache bush like a frightened rabbit, too afraid to move or breathe. Unsure of what else he had witnessed from the back of the wagon, but certain that his father had been murdered, he waited. Finally, when a covey of quail called to each other to round up for the night, he began to move. Cautious at first, he soon realized that Santos had left the area and had stolen the wagon full of goods. He ran north and did not stop running until he smelled smoke coming from a chimney, and then saw a cabin with a lit candle in the window.

The owner of the cabin had three dogs, all howling fiercely. Although the boy was frightened, his hunger fueled his resolve and spurred him to approach the cabin. The door swung open and a large man armed with a rifle bellowed, "Who's out there?"

The boy, overwhelmed with emotion and exhaustion wailed, "My father was murdered by a bloodthirsty outlaw."

A small woman appeared abruptly from the cabin. "What's this all about?"

The boy, surrounded by a pack of hounds, was unsure how to proceed, until the woman took him by the arm and shepherded him inside the house.

Several children descended from the loft of the crudely built cabin and were talking all at once.

The man shouted, "Quiet, damn you! Can't you see this child is in distress?"

The woman took the young boy to her bosom, holding him tenderly as he sobbed, and he told her the story of Santos murdering his father, and the four dead Mexican soldiers.

"We all need to be on the lookout for that bloodthirsty outlaw."

CHAPTER SEVENTEEN
Molly "Pumpkin" O'Rourke

June 6, 1840, 3:00 a.m.

Johnny Doyle, a compulsive gambler and alcoholic, had his only piece of good luck one night when he passed out in a drunken stupor in Flannery's Bar. Flannery's was the preferred gambling and drinking tavern for the criminal element in Dublin, Ireland.

Johnny heard voices in the wee hours of the morning, coming from the room behind the bar. At first he thought he was dreaming, but the voices persisted and he realized he was not alone. He was sure he recognized one of the voices—Paddy, who had been serving him at the bar for years.

"Paddy, are you sure you have the right combination?" said the well-known burglar Billy Murphy in a low voice.

"Of course, I've seen Big Mike put money in here many times when he didn't know I was watching. Let me see," as the excited Paddy, or Patrick O'Rourke, the burly bartender of Flannery's, elbowed Billy out of the way.

"How do you know we have the right combination?"

"Because he keeps the numbers written on the wall behind the Pope's portrait."

Paddy carefully entered the combination, and after the last tumbler clicked, he slowly opened the safe.

"Jesus, Mary, and Joseph!" Billy exclaimed, clearly astonished at the amount of cash they found.

Johnny Doyle's sudden movement, knocking over a chair, startled the two thieves. "Who's there?" Paddy turned toward the noise.

Billy pulled his pistol from his coat pocket and raised a lantern. The light, cascading through the open door to the space beyond the bar, fell upon Johnny's distorted face.

"Get in here, Johnny! What are you doing here, you old drunkard?" Paddy fixed Johnny with a menacing glare, and he sidled trembling into the room. One glance at the two faces told him he was in acute danger.

Billy cocked his pistol, "Let's shoot him right here."

"We don't want to alert anyone to our presence."

Billy shoved his pistol roughly into Johnny's ribs. "Get your hands up, you old bastard!" Paddy laid a hand on the pistol and faced the burglar, shaking his head and making calming motions with his other hand. "Billy, we need to talk. Let's go out the back and take him to my place."

The trio left the bar, after carefully erasing all signs of their recent theft. Billy still pressed the muzzle of his pistol against Johnny's back. "Move slowly, old man, or I'll blast you to smithereens."

Johnny, staggering a bit and occasionally stumbling, muttered curses interspersed with prayers and pleas for mercy as they went.

Upon entering Paddy's small dwelling, the thieves spread all the money on the table and admired the benefits of their hard work.

Johnny began to sober up, hoping to reason with the thieves to convince them to spare his life. "I have a plan, boys, that can serve all of us."

Paddy spoke in a scornful voice, "And what plan might that be, you drunk?'

"Now boys, when Flannery's opens up on Monday morning and they discover all the cash is gone, all hell will break loose. Paddy, you may very well be the prime suspect, and I expect, after they torture you, Billy's name will come out and you both will be killed."

The realization of the probable consequences of what they had done brought a look of panic to the thieves' faces. Johnny could see he was making headway, especially since Billy's pistol was now pointing to the floor. "I suggest you leave the country by ship immediately, going to America before they kill you both. Tomorrow is Sunday, the day the bar is closed. That will give you time to find a ship that's leaving before they discover their safe was burgled."

Paddy paused for the first time to think about the escape plan. "Big Mike could make inquiries on Monday, and find out that two men had suddenly boarded a ship bound for America."

Johnny expanded his plan. "Paddy, it would be easier to leave the country as a married man. I have a daughter, Molly, a real hard worker and a good cook too."

Suddenly, Paddy loomed over Johnny, fists clenched. "You're crazy, old man."

Billy raised the pistol. "Let's just shoot him and get it over with."

Johnny raised both hands, palms outward. "You boys will change your tune when they have you spread-eagled and start cutting off your privates."

The blood drained from both of the thieves' faces. Paddy's voice quavered a little. "Maybe your plan isn't such a bad idea. When can I meet your daughter?"

"Are you crazy, Paddy? Why should we give in to this blackmailer?"

"Billy, he's right. We didn't think the whole scheme through. When Big Mike discovers the cash missing, there will be blood. I expect to be long gone by then, and I would advise you to do the same."

They finally agreed to divide the swag into three equal parts, a tidy sum for each.

At daybreak, Johnny and Paddy headed to the wharves, boarded Johnny's small boat on the Liffey River, and rowed to find a ship that would be sailing soon. All they could find was a merchant ship headed to Texas, carrying supplies.

The Captain of the ship explained, "There's an Irish Colony in Texas called 'San Patricio' and my men will be unloading at Copano Bay close by. There's a nice farm near there, which I own and will sell to you, if you are interested. It even comes with a brother and sister to help you work the place.

"Johnny paid the sum the ship's Captain requested from his share of the ill-gotten gains. The Captain also agreed to provide a team and wagon at Copano Bay for Molly and Paddy to drive, with all their goods, to the ranch near San Patricio. He knew there would be a wagon waiting for him at the dock, so he could easily comply with the request by letting Paddy have it.

Johnny asked to speak to the Captain alone. During that brief dialogue, he had the Captain sign the ranch's deed over to Molly alone. He knew that Paddy was illiterate; his only experience with business matters was making change for customers at Flannery's.

"What's that all about—you talking to the Captain all private like?" Paddy asked, when Johnny returned.

"I wanted to make sure the Captain would look after you and Molly while aboard ship."

At noon on Sunday, while Molly was preparing tea, her father and a stranger entered the house. "Molly, I'd like to introduce you to my friend

Patrick O'Rourke, better known as 'Paddy.'"

The new friend's face darkened upon seeing Molly. He suppressed a gasp.

Molly Doyle was short and stout, with a large bust, broad hips and no waist, and with a thick and untamable mane of red hair. Her pale skin sported large freckles on her cheeks and nose, but her thick arms and legs promised strength and a capacity for hard work.

Johnny gently nudged Paddy. "Molly, Paddy has something he wants to ask you."

"Molly, I'm bound for America Monday morning, and your father told me you might like to join me as my wife."

Molly, clearly stunned as she stared at this handsome man, began to cry. Not wanting them to know that she was crying tears of happiness, all she could muster was an affirmative nod.

"Get to packing right now!" her future husband shouted.

Johnny took his daughter's arm. "Molly, I want you to have some of your mother's things from the bedroom."

The daughter and father walked into the bedroom, where they were out of Paddy's earshot, and he handed to her the deed to the ranch in Texas and a large sum of money, and whispered, "Guard this with your life!"

Sunday at four in the afternoon, Paddy and Molly had packed everything they could in a small cart. They walked to the dock, pulling the cart, and boarded Johnny's small boat, taking her possessions and leaving the cart behind. He rowed to the harbor.

Unknown to Paddy or her father, Molly had saved her money for years and had sewn her gold coins in the layers of her petticoats.

Once on board, Paddy found the Captain outside his cabin. "Captain, when do we embark for America?"

"We leave promptly at seven tomorrow morning."

Paddy sighed in relief, knowing the ship would depart before Flannery's opened on Monday.

Although the loving couple would never know it, after noon on Monday, Billy was never seen or heard from again.

When the ship was clear of the coast and in deep waters, Paddy asked the Captain to marry him and Molly. The ceremony was something the Captain rarely did, since most of his sailing career was on merchant vessels, but he agreed and married the couple.

After nearly eight weeks at sea, on August 2, the ship arrived at Copano Bay. Paddy had been drunk most of the time and only came to Molly one night during the voyage to consummate their marriage.

He was violent, cursing, and striking her at the least provocation, clearly regretting the bargain he had made. Molly, too, realized what a mistake she had made by entering into this hastily arranged pairing. But that one night of "love" had its effect. Paddy never knew that Molly was pregnant.

"Molly, how come you are sick every day? Is it the roiling of the ocean that's upsetting you?"

"I'm afraid the sea is having the best of me."

Due to a violent storm, the ship was forced to stay in the harbor an extra night before the crew and passengers could disembark on dry land. The morning after the storm, Finn, a member of the crew, pointed at Molly and snickered, "She looks kinda like a pumpkin. 'Ow'd you like to wake up next to that every morning?"

"I'd rather be flogged and thrown overboard," said his friend Jack.

"I heard Cap'n cleaned out 'er husband last night of everything they own."

Jack snorted. "Hell, I coulda' cleaned him out, too, with that deck of cards the Cap'n was usin'."

Molly overheard the remark. "Ye talkin' 'bout me Paddy?"

"Sorry, Missus, I don't wanna' be stickin' me nose in where it's none of me business."

Molly confronted the two sailors, "What 'ave you heard about Paddy?"

"Missus, we heard that Paddy had been drinkin' all night and the Cap'n won all his money."

Molly immediately walked to the O'Rourke cabin, and when she opened the door, she heard the still-drunken Paddy snoring. She shouted, "Wake up Paddy, it's time to leave the ship!"

Paddy grunted, "Me head, Molly, off with you!"

"Paddy, dear."

"Go away!"

Molly responded by emptying the pitcher of water from the washstand over Paddy's head. "Some fresh water to put you right as rain!"

"Goddammit, Molly!"

Molly then shattered the pitcher over Paddy's head. "Don't be takin' the Lord's name in vain, darlin'!"

The two crew members, hearing the sound of ceramic shattering, thought Molly was in danger and rushed to the room. They opened the door, saw the shards from the broken pitcher, and Paddy still in bed.

Finn tipped his cap to Jack. "Governor, that pumpkin really packs a wallop."

Finn told the two passengers they would be able to leave the ship that day, and they followed him, with Paddy scowling and sulking the whole time, and holding his head. Molly, looking ashore, saw a wagon and team of horses waiting there, and turned to Finn, "Could ye help a poor woman retrieve our belongings from where they're stored down below?"

Finn, who had suddenly developed a healthy respect for Molly, agreed. "Yes'm, I reckon you paid the Cap'n for this voyage and that includes the unloadin'." He turned to his companion. "Jack, hop to it!"

They loaded the goods from the ship into the rowboat, and brought Molly, Paddy, and their belongings to shore and placed them in the wagon. Paddy emptied the remnants of the whisky bottle on the way.

Jack dusted his hands and slapped his thighs after the load was secure. "You're headed for the Cap'n's ranch, aren't you?"

"Yes, but we don't know which way to go. Maybe you do?" Molly looked hopeful and produced a coin from her purse. She had foreseen the need of a tip here and there.

"I can help you there." Finn produced a wrinkled scrap of dirty paper from a pocket and a stub of pencil from another. Using the side of the wagon as his desk, he drew a crude map with directions to her new home. They also placed Paddy, by now too drunk to know where he was, in the back of the wagon.

Molly pressed a second coin into Finn's hand. "Thank you for all your help!" She climbed onto the driver's seat and confidently drove the wagon in the direction indicated on the map.

Finn and Jack watched her go with smiles on their faces.

After they had traveled two or three miles, the wagon hit a rut and Paddy awoke, still angry with his wife. He stood up in the wagon, cursing her, and tried to strike her with his fist, but at that very moment, the wagon hit a deeper rut, launching him out. He landed on a large rock, which shattered his skull. He died on the spot.

Molly got out of the wagon, examined the body, and made the sign of the cross. She prayed, "God, I am pregnant and now a widow. Please tell me your plan for me." Immediately, she realized there was only one course of action: continue to the ranch.

She needed to get her dead husband into the wagon. She pulled off her shawl and wrapped his head and upper body in it, to keep his blood from getting on her. She bent and pulled the body onto her back, got up, and dumped it roughly into the back of the wagon. She heaved a sigh, dusted herself off and wiped at a few blood spots, then climbed back into the driver's seat and headed to her new home.

Upon reaching the ranch, after five days of hard travel with a now badly decomposing Paddy, she was pleasantly surprised at how well-kept the place was. She saw beautiful orchards, the weeds and grass scythed to make a lawn around the trees, a carefully tended garden with an abundance of vegetables, a substantial stone house, and fat livestock grazing on the other side of the fence. In the distance, she saw a thick line of trees, meaning some type of water was just behind the trees. She looked at her map and saw that the wavy line represented water and was marked the Nueces River, one of the boundaries of her ranch.

Hearing the noise outside, María Zaragoza came out the front door and stood in the front yard to see what was happening. She gasped when she saw the body and smelled the foul odor of decaying flesh.

Molly quickly explained, "I'm Molly O'Rourke, and the poor man in back of the wagon is, was, my husband. He stood up at the wrong time and when the wagon hit a rut he fell out and shattered his head, ye see. So here I am, a poor widow and pregnant I am, too. But I'm here because me father bought this ranch for me from the ship's Captain." She produced the Deed and María merely glanced at the document, quickly seeing that it was legal.

María introduced herself and began assisting Molly down from the wagon as a tall, handsome man approached them.

"Molly, this is Juan Carlos, my brother. He tends the orchard and many other things on this place. Juan, could you unload Molly's husband?"

"Paddy, his name is Paddy O'Rourke, and we've been married only a short while."

"Juan, could you take a shovel and bury Paddy under the big oak tree? I will bring some fresh linen to bury him in."

"Molly, come inside with me. I will give you some tea I make when people are emotional. In these parts I am a *curandera*, a healer."

The kindness, generosity, and efficiency of the caretaker couple stunned Molly. She felt like she was moving in a dream. She could only nod and follow María's instructions.

Molly learned that Juan Carlos and his sister had been born in Mexico City in 1805 and 1806, respectively. They were forced to leave the area because of political persecution. They had moved to San Patricio in 1838 and become caretakers of the small ranch owned by the ship Captain from Ireland.

María was a curandera by trade, utilizing the resources around her, and became very popular in healing the local Irish, the Tejanos, and even the Comanche. A Comanche chief had brought his young son to María, and she had recognized the symptoms of chicken pox, against which the Indians had no immunity. She healed him through her knowledge of local herbs, dosing him with aloe vera both inside and out.

Juan Carlos helped María to gather herbs. He set up an apothecary in the back room, where there were jars of garlic, damiana, wormwood, eucalyptus, chaparral, chamomile, oregano, passion flower, bricklebush, rue, sage, linden flowers, and aloe vera, all carefully labelled.

The first words that Juan ever spoke to Molly were, "I would like to carve a marker for your husband's grave. What did you say his Christian name was?"

Molly stammered, "Patrick, Patrick O'Rourke." The warmth of Juan's body, standing so close, made her blush and feel warm all over. Embarrassed by her reaction, she quickly left the room. When she left so abruptly, he regretted asking her the question, thinking she was still in mourning for her deceased husband.

During Molly's pregnancy, María taught her to make mesquite bean jelly, beer biscuits, and her wonderful pies made from the fruits in the orchards.

On March 4, 1841, Molly delivered twins and named them Ryan and Rose of Sharon.

María served as her midwife, and the babies came easily after she gave the prospective mother a sedative of herbs to help her relax.

Molly kept the twins in the kitchen, where they would stay warm and she could watch them while she cooked scrumptious meals for them, herself, María, Juan Carlos, and anyone who stopped there. Soon, Molly's ranch became a favorite eatery and stage stop for hungry travelers, and she saved as much money as she could from the enterprise.

Jesse and his men made it a point to stop at Molly's, even if they had to ride extra miles to get there. She always remembered their names, saw them riding up to the house, and set the table before they had time to come in the front door. Jesse enjoyed playing with Ryan and Rose, both of whom had their mother's gregarious personality.

September 12, 1842

Rachel was in the corral working horses, when the dogs began barking. A trail of caliche dust followed a fast moving rider approaching the ranch. Rachel picked up her rifle and watched the rider. When she recognized Martin Stein, the courier who delivered the mail, she leaned the rifle against a fence post. Martin moved away from the cloud of caliche, reached into his saddlebags, and produced a letter marked, "EXTREMELY URGENT." The letter was postmarked August 25, 1842.

"Mrs. McAlester, pardon my rudeness, but I have other deliveries scheduled so I'll be on my way," he said while tipping his hat.

A worried Rachel could only nod, "Mr. Stein, I will tell Jesse you came by."

Trembling, she opened the letter tentatively, afraid of the contents.

Dear Jesse,

I am still in shock from the event that happened yesterday.

Your father was tragically murdered in the horse barn by an unknown assailant, stabbing him viciously numerous times.

By the time you read this letter, we will have buried him in the Masonic cemetery. I urge you to come immediately with your wife and children.

Your loving mother,

Sarah McAlester

Rachel began shaking and trembling so hard that the children began wailing. "Come here children, gather around Momma." Rachel began hugging the children, and patted her pregnant stomach to reassure herself.

Jesse arrived that evening from a scouting mission. When he dismounted, Rachel was crying and clutching the letter.

As he read the letter, he began sobbing hysterically for the loss of his father and the guilt he felt for not seeing him again while he was still alive.

"Rachel, I need to pack my bags immediately and head for Copano Bay."

"Jesse, I have thought this through. Sarah has invited the children and me to visit, and we are all going." Jesse surveyed the room for the first time that evening, spotting a large number of bags ready for travel.

"Rachel, you're six months pregnant, you cannot chance a trip like that."

"I'm fine. We are going. I've made up my mind."

"You are a stubborn woman!"

The family arrived in Nashville on September 29th, where they were met by Sarah, John and Jane Allen, along with Mary.

After introductions and hugs all around, Jesse got right to the point. "Who killed Father?"

Not wishing to make a scene with people all around them, Sarah ushered Jesse and his family to a wagon.

"John will drive his wagon, and Mary will follow in ours."

When they arrived at the farm, Sarah led the way to the house and had everyone assemble in the living room.

"Jesse, I know how impatient you are, so I'll get right to it. They identified the murderer as Magnus McGruder." A stunned silence pervaded the room.

Rachel's face was drained of all color, but Jesse's was red with rage. He began to pace.

"After the murderer was arrested, the sheriff interrogated him. He confessed to both his identity and the crime."

"Mama, how can this have happened?"

"Unfortunately, Jesse, we will never know the complete story, because a mob broke into the jail three days after he was arrested and hanged him on the tree in front of the courthouse. Over two hundred men confessed to being responsible for the hanging."

In the following days, his mother and his wife did their best to calm Jesse.

His mother doted on their children, teaching them songs and telling stories about their father when he was a boy.

Sarah and Rachel quickly became good friends, watching the children play.

Sarah cooked meals and invited all the family and many friends to visit her youngest son, his lovely wife, and their children.

Jesse and his family departed on October 7th, arriving back at Rancho Verde on October 23rd.

CHAPTER EIGHTEEN
War Clouds

December 15, 1844

Jesse and Rachel sat at the kitchen table after washing the dinner dishes. The children were in bed, and quiet had settled over their home.

Stirring the coals in the fireplace, Rachel asked, "Jesse, do you think Texas will ever become a state?"

"I hope so, but as long as the Mexican government disavows Santa Anna's treaty with Texas, we will continue to battle with them."

"I've heard there is opposition to our becoming a state, because of the fear that we would allow slavery."

"That's true, but I believe that the United States is hell-bent on owning all the territory from the Atlantic to the Pacific."

Rachel reached across and squeezed her husband's hand.

"As soon as Mexico realizes how eager President Polk is to annex Texas to the Union, all hell will break loose."

Rachel glanced at the official letter lying on the table between them. The lamplight glimmered on the white paper, giving it an almost threatening prominence against the dark wood. "That's why you've received these orders, then. Naturally, the Rangers will have to be involved."

Jesse leaned back in his chair and nodded his head in resigned acceptance. "Yeah, if the United States and Mexico are going to fight over Texas, I expect we Rangers will be right in the thick of things."

"The kids and I can manage the horses and other stock while you're away, but I can tell you right now the children are going to be very upset."

"I plan to tell the children at breakfast."

"You know, Angus and Sarah are more aware than you realize."

"What about Buddy and Martha?"

"They're too young to realize what their Papa is doing, but they'll sense something is wrong."

"It can't be helped. When I swore my oath to be a Ranger, I intended to see it through and now, I am even more determined to do my duty and obey orders until Texas can be a safer place for all of our families."

"Your stubbornness will be the death of you."

"Rachel, you've been managing the ranch while I'm away, so you know more about the horses than I do. Liberty is getting a little old to go to war. Which of the four-year-olds are most promising for me to ride?"

"I like the colt out of Liberty and that Spanish mare, Ginger. He's over fifteen-and-a-half hands high and has a smooth gait. He won't bolt when he hears gunfire because Isaac and Tobe have already killed deer while riding him."

"What's his name?"

"We call him Thunder because the morning he foaled, the heavens opened up."

"I think I'll give Thunder a try in the morning. Can you have Tobe saddle him for me first thing, right after breakfast? When I get back from trying him out, I want to have lunch in our cabin—all of us, and the Rangers. Will that be a problem for you? You will be cooking for a lot of folks."

"I will make y'all a meal fit for a king."

Breakfast was already over, the older children finishing the chores, when Rachel opened the back door and shouted, "Tobe, wherever you are, saddle Thunder for Jesse!"

Jesse scarcely had time to get up from the table when Tobe called from beyond the porch. "Jesse, your horse is waitin'."

As he mounted Thunder, he thanked Tobe. "I'll be gone about an hour, I expect. I need to check his gaits, his stamina, and whether he can jump. I need a horse as powerful as Liberty used to be, if I'm going to lead a squad of Rangers."

Jesse returned mid-morning with a big grin, and waved at Rachel as he passed the porch.

Before he could dismount, she met him at the corral.

"I love seeing you smile like that."

"Rachel, the plan to breed Liberty to the Spanish mustangs has worked out better than I would ever have imagined."

Rachel turned to Tobe. "Take Thunder to the barn, cool him off, give him oats, water and curry him down, please."

"Yes, ma'am."

"Jesse, let's sit and have a cup of coffee and tell me about your ride."

"Thunder has the best gait and stamina of any horse I've ever ridden."

"You think this is the horse of the future we've been hoping for?"

"You have done a great job with the horses. I give you all the credit. This is what we've dreamed of and now it is real. If all the other horses sired by Liberty can even get close to Thunder in ability, then yes, this is the horse of the future for the southwest."

Hearing whooping and yelling, the rest of the family came running to the cabin to see what the ruckus was about. They found the couple dancing, with Jesse swinging her in the air. After a few turns around the kitchen-dining-living room, Jesse took her hand and led her back to the table and the cooling cups of coffee. After cheering the dancers, the rest of the family left to allow the couple to have a quiet moment.

"When we get called up to fight, and I'm certain that will happen, I'm going to have our Ranger unit riding our stock," Jesse said. "When the Brass realizes their stamina, smooth gait, and ability to withstand the climate, they'll clamor for more. Since Quill Parker and Rube Reynolds got killed in battle with the Comanche and poor Bonner Pickens died of consumption, we have only five of the original Rangers left in our unit."

"Yes, that leaves Dob, Choc, Chato, and the Holley brothers."

"Right, Rachel. So we need five of the best mounts for my men, and remember when picking, Chato likes a mount to be a little wild and wooly.

"And you do remember that the entire family and the Rangers will all be here for dinner."

"Jesse McAlister, I haven't lost my mind yet. I suggest instead of sitting around here and giving orders, you hurry to the chicken yard and start wringing necks *muy pronto*," winking and pinching his butt.

"You're worse than any commanding officer."

"Just don't forget who is really in charge here."

After the food was consumed and the dishes cleared, Jesse rose and made an announcement. "I've invited you here to discuss the upcoming war with Mexico.

"Texas has not been safe since the Treaty of Velasco was signed and then reneged by the Mexicans. General Rafael Vasquez raided San Antonio in March of '42.

"Six months later, General Adrian Woll, along with his troops, captured many prominent citizens of San Antonio, including the City Council, and assigned a body of cavalry to march them all the way to Perote prison in Mexico.

"My point is that the Mexican government will continue harassing us in attempts to regain their territory. That's about to change!

"You all know that James Polk was elected President last month. Our spies have already informed us that the Mexican government is saber-rattling, and it's only a question of time until hostilities begin.

"Since Texas is squarely in the target, it is up to us to assist the American army by serving as Texas State Volunteers, who know the geography and logistics of Texas and Mexico."

Hamp interjected. "Jesse, when do you anticipate this happening?"

"I expect after Polk is sworn in, the politicking will begin."

"What do you mean by that?"

"I mean Mexico will never give up Texas without a fight." He grimaced. "I open the floor for other questions—Yes, Choc."

"Do you think we can lick 'em in a couple of months?" Everyone hooted and hollered.

"Chato, you know the land down there, what's your opinion?"

"We'll be fighting on their territory. They'll have the people behind them, including guerilla forces from most of their villages. It will be difficult to keep a large army fed, housed, and have clean water."

"Then you will be invaluable in knowing where the water is, the mountain passes to elude possible ambushes, and reconnoitering the enemy for troop strengths and movements."

"Does this mean I'll get a promotion and better pay?"

"I expect the United States Treasury has deeper pockets than our government."

"Tobe and Isaac, I want you to take the men out to the corrals to choose the new mounts we are providing them."

"No offense, Lieutenant, but we all like our own mounts."

"Chato, all I'm asking is for you to inspect the mounts, try them out, and see how they fit you."

Upon seeing the horses, they yelled "Whoopee," whistled, and spent moments in total admiration. Four horses were tethered to the corral fence, and Tobe strained to hold a well-muscled sorrel stallion. "Chato, Jesse asked me to hold this one for you because he's a little wild."

Chato ran to the sorrel, followed by the four other young men, who almost knocked each other down rushing to the horses. There were no fisticuffs because all the horses were equally praiseworthy. The young Rangers rushed to get their saddles and other things they needed off their old mounts, and then saddled the new horses like excited schoolchildren.

After riding for an hour or so, they returned, and each one asked Jesse what was to become of their old mounts.

"We'll keep them in the corral, and Tobe and Isaac can take care of them while we're gone. Men, if you don't have any further questions, you are excused. I'd like to speak with my family alone." Jesse left the group and went back inside his house.

Before he had a chance to talk to his family, Dob followed him in and approached him. "Jesse, I have some business that needs my attention. I'll be gone for a few days."

"Of course, I understand." Dob left the cabin, mounted his horse and rode to San Antonio.

Jesse put his hand on his wife's shoulder and gazed into her eyes. "Rachel, I expect you and Martha, along with Tobe and Isaac, to run the place, while I am gone. Greta and Bertie, please help attend to the children."

"Jesse McAlester, do you expect to drag my husband, with his bad leg, all over Mexico to fight when we need him here?"

Hamp's face now red. "Martha, I'm perfectly able to ride with Jesse and the boys."

"If you'll excuse us, I would like to speak with Hamp in the barn alone."

The two men walked out the door and headed to the barn. "Jesse, why the secrecy?"

"If anything were to happen to you, Martha would never forgive me, and don't forget she's already lost one husband to war."

An obviously relieved Hamp replied, "If you think it's for the best for me to stay here and protect the ranch, you can count on me, but you have to promise me you will watch over Dob."

"I will, and I trust you more than anyone in the world to protect my family."

Two days later, Dob returned. The McAlester family hurried to greet him, and was surprised to see he had two young pups squirming, yapping, and peering out from his jacket.

"Dob, what in tarnation are you doing with those pups?"

"Jesse, it's time you started training dogs again. I've heard tales of your Blue Paul Terriers and what rascals they were. These little fellers are just what you need to protect this place when we are gone."

Buck sauntered toward the pups and they growled at him. Buck snapped back, but the pups were unfazed.

"Isaac, you better get Buck away from the pups before they go after him."

The entire family erupted in laughter, and then scrambled to have their turn to hold the pups.

"Uncle Dob, what kind of pups are these?"

"I bought them from a saloon keeper in San Antonio. He calls them American bulldogs, but as you can see, they bear no resemblance to a bulldog. Jesse, I want you to have them as a present from me. You have the naming rights."

Jesse was pleased to hear Dob speak so much to the family, and very grateful for the new pups. He held up the red male pup, who was struggling his best to be released and barking as loud as he could.

Everyone laughed and called out names: "Prince...Tex..." and finally, because of the pup's ferocity, someone yelled, "Comanche."

Rachel yelled, "We gotta have one good Comanche on this place."

Jesse replied, "With all due respect, Rachel, I have the naming rights. I christen him Jackson, after Old Hickory, and we'll call him Jack."

"What are you going to name the other pup?" screamed the children.

"The saloon keeper told me his color is brindle," Dob said. "I don't know anything about that color, but he looks like a Tiger to me."

Jesse replied, "Well, I think Teddy is a better name."

"Then Teddy it is!"

Later in the day, Rachel watched Jesse teaching the pups to smell one of the dead Indian's breechcloths from the battle at the cabin when Gray Wolf was killed.

"Why are you doing that with the pups?"

"I want them to know that smell, so when the Comanche try to raid our place, they will alert the family."

Rachel smiled, realizing the pups' presence meant Jesse would stay longer at the ranch.

CHAPTER NINETEEN
Mexican-American War

July 25, 1845

President Polk ordered four thousand troops to assemble in Corpus Christi under the leadership of General Zachary Taylor, also known as "Old Rough and Ready." Jesse, Dob, the Holley twins, Chato, and Choc had received their orders to report to General Taylor to begin training the troops in guerrilla warfare. When they arrived, Jesse asked to see the General and was taken to his tent. When Jesse saw Taylor, he was surprised by the General's appearance: Old Rough and Ready had the physical appearance and garb of an elderly farmer.

"General Taylor, Texas Ranger Lieutenant Jesse McAlester reporting for duty, sir."

"Lieutenant, I want you and your men to get the troops here trained up. Then your next mission will be to scout south of the Nueces River. It is imperative that we have intelligence of troop movements and the weapons they will be using, especially their cannons."

"Will that be all, sir?"

General Taylor turned to an officer standing at ease near the wall of the tent. "Colonel Whiteside, assemble the men, so I may introduce these Texas Rangers who very well might help save the soldiers' lives. Lieutenant McAlester, accompany the colonel."

"Yes, sir."

As the troops came together, Jesse saw the troops line up in an orderly manner. Once they were gathered, Colonel Whiteside ordered them to stand at attention in rows by platoons of some twenty men, each with its Sergeants and Lieutenants.

General Taylor appeared and addressed the men. "As you well know, I'm General Zachary Taylor. You have my permission to call me 'Old Zach,' when I'm out of earshot, of course. I would like to introduce you to these rough-looking men to my right."

Some men cheered and some jeered until the Sergeants patrolling the area where the men were standing barked, "You men show some respect, or you'll be on guard duty all night."

General Taylor, accustomed to the hardscrabble life in army camps, introduced the Rangers. "This fine-looking fellow to my right is Lieutenant Jesse McAlester. Next to him are Sergeant Dob Andrews, Privates Chato Obregón, Cager Holley, and Cuddy Holley, and on the end is Charlie Wilson, all from the Texas Rangers."

One of the troops yelled to the Holley twins, "I never knew there could be two people as ugly as you!"

The General bristled. "Sergeant Roark, arrest that man and find a wagon and shackle him to it." He made a motion as if brushing a fly away, then continued. "After lunch, the Rangers will demonstrate on horseback some defensive maneuvers that very well may save your lives." He turned to Jesse. "Lieutenant McAlester, I have established a number of targets in the training area for your exclusive use."

Many of the men cheered wildly, anticipating some entertainment, but most cheered for lunch.

In the cleared field after lunch, the Rangers lined up to begin demonstrating their riding skills to the Regulars. Jesse, mounted on Thunder so he would have a good view of the training area, announced, "Private Chato Obregón will now demonstrate the maneuver to shield oneself from enemy fire."

Chato rode his horse to the far end of the field, wheeled around and raced toward the men, simultaneously dropping his entire body to the left, then to the right side of his mount. He whipped out a Walker Colt revolver from his holster, placed five out of six shots near the center of the target, and came to a sliding stop at the end of the field.

Demonstrations of other tactics continued until the regular soldiers were whooping and hollering "huzzahs" and "hip hip hoorays" for the Rangers. At the end of the demonstration, the Rangers lined up in front of Jesse.

"Good work, men. I want Dob and Chato to accompany me to scout for the Mexican army down by the Nueces. Cager, Cuddy, and Choc, I want you to continue working with these troops and teach them as much horsemanship and shooting skill as possible. Don't worry—you're going to see plenty of action."

After a week of reconnoitering, Jesse, Chato, and Dob returned to camp. Jesse reported to General Taylor, standing at attention while saluting him.

The General looked up from the map of Texas he had been examining. "At ease, Lieutenant. What were the conditions down south?"

"General, the Mexicans are crossing the Rio Grande and appear to be setting up areas to ambush our troops."

A crease appeared in Taylor's forehead and he stroked his chin. "Ambushes, you say. Are they operating above the Nueces River?"

"No, sir, but they appear to want to challenge us if we go below the Nueces. We tested them one day, and they immediately began massing on the other side of the river."

The General's lips widened in a grim smile. "Well, I expect them to be mad as hornets when we build the fort at the tip of Texas." He stood and paced back and forth for a moment. Then, he suddenly asked, "Lieutenant, where did you and your men obtain your horses? They are very impressive."

"Our horses were bred and trained at my ranch, sir."

"Is that so? Would you have more horses available to sell to the U.S. Army?"

"Yes, sir, we do."

"They must be of the same caliber and trained as well as yours."

"That's not a problem at all, sir."

"Please speak with Captain Jennings about the details. He's waiting outside my tent."

"Yes, sir! Will that be all, General?"

"Lieutenant, I understand you have a family obligation at your home. Do you think two weeks' leave will suffice?"

"Yes, sir. My wife and children will really appreciate that, and while there, I will personally inspect and select the proper horses for the Army to purchase." After a brief discussion with his men, Jesse rode Thunder straight home.

The dogs started barking while six-year-old Angus was playing in the yard, and his sharp ears picked up the sound of a trotting horse in the distance. He ran for the house.

"Mama! Mama! Papa's coming home!"

Jack and Teddy ran to meet Jesse, running circles around Thunder as the horse walked to the house.

Rachel hurried out onto the porch, as fast as her nine-months-pregnant body would allow. She leaned on the porch railing, listening. She knew Jesse's shape long before she could distinguish his features. He sagged in the saddle. It had been a long trip. As soon as he was within shouting distance, she waved her apron and shouted.

"Jesse, darlin', welcome home!"

He straightened, waved back and shouted, "You're a beautiful sight, Rachel!"

Thunder stopped by himself when they reached the porch. Jesse dismounted with a groan, and the couple fell into each other's arms. Rachel pushed off his hat and ran her fingers through his dusty, sweaty hair as she kissed him, while Jack and Teddy moved in for some attention.

"Darlin', you've been riding hard. And Thunder looks just as bedraggled as you do!"

By this time, Hamp, Martha, Tobe, Greta, Bertie, and Sarah, who was now four years old, had all gathered around and the romantic moment of arrival was past. Jesse hugged everyone.

Tobe took the stallion's reins. "Jesse, I'll take Thunder to the barn and feed and water him."

Jesse filled the basin with water and washed his face, hair, and hands. He and Rachel then disappeared into the house.

Rachel set to work, with the help of Martha, Greta, and Bertie, to cook Jesse's favorite dinner of fried chicken, mashed potatoes, gravy, fresh biscuits, and cold buttermilk. Meanwhile, Jesse knelt to greet the younger children.

"Buddy! How's my big boy!" Little Jacob wrapped his arms around his father's neck. He was called "Buddy," a nickname bestowed on him by big brother Angus. Little Martha toddled over. "Pa! Pa!" she cried. Jesse pulled her to him, rose with both children in his arms, and settled in the rocking chair to watch his family preparing supper.

"I'm so hungry, I could've eaten Thunder! And by the way, the military wants twenty of our horses for the high-ranking officers. How many are trained and ready for delivery?"

Rachel paused in peeling the sweet potatoes. "Oh, Jesse! What wonderful news! Just what we've been working for all these years. We have sixteen four-year-olds that are fully trained, and four three-year-olds that just need a bit more polishing."

Rachel's dinner was most enjoyable and was topped off with fresh apple pie. There were few leftovers.

After dinner and getting the children settled down in bed, Jesse and Rachel walked arm in arm on the banks of Verde Creek to the exact spot where they were married, and Jesse gently put his hands around his wife's face. "You are the most beautiful woman in the world. I knew that when I first saw you and that fact has never changed. We can be thankful that our children are healthy and smart."

"We will all be relieved when you can finally settle down and quit Rangering."

After a tender kiss, he could tell she was drooping a bit. "How are you feeling?"

"I think we should go home. I'm feeling a little tired."

He carried her home and did not mind that she was heavier than when they were married because she was carrying their beloved unborn child.

The next day, September 4, 1845, Ben McAlester was born. When he arrived, he screamed so loudly that Rachel told Jesse, "He's either going to be a politician or a preacher."

When Jesse held him for the first time, he whispered into the baby's tiny ear, "I love you, my dear young son, and I will always love and protect you. When you grow up, I will teach you the secret of the foal's milt and you will be the best rider in the world."

Jesse and Rachel had some quiet time together. He helped her with the children and the training of the horses.

Leaving his family was extremely difficult this time, but he was pleased that he had been home for Ben's birth.

Thereafter, Jesse regularly received requests to buy horses for the military and others as word of his sturdy, magnificent, well trained horses spread throughout Texas and beyond. He always told the buyers and anyone else who would listen that without his wife, they would not be able to continue in the horse business.

On December 29, 1845, Texas was annexed as the 28th state in the United States of America, even though Texas did not formally accede their sovereignty to the United States until February 19, 1846. There was joyful cheering, as well as celebrations in the major cities of Texas, which was contrasted strongly with the gloom pervasive throughout Mexico.

Rachel said to her children, "We're going to have a party and invite all our neighbors!" The children jumped up and down and yelled, "Yeah!" "Hurrah!" "Can I help, Mama?"

After the well-attended party, Rachel said, "Children, you were a great help," and she hugged them one by one.

Upon returning to Corpus Christi, Jesse was summoned to General Taylor's tent.

"Lieutenant McAlester reporting for duty, sir."

"I have been instructed by the State of Texas to advise you that you have been promoted to Captain for your amazing efforts in this war. Congratulations, Captain."

Jesse, eyebrows raised, stared at the General.

Jesse saluted, did an about face, exited the tent on a cloud, and sought out his fellow Rangers. He found them on the field, training General Taylor's cavalry. "Sergeant Andrews!"

"Hold on a minute, Jesse, we've all been promoted! I'm now Lieutenant Andrews. Chato, Cuddy, Cager, and Choc are now all Sergeants."

Jesse did not miss a beat. "In the morning, Lieutenant, I want you and all of our newly promoted Sergeants up at dawn to reconnoiter the area south of the Nueces."

"Sounds dangerous, do you expect us to run into any of the Mexican army?"

"Probably. But we're there to scout, not shed blood!"

March 28, 1846

The American Army, led by General Taylor, moved to the tip of Texas to establish the Rio Grande as the southern boundary of the state, and the United States. Port Isabel became a strategic location for the Mexican-American War. Supplies and men could easily be transported to that location under the protection of the United States Navy.

"Jesse, how long do you think we'll be in this wretched place?"

"Dob, I have orders to scout for a new fort site to establish our cannon emplacements. We need to find a place where the infantry will be well protected, and the artillery can easily bombard the town of Matamoros."

While scouting for a place to build a fort, Jesse and his Rangers saw increased activity from the Mexicans coming north of the Rio Grande. As the dust settled, the scouts observed large groups of mounted dragoons, Lancers, and hundreds of infantry being assembled.

"Men, I want you to return to camp. Dob, when you arrive, immediately report to General Taylor that we have found a site for the fort directly across from Matamoros. You might also mention that the Mexicans are building their strength north of the Rio Grande. That new fort will surely see some lively action—I hope not too soon."

"Aren't you going with us, Jesse?"

"No, I'm staying here for a few more days."

Jesse was still there when the Army engineers arrived, well protected by the U.S. infantry.

They brought an artillery contingent of four fourteen-pounders, and hastened to construct the fort, using dirt found in the area. Jesse could do only limited scouting while construction was going on. Major Jacob Brown, in charge of the artillery, immediately moved his troops inside the ruggedly built fort, naming it Fort Texas, and awaited further orders.

April 25, 1846

Seventy U.S. Dragoons sallied forth without guidance from the Rangers. They were ambushed, and to a man they were killed or captured while scouting the disputed area. Three days later, Jesse and a company of Rangers rode to Port Isabel to warn General Taylor about a large force of Mexican soldiers approaching. Chato, returning from a lone scouting excursion, had reported this danger the night before.

Fog blanketed the coast the next morning. The company of Texas Rangers, including Jesse, Dob, Chato, Cager, Cuddy, and Choc, took the best road north to Port Isabel. They had covered about half the distance when Chato spoke in a near whisper.

"Jesse, did you hear that?"

"What? I didn't hear anything beyond the noises we're making."

"A click, like a gun being cocked."

"I trust your ears." He turned to the other men. "Dismount and prepare for an attack!" They reined in at once, but simultaneous gunfire erupted from both sides. They had ridden into an ambush. Among the ghostly clumps of brush at the roadside, Mexican soldiers had been hiding their positions now revealed by blazing rifle fire.

Chato never got a foot on the ground. Mortally wounded, he fell sideways into a hole full of water. The men behind Jesse cried out or cursed as Jesse flattened himself in the hole with Chato, where the water became ever-increasingly crimson with his friend's blood. He placed his hand on Chato's neck and felt the jugular vein. No pulse. He waited.

The firing ceased. There was utter silence. Then Jesse heard the slap of wet brush against the cloth of britches, the clump of approaching boots. He held his position and his breath, hoping that Chato's blood would make the Mexicans believe they both were dead. Someone poked him in the back with a rifle barrel. Jesse didn't react. Not a move, not a quiver.

After a quick inspection tour, the Mexican officer gave a brief assessment and command. *"Estan todos muertos. ¡Buen trabajo, amigos! Ahora vámonos de aquí."* "They're all dead. Good work, friends! Now let's get out of here."

Jesse could breathe again, but remained still until the shadowed shapes of the soldiers were no longer visible, the noise of their horses fading into silence. He rose, soaked through with water and blood, and called. "Choc! Cager! Cuddy! Dob!"

A lone figure staggered to his feet. "Jesse! You're alive! It's me, Dob."

Dob came close, and Jesse could see that a bullet had creased the side of his skull. The wound was still bleeding freely. "Here, Dob, I've got a clean bandana."

He quickly made a bandage and tied the cloth around Dob's head. "I guess you were bleeding so much they thought they'd shot you through the head."

"Yeah. And I played dead pretty good, too. But Cager and Cuddy were killed instantly."

Jesse turned a full circle, surveying the scene, still heavy with fog. "Where's Choc? Oh, no! There he is, tangled in that bush. His horse must've dragged him. And there's his horse, a few yards away. Dead, too."

Dob placed a hand on Jesse's shoulder. "We have lost six men today and others are wounded."

Jesse's voice quavered, and tears filled his eyes. He was silent until he could gain control again. He realized he was always lucky, but felt extremely guilty for the loss of his men.

When the mournful cavalcade of Rangers finally reached Port Isabel, Jesse warned General Taylor of the approaching Mexican Army.

May 3, 1846

The Mexican army, with artillery and batteries positioned in Matamoros, bombarded Fort Texas, resulting in the death of Major Brown. Fort Texas was later renamed Fort Brown after its hero, Major Jacob Brown.

Five days later, on May 8, the Battle of Palo Alto took place on the coastal plains near Brownsville. Amidst sand, chaparral, and a blistering sun, the two armies met. This battle was an American victory due largely to better weapons, munitions, and the famous Flying Artillery, which was mobile and could be repositioned very quickly to execute devastating cannon fire on the flanks of the Mexican troops, decimating their forces.

Resaca de la Palma

On May 9, the two armies fought the Battle of Resaca de la Palma.

On the same day, Jesse was summoned to General Taylor's tent and upon entering stood at attention.

"Captain McAlester reporting for duty, sir."

"At ease, Captain. After the whipping we gave General Arista yesterday, I thought he would retire south of the Rio Grande. Instead, this morning he positioned his men about five miles from here in a dry riverbed with heavy growths of chaparral on either side making it difficult to spot his troops. I want you to affix your bayonets, use swords, or whatever means are necessary to drive those troops from their position."

"We will handle that!"

"The Mexicans have their backs to the river and their cannons pointed on the road toward us. Before you attack, our cannon will pepper the Mexican infantry hidden in the undergrowth to soften them up."

Jesse assembled his men and delivered their instructions and positions.

He and his men came as close as they dared. Immediately, the enemy's onslaught of bullets overwhelmed them. Some of the Mexican soldiers hidden in the chaparral charged them, brandishing their knives and pistols at Jesse and his men, who were clearly outnumbered. The hand to hand combat was the fiercest Jesse had witnessed.

General Taylor was forced to send Captain Charles May and his Dragoons to capture the enemy's cannon.

Captain May gave orders, "Come on men. Follow me and we'll surely prevail."

The Dragoon's charge was met with withering artillery fire and a deadly crossfire from the Mexican infantry, forcing the Dragoons in a full-fledged flight back to the American lines.

"Damn their hides for not carrying out my mission. Captain Donovan, do you think your boys can complete the mission?"

"Yes, General, but to escape from their cannons, we will outflank them pushing them from their hiding places into the river."

"Captain, I want you to join up with Captain McAlester and his men, or what's left of them, and push the Mexicans into the river. Then I want their cannons silenced."

Captain Donovan and his troops, along with Jesse and his men, arrived in the thick undergrowth. They drove the Mexican Infantry toward the river and successfully captured their cannons.

After the Mexican troops saw that they were outflanked, and their cannons were taken, they fled into the river in a panic and many of them drowned.

May 13, 1846

Public opinion of the Mexican-American War in the United States was deeply divided, with many viewing it as unjust aggression against a smaller, weaker foe. After Palo Alto and Resaca de la Palma, the tide turned in favor of war.

The time had come; therefore, President James Polk officially declared war against Mexico.

On May 18, General Taylor crossed the Rio Grande. In the city of Matamoros, Mexico surrendered to the Americans. Taylor, under orders from Washington, proceeded to march toward Monterrey.

"Jesse, do you think we'll see much action in Monterrey?"

"Dob, I expect this will be a different type of fighting than we're accustomed to."

"What do you mean?"

"I mean we won't be fighting in the open like we were at Palo Alto and Resaca de la Palma."

As it turned out, they weren't fighting at all. Jesse, Dob, and the other Rangers were furloughed.

Jesse returned home and trained Jack and Teddy by offering them a deer hide.

The dogs latched onto the hide as Jesse whirled it around and around, building their strength and tenacity.

He played with his children, spent quiet moments with his wife, and broke two horses and trained three others.

When their furlough ended, they left for Mexico, well rested.

September 21, 1846

Under a barrage of gunfire from rooftops and residences in the city of Monterrey, the Americans suffered staggering losses. Two days later, Captain Jesse McAlester stood at attention in General Taylor's headquarters.

"General, sir, if you will permit me, I would like to suggest another way of fighting in the city."

"Captain, you've been exemplary in combat. What is your suggestion?"

"Sir, I suggest we use the same tactics the Texians used at Bexar. We go from house to house from the inside, so we will not expose our troops to enemy fire."

Taylor turned to Colonel Whiteside. "Because our other strategies haven't worked, I order that we follow Captain McAlester's plan. Colonel, see that he receives all the help he requires. Captain, you are in charge."

"Yes, sir, I will have our men open holes in the houses, but I need a team of soldiers to enter the buildings and clear out any Mexican soldiers."

The General nodded at Colonel Whiteside. "That can be arranged."

"Dob, gather up some pick axes, sledgehammers, and any charges you can find. When you gain access into the buildings, I want you and your men to clear the Mexican soldiers shooting from the rooftops, so we can position our sharpshooters there."

The American losses were substantially reduced by using these "urban warfare" tactics.

The next day, General Pedro Ampudia asked for a cessation of hostilities.

Despite extreme objections from the Texas Rangers and President Polk, General Taylor agreed to a two-month armistice. He knew he had to resupply his army and attend to the wounded and dead.

"Jesse, why are we letting the Mexican army just walk out of here with their weapons?"

"Dob, General Taylor needs reinforcements, supplies, and munitions to keep this army moving. You can't fight on empty bellies. Our orders are to hold the city and let those snakes slither away. The good thing about this armistice is we can go back to the ranch and help Rachel."

President Polk was incensed about Taylor's actions, and the result was that some of General Taylor's best soldiers were removed and sent to Vera Cruz, crippling the core of his army and forcing him to rely on volunteers.

After two months at the ranch, Jesse bent down and said, "Jack, Teddy, I'm very proud of the way you're protecting the ranch." Both dogs, ears cocked, seemed to understand Jesse's praise, as he fed them some deer jerky from his pocket.

He selected five horses to take with him for the Army to buy.

Rachel was fearful for Jesse. "Please don't go back to fight. I am afraid you will be hurt. I need you here."

"Rachel, I love you, but I have to fulfill my duty."

"You also have a duty here."

Jesse's stubbornness came from his Scottish lineage. "Rachel, let me have a kiss."

"I'm not going to kiss a man that prefers fighting to being with his family."

Jesse mounted his horse to go back to battle the Mexican troops. He felt guilty about leaving Rachel and his children, and an ever-growing part of him wanted to stay at the ranch, but his adrenaline surged at the thought of more battles.

Battle of Buena Vista
February 23, 1847

On Tuesday, February 23, the American army was south of Saltillo. During the battle, Dob rode to Jesse's side. "The left flank is giving way, so I'm going to rally the boys to close it or we'll be surrounded."

"It appears that your compadre," Jesse said, motioning to a clearly agitated Lancer, "is singling you out for combat."

"Well, if it's a fight he wants, I'll give him hell!"

"Be careful of the lance," Jesse said, remembering his own previous encounter with a Mexican Lancer, and how it had cost him a thoroughbred horse.

The Lancer looked at Dob and screamed, "Gringo, I'm going to rip your balls off."

Lowering his lance, he charged straight toward Dob.

The Mexican cavalrymen who saw what was happening were cheering wildly, clamoring for a victory, but just as the Lancer was about to impale Dob, the Ranger put his foot in a leather strap and aligned his body on the right side of his horse, and the thrust found no purchase.

Dob wheeled his horse around before the Lancer could respond, grabbed the lance, and ran it through the now helpless Mexican.

Jesse and his mounted Rangers cheered wildly for Dob. There was a stunned silence from the Mexican cavalrymen as they realized the norteamericano had vanquished their hero.

Outnumbered by approximately 10,000 enemy troops, General Taylor was forced to retreat; his depleted forces, bereft of a large number of regulars, were fighting with unseasoned volunteers. The entire left flank of Taylor's little army was crumbling before the onslaught of Mexican troops. Hundreds of volunteers fled the field in disorganized chaos and headed north.

Just as all seemed lost for the Americans, Colonel Jefferson Davis and his mounted Mississippi riflemen began raking the Mexican lines with a deadly fusillade. The tide began to turn further when an American officer, sword drawn, rounded up several hundred of the deserting volunteers, forcing them back to the battle.

"Colonel Davis, thank God you arrived when you did, our whole left flank was being overrun and a lot of our men fled the field."

"Captain McAlester, damn the cowards that fled. I'm proud to have you and your Rangers on my side."

"Colonel, if your men will cover our retreat, I will rally our men to fall back, to live to fight another day. The Mexican Lancers and the local guerrillas have been lassoing stragglers, yanking them off their feet and dragging our soldiers through rocks and cactus."

Jesse and Dob fled the field when their mounts gave out, and the onrushing Mexicans, their escopetas loaded with heavy shot, blew Dob's head off. Jesse, trying to duck, was cut down by buck and ball, ripping his left shoulder apart. Just as he was about to be run through with a sword, he made one final desperate gambit: he simultaneously yelled and pointed out the Masonic ring that Santa Anna had given to him at Orozimbo.

"Gringo, are you offering me the ring before I kill you?"

"This is Santa Anna's personal ring, and I insist that you take me to him."

"Gringo, there's not much left of you to take, but I will humor you with an audience with the Generalissmo."

The mangled corpses of the American soldiers captured by the Mexicans were found butchered. Some were missing their heads, while others had their eyes gouged out and their private parts missing.

Word spread fast through the Mexican ranks of the capture of the famous Texas Ranger, finally reaching General Santa Anna. He requested to see the prisoner, and Jesse was marched to the General's tent.

"Captain McAlester—it's Captain now? Congratulations. Normally, I would receive you as a prisoner and send you to Perote Castle for imprisonment until we are victorious against your United States. But I remember that you treated General Almonte and me with respect and kindness at Orozimbo. I would like to extend the same courtesy to you. I see that you are still wearing the ring I gave you."

"Yes, General, it has been with me since Orozimbo."

"I'm going to have a small group of cavalry escort you back to your lines under a white flag and release you."

"That is very generous of you, General."

"Lieutenant Reyes, please get a detachment of your men and escort this soldier back to his lines."

"But General, are you sure this is wise? He is a Texas Ranger."

"How dare you question my judgment?" Santa Anna's eyes flashed with rage.

The American lines were close by, but before departing, Lieutenant Reyes huddled with his men out of earshot of Jesse.

While he was being escorted to his camp, Jesse heard the sound of pistols being cocked and the words, *"Adios, Rinche diablo."* "Goodbye, devil Ranger."

Jesse, gravely wounded, raced toward the American lines, but Thunder was shot dead and fell to the ground. Jesse was caught under the horse's body and passed out from the loss of blood.

The Mexican cavalrymen wheeled their mounts around and headed toward the Mexican lines.

Hearing the volley of gunfire, a squad of American Dragoons raced toward the sound, and upon discovering Jesse, pulled him out from beneath his dead horse. Realizing Jesse could not put any pressure on his leg, they carefully placed the severely wounded Ranger on one of their horses and headed toward a hospital tent. After two days, he regained consciousness.

When he awoke, a doctor was standing over him with a grim look on his face. "How bad is it, Doc?"

"Captain McAlester, we have bound your leg and cleaned your wounds as best we can in the field, but I fear you need better medical attention than we can give you."

"Will I live?"

"Your left shoulder and left lung have been badly damaged, and you may lose the limb and have reduced lung function."

"Please don't remove my arm."

"To save your arm, I'll send you back to Port Isabel. If you survive that trek, I'll have you put on a ship bound for New Orleans for proper treatment."

"Thank you, Doctor. I will do my part by staying alive." Jesse wrote Rachel about his ordeal and about Dob's death.

After surgery and months of convalescing in New Orleans, Jesse mustered out of the State of Texas Volunteer service, and was shipped to Corpus Christi, and then travelled over land by wagon to Rancho Arroyo Verde.

June 6, 1847

Jesse heard Teddy and Jack barking first, then he heard Rachel scream, "It's Jesse! He's back home!"

Suddenly Rachel, Martha, and Hamp, followed by the children, surrounded the wagon. Rachel cried tears of relief that her husband was home, and tears of sadness at the sight of his pale countenance. "You're nothin' but skin and bones!"

Jesse's face was also wet with tears. "I may be a bag of bones, but it was the thought of you and the family that kept my spirits up."

Unable to hug him due to the lingering tenderness in his left shoulder, she kissed him and whispered, "We've been praying for your safe return, and now our prayers are answered."

"Hamp, I'm so ashamed that I was not able to save Dob. His death weighs heavily on my conscience."

In the war with Mexico, the campaign shifted from the north to Veracruz, Mexico.

General Winfield Scott established a supply line from Veracruz to Mexico City. After almost six months of fierce fighting, Mexico City fell to General Scott and his troops on September 15, 1847.

The Treaty of Guadalupe Hidalgo was finally signed on March 6, 1848. The terms of the treaty required Mexico to cede over one-half of its northern territory to the United States.

CHAPTER TWENTY
New Rangers

Títo Ruiz was born in 1830 in a sleepy village north of the Rio Grande, and he was known as *"El Bastardo"* because his father was nameless. When he was seven, Títo asked his mother Pilar questions about his father.

"Why does my name have only your last name and not my father's too?"

"Títo, I'm ashamed to tell you this, but your father forced himself upon me and is a very violent man."

"Can you tell me anything else about him?"

"He was of medium size with dark eyes, and he had a tattoo of a scorpion on his left forearm," and she gestured on her arm where the tattoo was.

September 19, 1842

"Tito, they're stampeding the horses!" The first arrow pierced his mother's breast.

The Comanche who ran into their jacal was a fearsome sight, with half his face painted white, the other side black, but Tito was a brave young boy and protective of his mother. The warrior held his knife above the mother's head to scalp her when he was suddenly interrupted by Tito cutting his throat.

Huddled in the small adobe hut were his younger three sisters and two brothers. Although Tito wanted to help them, the Comanche were attacking so viciously that all he could do was dodge the warriors' arrows as he fled to the safety of the river.

Several hours later, the villagers, including Tito, carried lighted torches to examine the ruins of the village and the dozen mutilated corpses, to determine the names of the victims.

The next morning the *alcalde*, the mayor, gathered men for a burial detail. As the last shovel full of dirt fell, the *alcalde* began saying a prayer.

After the service, Tito remained at the gravesite, grieving for his mother and siblings, who were dead or captured by the Indians.

"Tito, what are your plans?" asked a man who was a good friend of the family.

He replied, while making the sign of the cross, "Señor, I have an uncle. He is my mother's brother. I will start for his rancho in the morning."

"Go with God."

The boy had no horse and no shoes, so he started out barefoot. After two days of hard traveling, he arrived at his uncle's ranch. When the dogs barked, his Uncle Carlos came out the front door. He looked astonished to see his nephew on foot, in bedraggled clothes, and very upset.

"Tito, is that you?"

He ran to the front door. "¡Sí, Tío!" He embraced his uncle.

After several days of rest, Tito stood before his uncle. "Tío Carlos, I'm ready to get started working on your rancho."

"All right. Today, I want you to work with Lucero. He is my most experienced vaquero. Go to the stables and tell him to give you anything you need to start working the horses."

After two months of hard work under the tutelage of Lucero, Tito had learned much; he became a good rider, and knew how to care for his uncle's horses. Feeling his confidence growing, he approached his uncle. "I would very much like to learn how to shoot. It may prove useful if we are attacked by the Indians."

Understanding that his nephew had scars in his heart from losing his mother and siblings in the Indian attack, Carlos said, "Tito, we have a fortress here with twenty-three hardened vaqueros, but I will teach you to shoot, for it is a skill you should know."

Within a year, Tito could ride, rope, and shoot as well as any of the vaqueros. On January 8, 1849, with a full moon in the sky, his future changed forever.

At first there was absolute silence, followed by the fierce barking of their pack of hounds, then silence again, followed by the ringing of the bell, signaling danger.

Outside the house, dozens of mounted Kiowa warriors, embellished with war paint, had begun killing everything they could find. A brave group of vaqueros attempted to fight back, but it was too late. The buildings were on fire from the flaming arrows.

With a shovel, Tito knocked a painted warrior from his horse, mounted the horse, and rode to the nearest ranch to warn them and seek help.

"Señor Villarreal, the painted savages were everywhere. I am lucky to be alive."

"Tito, calm down. Take this cup of mescal and get some rest. We will leave at first light."

The next morning, Tito walked through the smoldering ruins. All the residents were dead or missing, but Tito found the body of his uncle. He had been scalped and mutilated.

Señor Villarreal, making the sign of the cross, along with his vaqueros, asked, "Tito, did you see who did this terrible massacre?"

"Sí, Señor, it was the Kiowa. How may I seek my revenge?"

"If I were you, I would find the Ranger Jesse McAlester, and see if he will take you on as a Ranger."

"Where might I find this Jesse McAlester?"

"He lives on a ranch called Rancho Arroyo Verde, about four days ride north of here."

"*Muchas gracias*, I will gather what I can find and start there immediately."

"You will need a fresh horse. Take that bay over there."

"Gracias, Señor, I will pay you back as soon as I can."

Traveling almost day and night, Tito arrived at the McAlester place on the third day, exhausted and hungry, with his horse badly needing grain and water. He found Jesse in the barn.

Jesse, still favoring his left shoulder from the grievous wounds suffered at the Battle of Buena Vista, looked over the boy and his horse. He turned to Tito. "There's oats and water out back for your horse, and you can clean up at the basin on the porch."

"Señor, I am Tito Ruiz, and I have come to meet the famous Texas Ranger Jesse McAlester."

"I don't know about being famous, but I'm Jesse McAlester."

Tito was taken aback by Jesse's drawn appearance, unsure if he was the famous Texas Ranger. "Señor McAlester, I have come to be a Ranger, if you will accept me."

Jesse could see that Tito could hardly believe he was the Ranger he was seeking. "Son, I don't look like much these days, but I'm getting stronger every day."

"I'm so glad, how did you get your injuries?"

"I was shot through the shoulder at the Battle of Buena Vista—nearly cost me my left arm and part of my lung, and I was left for dead. My mount was killed. Fortunately for me, there was a fine surgeon from Philadelphia who saved my life in New Orleans."

Tito made the sign of the cross.

Immediately, Jesse's new horse, a beautiful white stallion reared up and began prancing on his hind legs.

"Muy bonito, Señor. What is his name?"

"I call him Zack in honor of General Zachary Taylor."

"Tell me about your background."

"When I was twelve, the Comanche raided our village, killing my mother and capturing my brothers and sisters. I have never known my father, but it is known that he is a bad man. My Uncle Carlos took me in and I worked for him until last week, when the Kiowa burned down his ranch, killed and scalped him, along with many other poor souls."

"So you are seeking revenge? The Rangers are plenty busy without blood matches, but if you can show me you can ride and shoot, I'll swear you in."

"Señor McAlester, I am grateful, and I will not disappoint you."

Jesse tested his riding and shooting skills, using the same procedures required for the other recruits. Tito passed with flying colors, and Jesse knew his fluent Spanish and knowledge of the terrain in South Texas would be of considerable help.

"Tito, raise your right hand and repeat after me."

Tito, smiling, repeated the Ranger's oath and Jesse pinned the badge on him.

Tito responded, "Thank you, Señor Jesse! Hurray!" and threw his hat in the air.

March 1849

Jesse and Títo were tracking some horse thieves near Corpus Christi Bay on a special assignment to discover where the stock was being loaded onto ships.

"Captain, look up ahead."

"I can see it. Looks like a big fire. Let's ride over there nice and easy like, until we know what we are up against."

As they slowly drew near the water, they saw what had once been someone's grass home, now only embers.

"Sir, this looks like the work of the Comanche." Tito slipped off of his big bay to examine the victims. "I count six men and three women dead."

Jesse examined the scalped and mutilated bodies. "Look at their large bows and arrows, probably used to hunt fish in the bay. These are *la genet gigantic*"—the giant people—"but many call them the Karankawas. The Comanche have killed most of them."

"Do they really eat the flesh of the people they kill to keep them from fighting in the next world?"

Before Jesse could answer, Tito cried out "Aaayyyyya," seeing a towering, solitary figure approaching cautiously in the bay, standing upright in his dugout canoe. He signaled to the imposing boatman that they came in peace. He responded with a fierce gesture, so the two Rangers prepared for battle.

When the Karankawa climbed out of his canoe, he walked past the two Rangers where they stood, tense and vigilant, and began examining the bodies of the members of his tribe. He began wailing, and cut himself with his war club, which was lined with shark's teeth.

"What should we do, Captain?"

"Not much we can do but stay ready in case he wants to attack us."

"Do you think he needs help in burying his people?"

"He might have a different way of doing things."

As the tide was receding, the Indian dragged the victims' bodies to the shore, and they were pulled toward the sea one by one.

Finally, the Rangers faced the huge Indian, and Títo said very slowly, "Me Títo, and this is Jesse."

Making a mess of the pronunciation of their names, he finally gave up and pointed to himself, "Me Kronk!" Kronk was a large man with a broad forehead. The Karankawa's custom of flattening their babies' foreheads was accomplished by using moss, cloth, and thin boards tied to the babies' heads for about one year.

Kronk was nearly seven feet tall, with coarse black hair, braided and hanging to his waist.

He had blue circles tattooed on his face, with a reed protruding through his nose. His neck was adorned with a string of small seashells. The only clothing he wore was a breechcloth of deerskin. He wore nothing to protect his head from the rain, or sun, and was barefoot. Kronk was an imposing figure, carrying a bow about six feet long with arrows about half that size.

Títo responded, "I'm going to call you Big Kronk," as the big Indian merely blinked.

"Títo, let's ride to Molly's to procure a horse for the big fellow. He can't be afoot."

"Whooee, I can hardly wait to get some of Molly's good food."

"Is he supposed to stay here or follow us?"

Jesse motioned for Big Kronk to follow, and he ran with long strides the sixteen miles to Molly's.

"Títo, I've never seen anybody that can cover ground like that," Jesse said. The younger man nodded his agreement.

When they reached Molly's, she met them at the front door and was quite startled by Kronk's size, as well as his tattooed face and the stick in his nose. Kronk immediately began staring at the pictures on the wall and seemed fascinated by them.

Ryan and Rose ran toward the Rangers and Big Kronk, and hugged everyone. "Gee mister, I've never seen anyone as big as you. Are you a giant?"

"Molly, this is Títo Ruiz, my new Ranger, and we haven't figured out what we're going to do with the big fellow yet."

The Rangers, trying not to smile, watched Big Kronk cautiously. He carefully lifted Rose until her head almost touched the ceiling. "Look Mama, I can touch the ceiling."

"Stop with this nonsense, and everyone follow me into the kitchen if you want a hot meal."

Kronk, unsure of what to expect, gently lowered Rose to the floor, and followed Jesse and Títo, who had been nervous about the Indian's action and continued to watch him closely.

Molly served one of her luscious meals. They consumed a leg of lamb and a large bowl of potatoes, washed down with cold buttermilk, along with two apple pies.

"Molly, that was a good meal, but we didn't want to impose on you like this." Kronk began rubbing his stomach and uttered the word *plá*— good.

Jesse repeated, *"Plá,"* while rubbing his stomach. "Well, now we know at least one word of his language. Molly, is there anything we can help you with while we are here?"

"Jesse, you can repay me by working some green horses that need breaking."

"I'm still recovering from my wounds from the war, but Títo here can oblige you." As Títo and Big Kronk left for the corrals, Jessie told Molly how they ran into the big Indian.

"That's a shame, and how did he get here without a horse?"

"He ran all the way from Corpus Christi Bay."

"Did you and Títo have a hard time following him?" They both laughed.

Títo broke three horses that day.

When Kronk expressed interest in mounting a horse, he fell off twice before he was able to wrap his long legs together under the horse's belly. Everyone was astonished!

The trio left the next day for Rancho Arroyo Verde. Kronk was content to hang back while trying to improve his riding skills.

"Títo, we need meat, and I can see a herd of deer in that grove of trees. I'm going to get us one," as Jesse removed his rifle from his scabbard.

Big Kronk slid off his horse and motioned for Jesse to move aside, growling, *"Ná-i ỳe dótn ahók"*—"I am going to kill deer." He unlimbered his six-foot bow and shot his three-foot arrow completely through the deer.

"Captain, I've never seen anything like that. How far do you reckon?"

"At least seventy-five paces!"

"Do you think you can teach him how to be a Ranger?"

"I expect he can teach us a thing or two."

CHAPTER TWENTY-ONE
German Immigrants

June 17, 1850

Karl Krueger and his new wife Hannah had been part of the German migration looking for new land in the Hill Country. Because of the political turmoil in Germany, they had decided to become a part of the German community promising cheap land in Texas.

Karl was not a farmer, but had tended sheep for all of his twenty-two years. He was a loner and sought out land more suitable for raising sheep rather than farming. His sixteen-year-old wife just wanted out of her abusive family life at home in Germany. After the long voyage, he had spoken with other Germans settling in the Hill Country, learning that many of the German immigrants were settling in a town called New Braunfels, Texas.

From the time he was twelve years old, Karl's father had apprenticed him to be a stonemason. The land where he was headed was well suited for both masonry and sheep ranching.

On the trip to New Braunfels, he bartered his masonry skills for a two-wheeled cart and three sheep. Hannah traded her seamstress skills for some bolts of strong cloth.

Their trip took ten days. The couple pushed their cart along the road, passing many beautiful springs, creeks, and rivers before achieving their destination of New Braunfels. The family of Fritz Guenther met them coming into town and invited them to stay in their barn that night.

"Thank you very much for your help," said Karl.

Gunther also gave the young couple directions to Herman Streicher, who could sell them land.

After arriving at Streicher's house and knocking on the door, a ruddy-faced man answered.

Karl asked, "Are you Herr Streicher?"

"Yes, I am."

"My name is Karl Krueger and this is my wife Hannah."

"I'm pleased to meet you both, and how may I be of service?"

"I was told you had land well suited for raising sheep that could be bought reasonably."

"That is true, but the land that is available is about six days' walk from here."

"We are not afraid of walking. How much does the land cost?"

"The land is very rocky so I can let you have it for fifty cents an acre."

"Hannah, how much money do we have in your satchel?"

"We have about a hundred dollars in gold."

Stretcher sold them one hundred and sixty acres, at fifty cents an acre. After exchanging the money for the Deed, the couple felt a warm glow at their success in acquiring the land.

Herr Streicher drew a crude map detailing the metes and bounds of the property, and they were satisfied from the physical description that they could find the spot. They acquired some dried venison, salted pork, and various spices, and set out for their new home, which was just shy of a hundred miles west of New Braunfels. The trip would take six days of hard walking and pushing the cart.

Karl had a fine German rifle, pistol, and a wooden box full of his hammers, chisels, and other masonry tools. Hannah had a sewing kit, some cloth, and very little else. What they did have was an intrepid spirit and the ability to adapt.

After six long days, they arrived at their property. They examined all of the physical signs that Herr Streicher had described to them in delineating the boundaries.

Hannah hugged her husband. "Oh Karl, I never dreamed that this land would be so beautiful."

"Hannah, I intend to build you a solid home. In examining the area, I would like to place the home near the stream, on that solid shelf of limestone near the giant oak tree. In the meantime, I will erect a temporary shelter for us."

"How long before you can build a permanent home?"

"With all the limestone here, I believe we can move in sometime in October."

The next day, Karl began making a crude lean-to from the smaller juniper trees. Hannah hauled water from a spring, and he shot his first white-tailed deer. Although it was hard work, they were able to eat what they wanted, and he built a primitive smoker to dry the rest of the meat for jerky. They were living on their own land, and they were happy.

On October 6, 1850, they set the last stone in their new home, and then celebrated with wine she had made from mustang grapes.

"Hannah, let's light the first fire in the fireplace tonight!"

Joseph Henry Matthews, born in the slums of Glasgow in 1827, worked his way from Scotland to the United States on a freighter bound for New Orleans. He was twelve years old when he killed for the first time, stabbing a man in New Orleans over a dispute. Unfortunately, the man he killed was the son of a prominent politician.

He fled to Texas, and at the age of twenty, joined the Texas Rangers to fight with General Zachary Taylor's army in Mexico. The first action he saw was in Monterrey in September 1847. He was thrown out of the Army for killing unarmed civilians, but faced no criminal proceedings. Matthews then joined a group of mounted Texans that embraced his style of guerrilla warfare.

With those men, he fought in the last battle of the Mexican-American War in Mexico City.

October, 1850

Joseph Henry Matthews, a killer with no conscience, had no war to fight, so he created a small gang of mercenaries to wage one against anyone who stood in their way. The Mexican government offered up to $50 per scalp for the marauding Comanche.

"Captain, what are we going to do when we run out of Comanche scalps?"

"I've been puzzling on that. I reckon we'll keep scalping greasers until the government finds out what we're doing."

"How so?"

"Did you notice the scalps on that last bunch of señoritas?"

"Yeah, so?"

"You ignorant fool. Ain't no difference!"

"What if their hair ain't black?"

"By damn, I'm tired of these questions," as he reached into his saddle bags and produced a bottle of black dye. "This will make a pink pig black."

All of the men laughed.

"I hope the law don't find out that it was us'n that done the killing instead of the Comanche."

"I already figured that. You still got that deerskin bag full of our Comanche booty?"

"All excepting their heads. They were so ripe the buzzards were circling."

"From now on, they will blame the Comanche for the killings because we will use bows and arrows."

"That's right smart, Matthews!"

"I won't tell you agin. You best call me Captain or commence to fighting."

The scalps began flowing like a river of blood, until the Mexican government announced there would be no more bounty money. They opened an investigation on the Matthews gang, and when it was completed, the authorities offered rewards for the gang, dead or alive.

"Captain, now's that we been chased out of Mexico, what are we going to do?"

"We're gonna keep scalping folks. Just not gonna get any money for it." Matthews glared down at the miscreant, who immediately took his leave.

The remaining members of the Matthews gang were the seasoned Mexican American War veterans Billy Davis, aka Tiny, William Kettler, aka Red Willie, Archibald McKenzie, aka Archie, and Robert Stewart. They were pursued by the Mexican army all the way to Acuna, Mexico, where the gang crossed the Rio Grande into the sleepy town of Del Rio. There the murderers pulled citizens from their homes to search for valuables. After the search, the females were raped, mutilated, and scalped.

The fires were still smoldering in the ruins of Del Rio when Jesse, Kronk, and Títo rode into town.

The citizens, deathly afraid of the Rinches Diablos, wailed at the sight of the Rangers, until a priest boldly walked to them and Títo had a pleasant conversation with the priest.

The priest cried, "The victims must be buried immediately and I will conduct a funeral for them."

Títo was given a firsthand account of the atrocities committed by the Matthews gang.

"Mount up, men!" Jesse leapt on Zack's back and the beautiful stallion bolted down the road.

"Captain, how much of a head start do you reckon?"

"I figure six hours."

Jesse, Títo, and Kronk had no problem determining which direction the gang was headed, with empty whiskey bottles, discarded items, and dead bodies leaving an obvious trail.

October 6, 1850

The Matthews gang rode seventy miles east of Del Rio, and upon finding a cabin, walked in on a couple eating breakfast. The gang pretended they meant no harm, until Joseph Henry drew his large Bowie from its sheath and laid its edge upon the woman's throat.

The husband howled, "We'll give you anything you want if you'll just leave us alone."

"We want to know if anybody in this area has any money."

"Not here, but there's a young German couple that strictly trades in gold."

"How far?"

"About thirty-five miles north of here. You can't miss it. It's a solid limestone house near a creek."

"Noooo!" shrieked the husband as Tiny slit his wife's throat, and said, "You're next!" Tiny had trouble cutting the man's throat because he was so large.

"Move out of the way, Tiny," Joseph Henry said. He pushed Tiny aside and cut the man's head off. "Peel their scalps and put 'em in the scalp bag," as they thundered out the door.

"I'll bet the German gal is a pretty young thing with yeller hair." Tiny licked his lips.

"Oh hell, Tiny, you ain't got no sense with womenfolk," said Archie. "I'd rather get some roasted meat, their horses, and their scalps, if I had my druthers."

Joseph Henry shouted, "Shut the hell up! I aim to get to that cabin by dark, if you damn fools can ride without falling off!"

At dusk, the outlaws came upon the bucolic setting of a sturdy limestone cabin with smoke coming from the chimney.

Joseph Henry motioned toward Red Willie. "Get this saddle blanket and put it on that chimney. That'll smoke 'em out!"

Karl poked a rifle through a slit in a wall to shoot one of the outlaws, but Matthews quickly grabbed the barrel and the shot sailed harmlessly through the air. Soon the couple emerged from the cabin, coughing and overcome by smoke.

Tiny, licking his lips, said, "Ain't you a pretty young thing, if we can wipe that smoke off of you!" Karl flailed at Tiny, but he was no match for the outlaw.

Jesse and the two other Rangers found the scalped and horribly mutilated couple killed by the Matthews gang.

"Títo, which way are these butchers heading?"

"Captain, I've got their trail. They are headed north."

"We need to leave pronto! We got some merciless killers, boys, and we better find them before they wipe out the whole country."

Steering Zack north, with the wind at their advantage, they rode to the next grisly scene, finding the mutilated, scalped German couple outside their cabin. Horses were tied up under a large live oak tree, but there was no other sign of the gang.

"Bad men," as Kronk unleashed his knife, "They will pay!"

"Men, try the door."

After minutes of straining, the men were unable to push the door open, so Jesse, with his bad shoulder, helped them. Finally, they got it slightly ajar. Apparently, all of the bandits had passed out from drunkenness and two were lying against the door.

The Rangers and Kronk were met by the hiss of dozens of angry rattlesnakes.

Jesse surveyed the scene. "Títo, light a torch and use it to get those rattlesnakes away." Three of the bandits, Red Willie, Archie, and Robert Stewart, punctured by dozens of rattlesnake bites, had died as they deserved, with panic and fear in their eyes.

Matthews and Billy Davis were found dead on the bed where they had sought refuge from the snakes, which were still buzzing and biting them.

Jesse prayed, "God has a way of dealing with merciless killers."

"Jesse, let's pray for the innocent couple while we bury them."

Kronk moved toward the couple. "Me get shovel."

"Let's bury them under the oak tree. Títo, get that torch, move the snakes, and drag those scum out. They've already caused too much trouble."

"What do we do with the outlaws' bodies?"

"Leave 'em to the wolves and buzzards. Get the gang's horses, and anything they might have stolen, so we can return them to the Ranger camp!"

Jesse noticed that the rattlesnakes had begun slithering back into a hole near the fireplace.

The German couple had not been aware they had built the cabin directly atop a rattlesnake den. Karl had thought leaving a hole near the hearth would be a good place to put the ashes. The snakes had been hibernating, and the heat of the fire tricked them into thinking that it was spring.

CHAPTER TWENTY-TWO
Road Agents

December 4, 1854

On a blustery winter day, the stagecoach was fully loaded with passengers and cargo for its scheduled run from San Antonio to San Patricio. Secured on top of the coach was a strongbox guarded by a burly man armed with a sawed-off double-barreled shotgun. The driver was familiar with the route and was ahead of schedule.

From atop a nearby ridge, hostile eyes watched the approaching vehicle. "Vicente, can you see the stage yet?"

"Sí, Santos, but there is an armed guard next to the driver."

"That must mean they are guarding a lot of money."

Vicente Suarez also known as *El Pecoso*, the freckled one, motioned to Santos and the gang to move toward the road, where they had conveniently placed a large log to obstruct the stagecoach's passage.

"Whoa there!" The driver reined in the horses. The guard, ever alert, cocked the twin hammers of his shotgun.

Three blasts from Santos and his gang blew the guard off the coach seat. He fell to the ground and lay motionless.

The driver held up his hands, "I give up. You can have whatever we have on board."

"I'll take your life." Santos gunned down the driver. He shouted an order. "Everyone out! Put your hands in the air where I can see them!"

"I want all of you to duck as soon as I exit the stage," whispered one bold passenger to the frightened ones. Santos had not reckoned on meeting up with William Lambert, an accomplished *pistolero* and veteran of the Mexican-American War.

Lambert exited the coach armed with a loaded Walker Colt .44 and blasted everyone in sight. Two bandits fell immediately, and Santos was shot though his shoulder. *El Pecoso* and the three remaining gang members made a hasty retreat into the thick scrub, while Santos was barely able to mount his horse to escape.

Jesse, Tito, and Big Kronk had been following the stagecoach and came upon the macabre scene.

Jesse dismounted and questioned William Lambert. "What's your name? What happened here?"

"My name's Lambert. William Lambert. As you see, bandits waylaid the coach, stopped it cold with that log across the road. They shot the driver and the guard immediately. They ordered us out with our hands up, and I didn't exactly follow orders."

Jesse nodded. "Yes. I see that. Thanks to you, Mr. Lambert, the passengers survived. If the bandits were led by a man named Santos, everyone would be dead without you. He always kills all his victims."

Jesse turned to his fellows. "Grab the bodies and tie them to the top of the coach. Mr. Lambert, you have done the State of Texas a big service today. I know y'all were headed to San Patricio, but I would advise returning to San Antonio to deliver these bodies and get a new crew for the stagecoach."

"I would like to help, Captain McAlester, in pursuing the outlaws."

"The best help you can render is to drive this stagecoach back to San Antonio so we can start tracking the gang."

"Well, sir, I will do that."

"Much obliged! Can you point out the direction that the gang took?" Even as Lambert was pointing the direction, Títo had picked up the trail.

Jesse held up a hand. "Wait, men. It's getting late. We'd better bed down here and pick up the trail in the morning."

They watched as Lambert expertly turned the coach and headed back in the direction of San Antonio.

The next morning, Títo pointed out the bandits' trail. "Captain, I make out four sets of tracks. Do you really think this is Santos and his gang?"

"From the description Lambert gave, I expect it is. How far do you figure we are behind them?"

"I reckon about twelve hours, give or take."

After tracking all day, Jesse and his men made camp for the night within twenty-five miles of San Patricio.

December 6, 1854

Títo turned from tracking the outlaws to signal Jesse. "Captain, the gang is heading straight toward Molly's ranch."

Kronk rubbed his belly. "We eat Molly's place."

Jesse abruptly halted Zack. "Títo, come here pronto!" Títo's eyes followed where Jesse was pointing. "I see it, too."

Jesse dismounted and examined the bandits' trail, observing hoof prints where another rider had merged with the gang. "It appears that Santos is bleeding. They have a good head start to Molly's."

Santos and *El Pecoso* arrived at Molly's ranch shortly after sunrise. Juan Carlos was working in the yard when Santos found him. He turned away, preparing to shout, but before he could warn Molly, Santos stabbed him in the back.

The grizzled Mexican bandit smelled a good aroma of something baking, peeked in the window, and saw Molly in the kitchen. He opened the back door carefully and slowly stepped toward Molly, watching her remove something from the oven. When he was about five feet from her, a creaking board alerted Molly to possible danger. She turned with the pie just as Santos lunged for her with his knife, and she threw the steaming hot apple pie at his face.

Momentarily stunned, and blinded by the pie burning his face and his eyes, he flayed about unsuccessfully with his knife, giving Molly time to rake his face and stab his eyes with her fingernails.

Finally, he stabbed her, fortunately missing her heart, but causing a serious wound nonetheless. She fell to the floor, bleeding profusely.

El Pecoso entered the house and found Santos flailing his hands in the air, with one eye already milky, and his face bleeding as if he had tangled with a wild animal. Realizing Santos was in no condition to be their leader, *El Pecoso* searched and found Molly's stash of money, and quickly abandoned the grizzled old bandit. He walked out the door and shouted, "Let's go men! Ride like hell out of here!"

Meanwhile, Santos, unable to comprehend his failure, stumbled out of the house and found his horse. He pulled himself onto the horse and gave him full rein, desperate to make his exit.

The bandits' dust had barely settled on the road when María, Ryan, and Rose pulled up in the wagon loaded with provisions. María wailed, "Noooo!" and jumped from the wagon and ran to Juan Carlos's body. Although clutching the cross Molly had given him, he was lifeless.

The twins ran to the house and found Molly's limp body in a pool of blood in the kitchen. They yelled, "María, help! Mama's been killed too!" María ran into the house and kneeling beside Molly, she found a weak pulse. "Let's get her to bed as gently as we can."

After getting her settled in her bed, María barked additional orders. "Ryan, go to the barn and gather all the spider webs you can find. Rose, bring me a lemon cut in two."

When Rose brought the lemon, María squeezed the juice on Molly's wound to disinfect it.

"Rose, go to the back room and bring me a comfrey poultice of leaves and roots to stop the bleeding. Also bring me a curved needle and some strong thread." Rose quickly returned with the requested items and nervously watched María applying the poultice.

Ryan rushed in with a handful of spider webs and saw María carefully sewing his mother's skin back together. He whispered, "Will Mama live?"

María made the sign of the cross and gently applied the spider webs to the sutured area. "Rose, get me some new linen to protect the wound. Ryan, go into the back room and bring me some linden flower to make her a hot tea so she can rest."

They heard the pounding sounds of horses' hooves on the road, and feared the worst.

Looking out the window, they were relieved to see Jesse, Títo, and Kronk swing off their horses, run to Juan Carlos's bloody body, then rush into the house, finding Molly in bed being attended to by María, Rose, and Ryan.

"María, what happened?"

"Jesse, we came home with supplies and found my brother dead in the yard and Molly in a pool of blood in the kitchen."

"Mr. McAlester, I just checked the box where Mama kept her money hidden," Rose said and pointed to the empty box.

"Well, we know who did this. We've been tracking Santos and his gang since yesterday. So sorry we didn't catch up with that cutthroat band of killers before they got here. Títo, I want you to scout, find them, and report their location to me. Be careful. Santos is dangerous."

Títo left quickly. The bandits were easy to track, and Títo soon reported to Jesse, "Captain, they are just sitting around the campfire, as casual as you please. I couldn't see clearly, but Santos didn't seem to be there among them."

"Men, cinch up your saddles, check your weapons, and let's ride!"

Títo led the way, and when Jesse saw the gang from a distance, he shot the bandit closest to him and was surprised when he didn't fall.

Títo and Kronk shot as they rode through the camp, and then noticed the arrows protruding from the gang's bodies.

Títo exclaimed. "Captain, looks like the Comanche got here first!"

They inspected the group around the dying campfire. *El Pecoso* and the other bandits had been scalped and mutilated. The Comanche had played a final joke by placing the bandits' sombreros on their scalped heads.

"Captain, they took their scalps and stole their weapons, but left the stolen money."

"Títo, put the money in your saddlebags. You know everyone loves Molly, even the Comanche. Looks like they did our job for us, but where's Santos?"

"Captain, Santos is losing a lot of blood. He couldn't have gone far."

Títo and Kronk crisscrossed the area until they found Santos's trail. They followed it to a watering hole, where they surprised him while he was washing his face. His pain distracted him enough so that Kronk came up behind him undetected. The big Indian pounced and pinned the outlaw in his powerful arms.

Without much of a struggle, they tied Santos's arms behind him and then saw his scalded face, with traces of dried apple pie still clinging to his skin, along with cuts, some of which were still bleeding. His left eye was cloudy.

Jesse looked closer at the bandit's face. "Santos, looks like you've been fighting with a wildcat."

Santos spat at Jesse. "So Ranger, you have finally caught up with me. Maybe the gringo from the stagecoach that shot me should have your job. I do not think the people of Texas are well protected by you, this *pendejo*, and that dumb Indian."

"We're here to mete out justice."

"Go to hell, McAlester! It was much pleasure to kill the dog Juan Carlos and his nursemaid Molly."

"Well, I've got news for you. Molly is still alive and I think she was the wildcat who attacked your face. If we knew you liked apple pie so much, we would have brought you some fresh buttermilk to go with it." The Rangers laughed.

"Títo, get his horse, and Kronk, get the rope ready."

Santos continued bragging even as he was being hoisted by the big Indian. "People will still be afraid to go to bed at night when they remember Santos Barbosa."

Jesse shook his head. "I expect you're wrong about that. Not after we tell them how the pistolero on the stagecoach got the best of you when he shot you, how your face looked after Molly defended herself, and how now you've surrendered like a kitten. Kronk, lift him on his horse now. Tito, swing the rope over that limb and tighten the noose."

Santos cursed and screamed, "Tito, I know you. I know that birthmark on the bottom of your foot, because…"

Tito's eyes widened as he recognized the scorpion tattoo on Santos's left forearm. He looked up in horror into the man's face. Simultaneously, Santos kicked his horse and screamed, "I'm your *padre*."

Tito was aghast, too stunned to speak, watching Santos's neck snap and his body swinging violently. Still in shock, he cried out, "No! No! He couldn't have been my father!"

Jesse and Kronk looked at Santos's body, and then looked at each other, realizing that Tito did in fact bear a striking resemblance to the old bandit.

Tito fell to the ground and rocked violently back and forth, but Jesse and Kronk could only watch. Finally, Jesse spoke. "Do you want us to bury him?"

"Let the buzzards have him, I don't care what becomes of the body."

"How about his horse and his belongings?"

Tito sat up. "We should care for his horse and give his belongings to the government. When we return to Molly's place, we can give her the horse and the money his gang stole from her, and then give Juan Carlos a proper burial."

Jesse extended his hand and pulled Tito to his feet. They rode to Molly's place and followed his requests. When they arrived, they were exhausted, but heartily welcomed. Títo gave Ryan and Rose the money stolen by Santos's gang, along with Santos's horse.

"María, would you like for Títo and Kronk to dig a grave for your brother?"

"Jesse, yes, please. I've dressed him in white linen, but would prefer to bury him tomorrow. I would like for Molly to watch his burial, and I think she will be able to do so then."

"If you don't mind putting us up for the night, we would be honored to stay for the burial."

The Rangers awoke the next morning smelling coffee brewing and biscuits baking in the oven.

Jesse found María cleaning Molly's wounds, while Rose brushed her mother's hair. Although still weak, she was able to speak with Jesse and describe her struggle with Santos, and watch Juan Carlos' burial.

A few days later, Ryan painted a sign for Molly's place and hung it on the house. The sign read "Wildcat Inn." After she recovered fully, her business prospered because many folks wanted to see Molly, the woman who had defended herself against Santos Barbosa. Others just went to the Wildcat Inn for the wonderful food.

With the increased business, she hired more help and built a large cabin with a big kitchen, along with rooms for folks staying overnight. After the cabin's completion, she had a separate home built for her family and María.

She instructed a workman to remove the Wildcat Inn sign from her home and hang it from the roof of the large new cabin. The workman wanted to repair the sign or build a better one, but she stamped her foot and shouted, "The customer is always right! I want the old sign!" She got her way and, in the future, almost every visitor talked about the antique sign. Molly and the Wildcat Inn became quite famous. She trained Rose to follow in her footsteps.

May, 1856

The United States Camel Corps was established at the new U.S. Army post at Camp Verde, near Rancho Arroyo Verde. U.S. Secretary of War Jefferson Davis commissioned the project, and approximately seventy-five camels were sent to the post to provide transportation of supplies and a communication line with the western areas. The camels could carry more weight than horses or mules and were better acclimated to the terrain, making the project successful.

Since the fort was about two miles away from their home, Rachel and Jesse took their younger children, Martha and Ben, to see the camels, and Jesse escorted them to the corrals to get a better view. "Look, Mama!" "Wow!" "Papa, they are so big!" "Watch out, Papa, they're spitting at us."

The family was disappointed when the project was discontinued because the United States did not want to maintain the experiment after the Civil War.

When the camels were released, Jesse obtained two camels, Arthur and Humps, enjoyed by his children and grandchildren for many years.

CHAPTER TWENTY-THREE
Civil War

March 15, 1861

Jesse, now 48 years old with an arthritic right hand and a left shoulder that had become useless by that time, was approached by the State of Texas regarding the looming Civil War. His official notice was from Colonel Robert Ballantine in San Antonio, asking him to report on March 15, 1861.

"Colonel Ballantine, Captain McAlester reporting for duty, sir."

"At ease, Jesse, we don't have to be so formal here. I have reports from all over the state that the Kiowa and Comanche are raiding homesteads everywhere. It seems that we have some Yankee conspirators selling weapons, corn liquor, and information to the tribes in order to stir them up. Right now they are succeeding!"

"What can I do to help?"

"I know your left arm is stove up and you can't serve with the volunteers, but I'd like you to join the Home Guard to protect our settlers from Indian depredations. I know, everyone is clamoring to join the Confederacy, but don't you see, if we don't have seasoned Indian fighters, you won't have homes to come back to."

"I see your point, Colonel," Jesse said, as he mentally envisioned the potential raids on Rancho Arroyo Verde and the ranches nearby.

"I want you and every seasoned Indian fighter to form a squad to quell these potential raids."

"I can think of nineteen men I would choose to fight alongside me."

"Very good. What supplies and weapons will you need?"

"I had a notion why I was being called to San Antonio, so I prepared a list," he said, pulling it from his pocket and handing it to the Colonel.

"Jesse, this is a very extensive list, including a remuda of horses of your choosing."

"I understand, but the horses we breed are superior to any other stock that is available."

"I have, of course, heard of your horses, and I understand your wife has been very involved in the care and breeding of your stock."

"That's right, Colonel, I could not have developed this line of horses without her help."

"That's quite an admission."

"It's true. My Rangering caused regular absences from my home. Without her knowledge and skill, it would not have been possible."

"Jesse, give your complete list to the Quartermaster Sergeant, and I will see that we obtain the funds necessary."

"Rachel, darling, I have great news. The State of Texas is assigning me the position of Captain of the Home Guard, and I will be responsible for a squad of Rangers for the Home Front."

"Am I supposed to get excited that you could be killed around here, rather than in another state?"

"Well, I'd rather take my chances around here."

"I suppose you're right, since Angus and Buddy have already joined up with the Confederacy. I received a letter from Molly saying Ryan has signed up too, and will be departing soon. I blame your damned hide, for your foolishness in encouraging the boys to go to war. If anything happens to my boys, there'll be hell to pay on your part."

"Give me your hand and let's recite The Lord's Prayer," Jesse said. After the prayer, he smiled and said, "Now, here's the good news."

"Don't try to change the subject."

"Texas will purchase fifty of our best horses for the officers at one hundred-seventy-five dollars apiece."

"Darling, that is eight thousand, seven hundred-fifty dollars in gold. I can't believe it!" Tears rolled down Rachel's face.

"Why are you crying?"

"Because I'm so happy."

I'll never figure out women, Jesse thought.

Although the Comanche and Kiowa continued to raid, Jesse and his fellow Rangers of the Home Guard were feeling pressure from the Confederates to control the Germans that lived all around him.

June 9, 1862

"Rachel, the Confederates are giving me all kinds of hell since the war started. They think our German neighbors might try and release the Union prisoners at Camp Verde."

The plight of the Germans, already distrusted by the other Texans, worsened because they were thought to be Union sympathizers. An order came down to conscript the Germans into the Confederate Army. Many refused, and some sixty-one, including one Tejano who also did not believe in slavery, fled to an area north of Uvalde on the Nueces River on August 1, 1862, with others arriving on August 3.

August 10, 1862

A group of Germans camping on the banks of the Nueces River were made aware of the approaching Confederate soldiers. They repelled the initial onslaught, but were finally overwhelmed by a larger force, resulting in thirty-eight known dead. The Confederate soldiers executed many of the wounded.

The Civil War, unimaginably bloody, was responsible for many massacres, where neighbor killed neighbor, brother fought brother, father shot son.

In the following years, the McAlesters received three letters.

One from Molly: "I wanted to let you know that my dear son Ryan was killed on April 6, 1862 in the Battle of Shiloh...."

One from the Confederacy: "We regret to inform you that on September 20, 1863, Angus McAlester was wounded in action at the Battle of Chickamauga and succumbed to his injuries on November 25 of that same year. We send our condolences to his family."

Another from the Confederacy: "We regret to inform you that on June 3, 1864, Jacob McAlester was killed in action at the Battle of Cold Harbor. We send our condolences to his family."

In August 1865, Jesse led a group of men to recover the remains of the slaughtered Germans and the Tejano at the Nueces Massacre. They moved them to their final resting place in Comfort, Texas. A monument was erected there engraved with *"Treue der Union"*—"Loyalty to the Union"—and all the names of victims were also engraved on the monument.

It is the only Union monument erected in the South. The United States flag beside the monument flies perpetually at half-mast and has a light shining on it at night.

CHAPTER TWENTY-FOUR
Bandera Pass

In the winter of 1878, during a cold spell, Gus Lehman rode up on his old mare before daybreak and hallooed to the McAlester house.

Jesse opened the front door and stuck his head out. "Gus, get down off that horse and come on in by the fire!"

"I'd rather you get old Paint saddled up and follow me to a turkey roost."

"Give me time to throw on some warm clothes. I'll give some oats to Paint, and then I'll be a-rarin' to go." Jesse fingered his .32/40 Winchester rifle and slipped ten shells into his coat pocket.

Gus fidgeted. "Those turkeys won't wait all day. I've already packed some venison jerky and a canteen of water."

They walked together down to the barn. Jesse went to Paint's stall. "Come on, Paint, we're going to the Pass to get us some supper."

Paint whinnied and shifted his weight, and Jesse put on the blanket and heaved the saddle on the horse's back. Paint was still working on his oats when Jesse slid the rifle into the scabbard. After finishing his breakfast, Paint was fired up and eager for the trail.

Lehman was off at a trot when Jesse whispered to Paint, and they eased up to ride side by side.

"We're getting too old for this, Gus. What makes you think with your old eyes you can even shoot a turkey?"

"Cause they're sitting lined up in a tree, and a blind man could take 'em."

"We'll see how good those old eyes are."

They tied their horses at the base of Bandera Pass, and after a short walk, Gus pointed to a flock of turkeys sitting on a branch of a giant oak, silhouetted by the full moon setting behind them.

A metallic click came suddenly as Jesse chambered bullets in lightning fashion. A cacophony of gunshots: boom, boom, boom, was followed immediately by movement from the oak. Three turkeys toppled to the ground and others, squawking, flew away, and then all hell broke loose.

The deafening noise caused an explosion of bats to erupt in a juniper grove far above their heads.

"Gus, I've never seen bats on this side of the Pass." Thousands of bats were swirling out of the side of the hill. "I'm going up to take a look at their roost."

"We need to get those turkeys back to the house and get 'em cleaned. I don't wanna be fooling around with no blood suckers."

"I'm going up to the opening to see what's inside. I'd appreciate if you'd come up there with me in case there's any trouble."

"If you'd rather go chasing after some old bats, instead of going home to a hot breakfast, then let's git 'er done."

Jessie parted the mass of lower limbs on the ancient juniper, which was growing near the edge of a small cliff. "I can feel a draft of cold air. It's coming out of a cave right here behind the tree. Hand me that fallen juniper limb so I can make a torch."

Immediately upon entering the cave, Jesse swept the torch near the cave walls and discovered six skeletons.

"You're not going to believe your eyes. I've finally found the Comanche from our fracas in 1843."

"What? How do you know it's the Comanche?" Gus finally entered the cave.

"Because these bows, quivers, and lances all have Comanche markings."

Over the years, the weapons and skeletons had been scattered by the varmints and very little was intact.

"Turn around, Gus, there's a rawhide bag on the ledge above your head."

"You're right, and look here. There's another bow and six arrows."

They started coughing. They covered their faces with their bandanas because of the awful stench in the cave.

In the Battle of Bandera Pass, the Comanche had set up an ambush for the Texas Rangers, who were taken totally by surprise when a fusillade of arrows rained down upon them. The Rangers returned fire, and, as they had done in the past, the Comanche surged forward. As they moved forward, they were caught in the deadly fire of Paterson Colt revolvers.

The barrage of gunfire decimated the ranks of the Comanche. When the battle devolved into hand-to-hand fighting, the Comanche made a desperate and successful attempt to remove their dead and wounded from the field. The Rangers never knew how the enemy had managed to escape.

"Gus, I can see this one's been shot right between the eyes. Let's gather up all of their weapons and take them back to the ranch. We can get Ben to come back with a wagon and pick up anything we've missed."

Both men were coughing violently.

"I can't breathe, Jesse. Let's get out of here. I'm a lot more interested in getting out of here than in collecting a bunch of old bones and weapons from the Comanche."

They left most of the Indian souvenirs behind, only taking a sample of what lay in the cave. They rode back to Rancho Arroyo Verde with the three turkeys, but they coughed all the way. When they arrived at the ranch, Rachel noticed that Jesse was shivering.

"Are you going to be all right? Your face is flushed."

"I'm just tired from going up to the Pass. Gus and I climbed into the hills after some turkey, and when we shot, a few thousand bats flew out of an opening near the top."

"What in Heaven's name do you think you're doing climbing up those hills like some kind of billy goat?"

"We got carried away. We went up to see where the bats were coming from, and the next thing we knew, there was their cave, hidden behind an ancient juniper. It was easy to get inside, and we found weapons and skeletons from the Comanche we fought in our battle there in '43."

"I don't care anything about some old bones, but I do care about your getting sick at your age. Now lie down on the bed, and I'll bring you some hot tea and honey."

In the middle of the night, Jesse's breathing became more labored.

"Jesse, wake up. Your breathing is very loud and ragged. I'm going to send for the doctor at first light."

"I'll be all right, I wore myself out in the hills yesterday, and I'm paying for it now."

"I think it's more than that. When you came home last night, you had an awful smell about you."

"Well, it couldn't be helped. There were bat droppings everywhere, and the odor was horrible."

"I hope the old bones and the weapons you found were worth it."

"I'm having trouble breathing and talking right now, so do you mind if I go back to sleep?"

She could hear the racking sound of Jesse's lungs throughout the night and she became very worried.

When dawn broke, she quickly saddled Paint and rode to Ben's cabin. He and his wife Maggie were still asleep. Rachel knocked loudly and called, "Ben, wake up, son, your Papa's taken ill, and we need to get the doctor over to our place."

Maggie came to the door, hugging a dressing gown around her against the cold. "Rachel, what are you doing out in this cold weather without a coat? You'll catch your death of pneumonia!" She pulled Rachel inside the living room and closed the door.

"It's Jesse, honey. I'm afraid he already has it. Caught it yesterday up at Bandera Pass."

Ben appeared in his nightshirt, rubbing his eyes and yawning. "Mama, why are you up so early?"

"Ben, I want you to find Doc Harrell and bring him to our house as soon as possible."

A worried look on Ben's face belied his normally cool exterior. "I'm already gone, Mother, and I'll bring the Doc back before you know it."

Rachel lost no time galloping back to the ranch. She left Paint in the barn still saddled and ran to the house and into the bedroom. Luckily, the kettle she'd placed on the hook in the fireplace was steaming. She filled the smaller teakettle. "Jesse, wake up, darling, I need you to breathe some steam from the teakettle."

At noon, Ben and Doc Harrell arrived. "Mrs. McAlester, I would have been here sooner, but I was attending to old Gus Lehman."

"Doc, what's the problem with Gus?"

"I believe he has pneumonia. I gave him some herbal remedies, and advised his wife to not let him get out of the bed unless it was absolutely necessary."

"Jesse's through here, Doc."

As soon as Doc saw Jesse, he knew he was dealing with the same type of pneumonia Gus Lehman had. "Jesse, can you hear me?"

"Doc, I'm having a terrible time catching my breath."

"I understand you and Gus were at the Pass yesterday and discovered a bat cave?"

Jesse replied, each breath labored, "Yes, Doc, we were."

"Were y'all having trouble breathing inside the cave?"

Jesse nodded weakly, then passed out, and Doc Harrell summoned Rachel into the main room.

"I can offer you the same treatment I gave Gus, but I'm not sure it will help. Keep giving him steam, and I want you to make a drink of ground up garlic, milk, and water, and try to get him to drink it at least four times a day."

"Doc, I'm worried, do you think going into the cave with the bats was harmful?"

"I'm no scientist, but it seems to be a possibility."

Gus Lehman died on December 22, 1878.

Jesse's family gathered around him and prayed that he would survive. Rachel saw that her beloved husband was trying to speak and bent closer to Jesse's lips. "Texas" was the last word he said. After speaking that word, Jesse's breathing became shallower, and then stopped.

Jesse died on Friday, December 27, 1878. The family's clock was stopped at 9:18 p.m.

The McAlester family decided to put Jesse in the icehouse and cover him with straw until they could spread the word that the funeral would be held at the ranch on December 31, 1878.

The wagons began arriving on December 30, and their incoming number did not decrease until the next day. The crowd was estimated to be three hundred people. Rachel was impressed and grateful that folks thought that much of Jesse.

"Ben, I know the funeral was scheduled for ten o'clock, but I would like to delay until two o'clock to allow for stragglers to arrive."

"I agree, Mother. Sarah and Martha are going to help Maggie with Creed and Anne." Creed was six years old, and his sister, Anne McAlester, had been born on June 1, 1875.

Rachel laid a hand on her son's arm. "Do you have your eulogy prepared?"

"Yes, Mama, as soon as the preacher gets here, I'm going to address the crowd, and then let the preacher take over."

A contingent of Texas Rangers arrived, bringing a fully attired Scotsman to play "Amazing Grace" on his bagpipes. There was not a dry eye at the private cemetery.

CHAPTER TWENTY-FIVE
Ruth McAlester Mitchell

Recently retired from the Armstrong Browning Library on the campus of Baylor University in Waco, Texas, Ruth Mitchell looked around her house for projects because she had time on her hands.

She realized she needed a larger desk for all the projects she intended to start. She remembered the roll top she had inherited from her father, Creed McAlester, and went into one of her guest bedrooms to inspect it.

Then she went to the back door and spotted Ramón at work repairing the back fence.

"*Ramón, entrarias, necesito ayuda?*" "Ramón, would you come inside? I need some help." He had been her yardman, caretaker of her horses, and handyman for years.

"*Si, Señora Michell, estoy en camino.*" "Yes, Mrs. Mitchell, I'm on my way."

Once inside, she showed him the heavy old desk and asked him to pull it out from the walls so she could dust and polish it. He did, and asked her, "*Cualquier otra cosa?*" "Anything else?"

"Yes, get some lemonade from the fridge. I made it the way you like it."

"*Gracias, Señora Mitchell.*" He poured the lemonade into a plastic cup with ice.

"*Ramón, te lo he dicho un million de veces, no necesitas llamarme la Señora Mitchell. Ruth estara bien.*" "Ramón, I've told you a million times you don't need to call me 'Mrs. Mitchell.' 'Ruth' will be just fine."

"*Te he llamado la Señora Mitchell durante anos, es dificil cambiar los viegos habitos.*" "I've called you 'Mrs. Mitchell' for so many years—it's hard to change old habits."

"*Tienes razon sobre eso.*" "You're right about that."

"*Llamame cuando este listo para volver a poner el escritio.*" "Call me when you're ready to put the desk back."

She began cleaning the back of the desk, and saw something strange—a latch. She tried to turn it, but nothing happened and she could not budge that part of the desk. She examined the desk more thoroughly, but found no other latches, so she removed the drawers and discovered that one of them was shorter than the others. She got her flashlight and aimed it at the vacant area where the shorter drawer was. She gasped. Sure enough, there was a secret drawer with a second latch.

She got a long knife to reach to the end of the area and turn the second latch. Then she pulled out the secret drawer from the back of the desk.

The drawer held a beautiful carved box, engraved with the word "McAlester." Obviously, the contents had been important to someone in her family, probably her father.

"I've hit a gold mine!" she shouted.

She carefully opened the box and realized she needed to put on the pair of white gloves she always wore when handling historical documents.

Such documents usually had thin, brittle paper, which could easily tear.

She opened one of her bureau drawers and found the gloves.

With the gloves on, she removed the old folded paper, opened it, and saw that it was not just any letter, but the Mexican Lancer's letter, which she had heard about from her father and her grandfather.

Fantastic, I found the Mexican Lancer's letter! she thought. Then she read the beautiful cursive Spanish writing.

The mention of Popocatépetl reminded her of her travels, and the love language reminded her of the letters of Robert Browning and Elizabeth Barrett Browning that she had read and researched at the library.

The letter led her to remember her family telling the history of her great-grandfather, Jesse McAlester, who was a renowned soldier at the Battle of San Jacinto, a hero of the Mexican-American War, and a famous Texas Ranger.

She also thought about her great-great-grandfather, Angus Burns, a courier who was tragically killed at the Alamo by Antonio Vargas Delgado. *How intertwined our lives become, like the weave of a delicate silk scarf,* she thought.

She stood up and walked to the wall, where the last letter Angus Burns wrote to his wife hung. Her father had had the letter professionally mounted and framed, and had given it to her on her birthday. She had placed the framed letter in a place of honor in her home.

She wondered why the Mexican Lancer's letter was in the secret compartment, and then remembered her father's forgetfulness in the last year of his life. He must have forgotten where it was.

Knowing the importance of the letter to her family, she began to wonder about the descendants of the Mexican Lancer, Antonio Vargas Delgado.

Would they want his letter? Are any of his descendants alive? Isn't his family the rightful owner of the letter? What if his family rejects me and his letter because Jesse killed the man? But if she and her family had been able to forgive the Lancer for killing Angus, then it would be possible the Mexican family could do the same. She had always been told that time heals all wounds. It was a war after all.

She decided to take the risk, and return the Lancer's letter to his family.

After hours of research and then including the famous volcano, Popocatépetl, in her search, she discovered the living descendants of the Mexican Lancer.

After she contacted Alejandra, the great-great granddaughter of the Lancer, she made arrangements to fly to Mexico City. Upon arriving in Mexico City, she took the bus to Puebla and was amazed at the quality and service of the bus. Ruth had made arrangements for a car and driver to take her to the ranch of one of the descendants. The other Lancer's descendants were to meet her there.

The driver turned off the main road and drove down a lane with beautiful orange *(naranja)* trees on one side and avocado *(aguacate)* trees on the other. The lane turned and she could see an enormous barn and fenced area where Andalusians were being trained in dressage

Around another corner, she saw a magnificent house made of limestone with a red tiled roof and a large bronze monument inside the courtyard of the Mexican Lancer riding an Andalusian.

I can see Popocatépetl above the house! she realized. This beautiful sight confirmed she was at the right place.

When she got out and walked to the front door, a servant answered and said, "You are expected. Please follow me."

He led her through unbelievable rooms with elegant tapestries, large bronze statues, and long tables with beautiful, thick marble tops.

When she arrived in an enormous room with a high ceiling, she saw a number of people waiting for her. There were photos everywhere in the room, some of people and some of horses. A lance hung on the wall above the fireplace and large paintings of horses adorned another wall.

Alejandra stood up and walked toward her. She introduced herself and said, with a sweeping gesture, "All of the people here are members of my family, and we are honored that you have traveled to our home. In particular, I would like to introduce you to my brother Gabriel. Our great-great grandfather was a famous Lancer, and his death grieved his family and the workers here at the ranch. The family erected a monument in his memory. Now every year on his birthday, we say prayers and place flowers on the base of the monument in tribute to him."

Ruth was served an elegant piece of cake and strong coffee. She was invited to stay for lunch.

"Thank you so much for your hospitality. As you know, I have the letter from your great-great-grandfather." She handed the letter, protected in Mylar, to Alejandra, who was named after her great-great grandmother. Her brother Gabriel walked over to be the next in line to read the letter.

As Alejandra read the letter, tears brimmed in her eyes, and Ruth pulled a lace handkerchief from her purse and extended it to her. She not only took the handkerchief, but also Ruth's hand and held it firmly in a sign of friendship. At that moment, Ruth knew the letter's long journey was over and it had finally been delivered to the proper hands.

When Ruth arrived home, she thought about being the last generation of the McAlesters, and remembered all the happy times when her father, grandfather, and she had read the worn and faded letter written by Angus Burns to his wife, and reminisced about her family's history, and the love story of Jesse and Rachel.

What am I going to do with Jesse's personal effects?

First, she had them appraised and learned they were of great value. Several museums approached her, interested in expanding their Texana collections.

Before she made her decision, and thinking about the bronze statues she saw in Alejandra's home, she commissioned a life-size bronze statue of Jesse McAlester astride a horse, modeled after Ruth's favorite horse. When it was finished, she donated it, along with the leather saddlebags originally belonging to Angus Burns and after his death to Jesse McAlester, to the Texas Ranger Museum in Waco. She also gave Jesse's Ranger badge to the museum.

At the reception for the donations, Ruth was asked to speak, and she ended her speech with these words, "Our ancestors were courageous men and women, who fought for their beliefs. But above all, they loved and sacrificed for their families."

CHAPTER TWENTY-SIX
Anomaly

October 1985

The Curator of the Texas Ranger Museum in Waco, Dr. Stephen R. Callaway, was looking for new items to display in the museum.

On the donation list was a pair of saddlebags that had belonged to Ruth Mitchell's great-great grandfather Angus Burns, a courier from the Alamo who was killed outside the walls of the fort.

Upon examination of the saddlebags, under the scrutiny of an overhead lighted magnifying glass, he could barely discern a large scrolled "B," on either side of each bag.

Interesting, he thought. *I believe these may be worth running through the CT scan at the hospital to examine them more thoroughly. They have been very kind to allow us to use this technology in the past.*

Dr. Callaway called the Hillcrest Hospital, and upon speaking with the CT technician, arranged to deliver the bags the next day.

The following morning, after delivering the saddlebags to the hospital, he drove to the museum, walked in, and worked in the archive room, examining the other donations from Mrs. Mitchell.

That afternoon, the telephone rang in the director's office, "Dr. Callaway, this is the CT scan tech from Hillcrest Hospital and the results are in on the saddlebags."

"Did you find anything interesting?"

"Well, my colleague and I detected an anomaly on the inside of the saddlebags."

"Do you know what it is?"

"No, sir, it seems that you will actually have to open up the area in question to discover the contents."

"I will send someone from my office to pick up the bags. Please don't discuss your findings with my staff member."

"No problem, sir, but I have attached a sticky note on the area with the anomaly for your benefit."

"I would appreciate it, if you could put them in a box, and seal the box before my staff member arrives."

"Will do."

The technician chuckled after the phone call, "Man, that guy is really paranoid."

The intern, Angela Norris, who was working for a semester in the museum, was walking by his office, and Dr. Callaway said, "Why don't you run down to the hospital and fetch the box that I delivered to them earlier today."

After picking up the sealed box and delivering it to her boss, she returned to her desk.

Dr. Callaway advised the receptionist, "I'm going to be in the archive room, and I don't wish to be disturbed."

"Yes, sir, I'll hold your calls until you get back."

He carefully opened the box, placing the saddlebags on the table directly beneath his overhead magnifying glass. Putting on his white gloves, he removed the sticky note, and with a small seam ripper, gently removed the fine stitching on the inside. With a special pair of forceps, he carefully removed a very thin leather pouch. From the pouch, he then removed a letter, still with the red wax seal intact with the letter "B" impressed in the wax. Unable to contain himself, he turned on a hair dryer, which he kept for this purpose in the archive room, at a low setting to loosen the seal, and carefully removed it in one piece so he could later reattach it. Gently unfolding the letter, he read it. "By damn, this is the most incredible thing that I have ever seen!"

February 28, 1836

General Houston,

    I am growing weaker each day, and I wish to convey an important message that could very well save Texas. I have been in possession of a very large amount of gold and silver. I have hidden the cache in a cave approximately 4 miles east of the Alamo. I am enclosing a map, along with this letter, inside my saddlebags in a secret compartment that will lead you to the cave, and a detailed description where I buried the treasure inside.

    Your obedient servant,

    James Bowie

A crudely drawn map was on the second page of the letter.

Angela, growing suspicious upon hearing Dr. Callaway's exclamation, moved closer to the door. She heard the safe door shut, and rushed back to her desk, now even more curious.

She saw Dr. Callaway, who was red-faced and sweating, obviously very agitated when he came out of the archive room and told the receptionist, "I don't wish to be disturbed for the remainder of the day."

"Yes, sir, I will make sure of that."

As Dr. Callaway entered his office, and closed and locked his door, Angela made a bold move. Holding an empty folder, she entered the archive room. She saw that the lights were still on above the exam table, and the saddlebags were on the table, along with a seam ripper. She carefully looked inside the bags. There was now a void exposing a hidden compartment. *Interesting, I wonder what he found.*

Passing by the safe, she pulled on the lever, and to her astonishment, it opened. She discovered the small leather pouch and a letter written in bold cursive and a map. Carefully, she placed the letter and map in her folder and casually walked to the copy room in the back of the building.

Not wishing to get caught, she made a copy of the letter and the map as fast as possible, returned the originals to the safe, closed the door, and spun the combination to lock it.

She returned to her desk, placed the precious copies in her backpack, and waited to leave for the day.

Regaining his composure, the director processed the information that the saddlebags had belonged to James Bowie, and not Angus Burns.

Now, how can I find that cave, and remove the contents without being detected?

That night, in her small apartment, Angela placed the copies of the letter and map on her kitchen table and read the letter, three times. Then she looked at the copy of the map, staring at it until it was burned into her memory. She smiled and began to form a plan.

Sharing the same birthday—day, month, and year—**James and Pamela Nelson** lead captivating lives and both are cancer survivors. Before retirement Pamela led an interesting career as an attorney and James received a degree in history, embarking on a successful career as a real estate investor. They live in San Antonio, Texas, with their Maltese dogs, Molly and Allie. Passionate about Texas history, they spend much of their free time reading and collecting artifacts.